# CHRONICLES OF THE CANONGATE

By Sir Walter Scott, Bart.

INTRODUCTION TO CHRONICLES OF THE CANONGATE.

The preceding volume of this Collection concluded the last of the pieces originally published under the NOMINIS UMBRA of The Author of Waverley; and the circumstances which rendered it impossible for the writer to continue longer in the possession of his incognito were communicated in 1827, in the Introduction to the first series of Chronicles of the Canongate, consisting (besides a biographical sketch of the imaginary chronicler) of three tales, entitled "The Highland Widow," "The Two Drovers," and "The Surgeon's Daughter." In the present volume the two first named of these pieces are included, together with three detached stories which appeared the year after, in the elegant compilation called "The Keepsake." "The Surgeon's Daughter" it is thought better to defer until a succeeding volume, than to

"Begin, and break off in the middle."

I have, perhaps, said enough on former occasions of the misfortunes which led to the dropping of that mask under which I had, for a long series of years, enjoyed so large a portion of public favour. Through the success of those literary efforts, I had been enabled to indulge most of the tastes which a retired person of my station might be supposed to entertain. In the pen of this nameless romancer, I seemed to possess something like the secret fountain of coined gold and pearls vouchsafed to the traveller of the Eastern Tale; and no doubt believed that I might venture, without silly imprudence, to extend my personal expenditure considerably beyond what I should have thought of, had my means been limited to the competence which I derived from inheritance, with the moderate income of a professional situation. I bought, and built, and planted, and was considered by myself, as by the rest of the world, in the safe possession of an easy fortune. My riches, however, like the other riches of this world, were liable to accidents, under which they were ultimately destined to make unto themselves wings, and fly away. The year 1825, so disastrous to many branches of industry and commerce, did not spare the market of literature; and the sudden ruin that fell on so many of the booksellers could scarcely have been expected to leave unscathed one whose career had of necessity connected him deeply and extensively with the pecuniary transactions of that profession. In a word, almost without one note of premonition, I found myself involved in the sweeping catastrophe of the unhappy time, and called on to meet the demands of creditors upon commercial establishments with which my fortunes had long been bound up, to the extent of no less a sum than one hundred and twenty thousand pounds.

The author having, however rashly, committed his pledges thus largely to the hazards of trading companies, it behoved him, of course, to abide the consequences of his conduct, and, with whatever feelings, he surrendered on the instant every shred of property which he had been accustomed to call his own. It became vested in the hands of gentlemen whose integrity, prudence, and intelligence were combined with all possible liberality and kindness of disposition, and who readily afforded every assistance towards the execution of plans, in the success of which the author contemplated the possibility of his ultimate extrication, and which were of such a nature that, had assistance of this sort been withheld, he could have had little prospect of carrying them into effect. Among other resources which occurred was the project of that complete and corrected edition of his Novels and Romances (whose real parentage had of necessity been disclosed at the moment of the commercial convulsions alluded to), which has now advanced with unprecedented favour nearly to its close; but as he purposed also to continue, for the behoof of those to whom he was indebted, the exercise of his pen in the same path of literature, so long as the taste of his countrymen should seem to approve of his efforts, it appeared to him that it would have been an idle piece of affectation to attempt getting up a new incognito, after his original visor had been thus dashed from his brow. Hence the personal narrative prefixed to the first work of fiction which he put forth after the paternity of the "Waverley Novels" had come to be publicly ascertained; and though many of the particulars originally avowed in that Notice have been unavoidably adverted to in the Prefaces and Notes to some of the preceding volumes of the present collection, it is now reprinted as it stood at the time, because some interest is generally attached to a coin or medal struck on a special occasion, as expressing, perhaps, more faithfully than the same artist could have afterwards conveyed, the feelings of the moment that gave it birth. The Introduction to the first series of Chronicles of the Canongate ran, then, in these words:—

## INTRODUCTION.

All who are acquainted with the early history of the Italian stage are aware that Arlecchino is not, in his original conception, a mere worker of marvels with his wooden sword, a jumper in and out of windows, as upon our theatre, but, as his party-coloured jacket implies, a buffoon or clown, whose mouth, far from being eternally closed, as amongst us, is filled, like that of Touchstone, with quips, and cranks, and witty devices, very often delivered extempore. It is not easy to trace how he became possessed of his black vizard, which was anciently made in the resemblance of the face of a cat; but it seems that the mask was essential to the performance of the character, as will appear from the following theatrical anecdote:—

An actor on the Italian stage permitted at the Foire du St. Germain, in Paris, was renowned for the wild, venturous, and extravagant wit, the brilliant sallies and fortunate repartees, with which he prodigally seasoned the character of the party-coloured jester. Some critics, whose good-will towards a favourite performer was stronger than their judgment, took occasion to remonstrate with the successful actor on the subject of the grotesque vizard. They went wilily to their purpose, observing that his classical and Attic wit, his delicate vein of humour, his happy turn for dialogue, were rendered burlesque and ludicrous by this unmeaning and bizarre disguise, and that those attributes would become far more impressive if aided by the spirit of his eye and the expression of his natural features. The actor's vanity was easily so far engaged as to induce him to make the experiment. He played Harlequin barefaced, but was considered on all hands as having made a total failure. He had lost the audacity which a sense of incognito bestowed, and with it all the reckless play of raillery which gave vivacity to his original acting. He cursed his advisers, and resumed his grotesque vizard, but, it is said, without ever being able to regain the careless and successful levity which the consciousness of the disguise had formerly bestowed.

Perhaps the Author of Waverley is now about to incur a risk of the same kind, and endanger his popularity by having laid aside his incognito. It is certainly not a voluntary experiment, like that of Harlequin; for it was my original intention never to have avowed these works during my lifetime, and the original manuscripts were carefully preserved (though by the care of others rather than mine), with the purpose of supplying the necessary evidence of the truth when the period of announcing it should arrive. [These manuscripts are at present (August 1831) advertised for public sale, which is an addition, though a small one, to other annoyances.] But the affairs of my publishers having, unfortunately, passed into a management different from their own, I had no right any longer to rely upon secrecy in that quarter; and thus my mask, like my Aunt Dinah's in "Tristram Shandy," having begun to wax a little threadbare about the chin, it became time to lay it aside with a good grace, unless I desired it should fall in pieces from my face, which was now become likely.

Yet I had not the slightest intention of selecting the time and place in which the disclosure was finally made; nor was there any concert betwixt my learned and respected friend LORD MEADOWBANK and myself upon that occasion. It was, as the reader is probably aware, upon the 23rd February last, at a public meeting, called for establishing a professional Theatrical Fund in Edinburgh, that the communication took place. Just before we sat down to table, Lord Meadowbank [One of the Supreme Judges of Scotland, termed Lords of Council and Session.] asked me privately whether I was still anxious to preserve my incognito on the subject of what were called the Waverley Novels? I did not immediately see the purpose of his lordship's question, although I certainly might have been led to infer it, and replied that the secret had now of necessity become known to so many people that I was indifferent on the subject. Lord Meadowbank was thus induced, while doing me the great honour of proposing my health to the meeting, to say something on the subject of these Novels so strongly connecting them with me as the author, that by remaining silent I must have stood convicted, either of the actual paternity, or of the still greater crime of being supposed willing to receive indirectly praise to which I had no just title. I thus found myself suddenly and unexpectedly placed in the confessional, and had only time to recollect that I had been guided thither by a most friendly hand, and could not, perhaps, find a better public opportunity to lay down a disguise which began to resemble that of a detected masquerader.

I had therefore the task of avowing myself, to the numerous and respectable company assembled, as the sole and unaided author of these Novels of Waverley, the paternity of which was likely at one time to have formed a controversy of some celebrity, for the ingenuity with which some instructors of the public gave their assurance on the subject was extremely persevering. I now think it further necessary to say that, while I take on myself all the merits and demerits attending these compositions, I am bound to acknowledge with gratitude hints of subjects and legends which I have received from various quarters, and have occasionally used as a foundation of my fictitious compositions, or woven up with them in the shape of episodes. I am bound, in particular, to acknowledge the unremitting kindness of Mr. Joseph Train, supervisor of excise at Dumfries, to whose unwearied industry I have been indebted for many curious traditions and points of antiquarian interest. It was Mr. Train who brought to my recollection the history of Old Mortality, although I myself had had a personal interview with that celebrated wanderer so far back as about 1792, when I found him on his usual task. He was then engaged in repairing the Gravestones of the Covenanters who had died while imprisoned in the Castle of Dunnottar, to which many of them were committed prisoners at the period of Argyle's rising. Their place of confinement is still called the Whigs' Vault. Mr. Train, however, procured for me far more extensive information concerning this singular person, whose name was Patterson, than I had been able to acquire during my own short conversation with him. [See, for some further particulars, the notes to Old Mortality, in the present collective edition.] He was (as I think I have somewhere already stated) a native of the parish of Closeburn, in Dumfriesshire; and it is believed that domestic affliction, as well as devotional feeling, induced him to commence the wandering mode of life which he pursued for a very long period. It is more than twenty years since Robert Patterson's death, which took place on the highroad near Lockerby, where he was found exhausted and expiring. The white pony, the companion of his pilgrimage, was standing by the side of its dying master the whole furnishing a scene not unfitted for the pencil. These particulars I had from Mr. Train.

Another debt, which I pay most willingly, I owe to an unknown correspondent (a lady), [The late Mrs. Goldie.] who favoured me with the history of the upright and high-principled female, whom, in the Heart of Mid-Lothian, I have termed Jeanie Deans. The circumstance of her refusing to save her sister's life by an act of perjury, and undertaking a pilgrimage to London to obtain her pardon, are both represented as true by my fair and obliging correspondent; and they led me to consider the possibility of rendering a fictitious personage interesting by mere dignity of mind and rectitude of principle, assisted by unpretending good sense and temper, without any of the beauty, grace, talent, accomplishment, and wit to which a heroine of romance is supposed to have a prescriptive right. If the portrait was received with interest by the public, I am conscious how much it was owing to the truth and force of the original sketch, which I regret that I am unable to present to the public, as it was written with much feeling and spirit.

Old and odd books, and a considerable collection of family legends, formed another quarry, so ample that it was much more likely that the strength of the labourer should be exhausted than that materials should fail. I may mention, for example's sake, that the terrible catastrophe of the Bride of Lammermoor actually occurred in a Scottish family of rank. The female relative, by whom the melancholy tale was communicated to me many years since, was a near connection of the family in which the event happened, and always told it with an appearance of melancholy mystery which enhanced the interest. She had known in her youth the brother who rode before the unhappy victim to the fatal altar, who, though then a mere boy, and occupied almost entirely with the gaiety of his own appearance in the bridal procession, could not but remark that the hand of his sister was moist, and cold as that of a statue. It is unnecessary further to withdraw the veil from this scene of family distress, nor, although it occurred more than a hundred years since, might it be altogether agreeable to the representatives of the families concerned in the narrative. It may be proper to say that the events alone are imitated; but I had neither the means nor intention of copying the manners, or tracing the characters, of the persons concerned in the real story. Indeed, I may here state generally that, although I have deemed historical personages free subjects of delineation, I have never on any occasion violated the respect due to private life. It was indeed impossible that traits proper to persons, both living and dead, with whom I have had intercourse in society, should not have risen to my pen in such works as Waverley, and those which followed it. But I have always studied to generalize the portraits, so that they should still seem, on the whole, the productions of fancy, though possessing some resemblance to real individuals. Yet I must own my attempts have not in this last particular been uniformly successful. There are men whose characters are so peculiarly marked, that the delineation of some leading and principal feature inevitably places the whole person before you in his individuality. Thus, the character of Jonathan Oldbuck, in the Antiquary, was partly founded on that of an old friend of my youth, to whom I am indebted for introducing me to Shakespeare, and other invaluable favours; but I thought I had so completely disguised the likeness that his features could not be recognized by any one now alive. I was mistaken, however, and indeed had endangered what I desired should be considered as a secret; for I afterwards learned that a highly-respectable gentleman, one of the few surviving friends of my father, and an acute critic, [James Chalmers, Esq., Solicitor at Law, London, who (died during the publication of the present edition of these Novels. Aug. 1831.)] had said, upon the appearance of the work, that he was now convinced who was the author of it, as he recognized in the Antiquary of Monkbarns traces of the character of a very intimate friend of my father's family.

I may here also notice that the sort of exchange of gallantry which is represented as taking place betwixt the Baron of Bradwardine and Colonel Talbot, is a literal fact. The real circumstances of the anecdote, alike honourable to Whig and Tory, are these:—

Alexander Stewart of Invernahyle—a name which I cannot write without the warmest recollections of gratitude to the friend of my childhood, who first introduced me to the Highlands, their traditions, and their manners—had been engaged actively in the troubles of 1745. As he charged at the battle of Preston with his clan, the Stewarts of Appin, he saw an officer of the opposite army standing alone by a battery of four cannon, of which he discharged three on the advancing Highlanders, and then drew his sword. Invernahyle rushed on him, and required him to surrender. "Never to rebels!" was the undaunted reply, accompanied with a lunge, which the Highlander received on his target, but instead of using his sword in cutting down his now defenceless antagonist, he employed it in parrying the blow of a Lochaber axe aimed at the officer by the Miller, one of his own followers, a grim-looking old Highlander, whom I remember to have seen. Thus overpowered, Lieutenant-Colonel Allan Whitefoord, a gentleman of rank and consequence, as well as a brave officer, gave up his sword, and with it his purse and watch, which Invernahyle accepted, to save them from his followers. After the affair was over, Mr. Stewart sought out his prisoner, and they were introduced to each other by the celebrated John Roy Stewart, who acquainted Colonel Whitefoord with the quality of his captor, and made him aware of the necessity of receiving back his property, which he was inclined to leave in the hands into which it had fallen. So great became the confidence established betwixt them, that Invernahyle obtained from the Chevalier his prisoner's freedom upon parole; and soon afterwards, having been sent back to the Highlands to raise men, he visited Colonel Whitefoord at his own house, and spent two happy days with him and his Whig friends, without thinking on either side of the civil war which was then raging.

When the battle of Culloden put an end to the hopes of Charles Edward, Invernahyle, wounded and unable to move, was borne from the field by the faithful zeal of his retainers. But as he had been a distinguished Jacobite, his family and property were exposed to the system of vindictive destruction too generally carried into execution through the country of the insurgents. It was now Colonel Whitefoord's turn to exert himself, and he wearied all the authorities, civil and military, with his solicitations for pardon to the saver of his life, or at least for a protection for his wife and family. His applications were for a long time unsuccessful. "I was found with the mark of the Beast upon me in every list," was Invernahyle's expression. At length Colonel Whitefoord applied to the Duke of Cumberland, and urged his suit with every argument which he could think of, being still repulsed, he took his commission from his bosom, and having said something of his own and his family's exertions in the cause of the House of Hanover, begged to resign his situation in their service, since he could not be permitted to show his gratitude to the person to whom he owed his life. The duke, struck with his earnestness, desired him to take up his commission, and granted the protection required for the family of Invernahyle.

The chieftain himself lay concealed in a cave near his own house, before which a small body of regular soldiers were encamped. He could hear their muster-roll called every morning, and their drums beat to quarters at night, and not a change of the sentinels escaped him. As it was suspected that he was lurking somewhere on the property, his family were closely watched, and compelled to use the utmost precaution in supplying him with food. One of his daughters, a child of eight or ten years old, was employed as the agent least likely to be suspected. She was an instance, among others, that a time of danger and difficulty creates a premature sharpness of intellect. She made herself acquainted among the soldiers, till she became so familiar to them that her motions escaped their notice; and her practice was to stroll away into the neighbourhood of the cave, and leave what slender supply of food she carried for that purpose under some remarkable stone, or the root of some tree, where her father might find it as he crept by night from his lurking-place. Times became milder, and my excellent friend was relieved from proscription by the Act of Indemnity. Such is the interesting story which I have rather injured than improved by the manner in which it is told in Waverley.

This incident, with several other circumstances illustrating the Tales in question, was communicated by me to my late lamented friend, William Erskine (a Scottish judge, by the title of Lord Kinedder), who afterwards reviewed with far too much partiality the Tales of my Landlord, for the Quarterly Review of January 1817. [Lord Kinedder died in August 1822. EHEU! (Aug. 1831.)] In the same article are contained other illustrations of the Novels, with which I supplied my accomplished friend, who took the trouble to write the review. The reader who is desirous of such information will find the original of Meg Merrilies, and, I believe, of one or two other personages of the same cast of character, in the article referred to.

I may also mention that the tragic and savage circumstances which are represented as preceding the birth of Allan MacAulay in the Legend of Montrose, really happened in the family of Stewart of Ardvoirlich. The wager about the candlesticks, whose place was supplied by Highland torch-bearers, was laid and won by one of the MacDonalds of Keppoch.

There can be but little amusement in winnowing out the few grains of truth which are contained in this mass of empty fiction. I may, however, before dismissing the subject, allude to the various localities which have been affixed to some of the scenery introduced into these Novels, by which, for example, Wolf's Hope is identified with Fast Castle in Berwickshire, Tillietudlem with Draphane in Clydesdale, and the valley in the Monastery, called Glendearg, with the dale of the river Allan, above Lord Somerville's villa, near Melrose. I can only say that, in these and other instances, I had no purpose of describing any particular local spot; and the resemblance must therefore be of that general kind which necessarily exists between scenes of the same character. The iron-bound coast of Scotland affords upon its headlands and promontories fifty such castles as Wolf's Hope; every county has a valley more or less resembling Glendearg; and if castles like Tillietudlem, or mansions like the Baron of Bradwardine's, are now less frequently to be met with, it is owing to the rage of indiscriminate destruction, which has removed or ruined so many monuments of antiquity, when they were not protected by their inaccessible situation. [I would particularly intimate the Kaim of Uric, on the eastern coast of Scotland, as having suggested an idea for the tower called Wolf's Crag, which the public more generally identified with the ancient tower of Fast Castle.]

The scraps of poetry which have been in most cases tacked to the beginning of chapters in these Novels are sometimes quoted either from reading or from memory, but, in the general case, are pure invention. I found it too troublesome to turn to the collection of the British Poets to discover apposite mottoes, and, in the situation of the theatrical mechanist, who, when the white paper which represented his shower of snow was exhausted, continued the storm by snowing brown, I drew on my memory as long as I could, and when that failed, eked it out with invention. I believe that in some cases, where actual names are affixed to the supposed quotations, it would be to little purpose to seek them in the works of the authors referred to. In some cases I have been entertained when Dr. Watts and other graver authors have been ransacked in vain for stanzas for which the novelist alone was responsible.

And now the reader may expect me, while in the confessional, to explain the motives why I have so long persisted in disclaiming the works of which I am now writing. To this it would be difficult to give any other reply, save that of Corporal Nym—it was the author's humour or caprice for the time. I hope it will not be construed into ingratitude to the public, to whose indulgence I have owed my SANG-FROID much more than to any merit of my own, if I confess that I am, and have been, more indifferent to success or to failure as an author, than may be the case with others, who feel more strongly the passion for literary fame, probably because they are justly conscious of a better title to it. It was not until I had attained the age of thirty years that I made any serious attempt at distinguishing myself as an author; and at that period men's hopes, desires, and wishes have usually acquired something of a decisive character, and are not eagerly and easily diverted into a new channel. When I made the discovery—for to me it was one—that by amusing myself with composition, which I felt a delightful occupation, I could also give pleasure to others, and became aware that literary pursuits were likely to engage in future a considerable portion of my time, I felt some alarm that I might acquire those habits of jealousy and fretfulness which have lessened, and even degraded, the character even of great authors, and rendered them, by their petty squabbles and mutual irritability, the laughing-stock of the people of the world. I resolved, therefore, in this respect to guard my breast—perhaps an unfriendly critic may add, my brow—with triple brass, [Not altogether impossible, when it is considered that I have been at the bar since 1792. (Aug. 1831.)] and as much as possible to avoid resting my thoughts and wishes upon literary success, lest I should endanger my own peace of mind and tranquillity by literary failure. It would argue either stupid apathy or ridiculous affectation to say that I have been insensible to the public applause, when I have been honoured with its testimonies; and still more highly do I prize the invaluable friendships which some temporary popularity has enabled me to form among those of my contemporaries most distinguished by talents and genius, and which I venture to hope now rest upon a basis more firm than the circumstances which gave rise to them. Yet, feeling all these advantages as a man ought to do, and must do, I may say, with truth and confidence, that I have, I think, tasted of the intoxicating cup with moderation, and that I have never, either in conversation or correspondence, encouraged discussions respecting my own literary pursuits. On the contrary, I have usually found such topics, even when introduced from motives most flattering to myself, Rather embarrassing and disagreeable.

I have now frankly told my motives for concealment, so far as I am conscious of having any, and the public will forgive the egotism of the detail, as what is necessarily connected with it. The author, so long and loudly called for, has appeared on the stage, and made his obeisance to the audience. Thus far his conduct is a mark of respect. To linger in their presence would be intrusion.

I have only to repeat that I avow myself in print, as formerly in words, the sole and unassisted author of all the Novels published as works of "The Author of Waverley." I do this without shame, for I am unconscious that there is any thing in their composition which deserves reproach, either on the score of religion or morality; and without any feeling of exultation, because, whatever may have been their temporary success, I am well aware how much their reputation depends upon the caprice of fashion; and I have already mentioned the precarious tenure by which it is held, as a reason for displaying no great avidity in grasping at the possession.

I ought to mention, before concluding, that twenty persons, at least, were, either from intimacy, or from the confidence which circumstances rendered necessary, participant of this secret; and as there was no instance, to my knowledge, of any one of the number breaking faith, I am the more obliged to them, because the slight and trivial character of the mystery was not qualified to inspire much respect in those entrusted with it. Nevertheless, like Jack the Giant-Killer, I was fully confident in the advantage of my "Coat of Darkness;" and had it not been from compulsory circumstances, I would have, indeed, been very cautious how I parted with it.

As for the work which follows, it was meditated, and in part printed, long before the avowal of the novels took place, and originally commenced with a declaration that it was neither to have introduction nor preface of any kind. This long proem, prefixed to a work intended not to have any, may, however, serve to show how human purposes in the most trifling, as well as the most important affairs, are liable to be controlled by the course of events. Thus we begin to cross a strong river with our eyes and our resolution fixed on that point of the opposite shore on which we purpose to land; but gradually giving way to the torrent, are glad, by the aid perhaps of branch or bush, to extricate ourselves at some distant and perhaps dangerous landing-place, much farther down the stream than that on which we had fixed our intentions.

Hoping that the Courteous Reader will afford to a known and familiar acquaintance some portion of the favour which he extended to a disguised candidate for his applause, I beg leave to subscribe myself his obliged humble servant,

WALTER SCOTT. ABBOTSFORD, OCTOBER 1, 1827.

Such was the little narrative which I thought proper to put forth in October 1827; nor have I much to add to it now. About to appear for the first time in my own name in this department of letters, it occurred to me that something in the shape of a periodical publication might carry with it a certain air of novelty, and I was willing to break, if I may so express it, the abruptness of my personal forthcoming, by investing an imaginary coadjutor with at least as much distinctness of individual existence as I had ever previously thought it worth while to bestow on shadows of the same convenient tribe. Of course, it had never been in my contemplation to invite the assistance of any real person in the sustaining of my quasi-editorial character and labours. It had long been my opinion, that any thing like a literary PICNIC is likely to end in suggesting comparisons, justly termed odious, and therefore to be avoided; and, indeed, I had also had some occasion to know, that promises of assistance, in efforts of that order, are apt to be more magnificent than the subsequent performance. I therefore planned a Miscellany, to be dependent, after the old fashion, on my own resources alone, and although conscious enough that the moment which assigned to the Author of Waverley "a local habitation and a name," had seriously endangered his spell, I felt inclined to adopt the sentiment of my old hero Montrose, and to say to myself, that in literature, as in war,—

"He either fears his fate too much,
  Or his deserts are small,
    Who dares not put it to the touch,
      To win or lose it all."

To the particulars explanatory of the plan of these Chronicles, which the reader is presented with in Chapter II. by the imaginary Editor, Mr. Croftangry, I have now to add, that the lady, termed in his narrative, Mrs. Bethune Balliol, was designed to shadow out in its leading points the interesting character of a dear friend of mine, Mrs. Murray Keith, whose death occurring shortly before, had saddened a wide circle, much attached to her, as well for her genuine virtue and amiable qualities of disposition, as for the extent of information which she possessed, and the delightful manner in which she was used to communicate it. In truth, the author had, on many occasions, been indebted to her vivid memory for the SUBSTRATUM of his Scottish fictions, and she accordingly had been, from an early period, at no loss to fix the Waverley Novels on the right culprit.

[The Keiths of Craig, in Kincardineshire, descended from John Keith, fourth son of William, second Earl Marischal, who got from his father, about 1480, the lands of Craig, and part of Garvock, in that county. In Douglas's Baronage, 443 to 445, is a pedigree of that family. Colonel Robert Keith of Craig (the seventh in descent from John) by his wife, Agnes, daughter of Robert Murray of Murrayshall, of the family of Blackbarony, widow of Colonel Stirling, of the family of Keir, had one son—namely Robert Keith of Craig, ambassador to the court of Vienna, afterwards to St. Petersburgh, which latter situation he held at the accession of King George III.—who died at Edinburgh in 1774. He married Margaret, second daughter of Sir William Cunningham of Caprington, by Janet, only child and heiress of Sir James Dick of Prestonfield; and, among other children of this marriage were the late well-known diplomatist, Sir Robert Murray Keith, K.B., a general in the army, and for some time ambassador at Vienna; Sir Basil Keith, Knight, captain in the navy, who died Governor of Jamaica; and my excellent friend, Anne Murray Keith, who ultimately came into possession of the family estates, and died not long before the date of this Introduction (1831).]

In the sketch of Chrystal Croftangry's own history, the author has been accused of introducing some not polite allusions to respectable living individuals; but he may safely, he presumes, pass over such an insinuation. The first of the narratives which Mr. Croftangry proceeds to lay before the public, "The Highland Widow," was derived from Mrs. Murray Keith, and is given, with the exception of a few additional circumstances— the introduction of which I am rather inclined to regret—very much as the excellent old lady used to tell the story. Neither the Highland cicerone Macturk nor the demure washingwoman, were drawn from imagination; and on re-reading my tale, after the lapse of a few years, and comparing its effect with my remembrance of my worthy friend's oral narration, which was certainly extremely affecting, I cannot but suspect myself of having marred its simplicity by some of those interpolations, which, at the time when I penned them, no doubt passed with myself for embellishments.

The next tale, entitled "The Two Drovers," I learned from another old friend, the late George Constable, Esq. of Wallace-Craigie, near Dundee, whom I have already introduced to my reader as the original Antiquary of Monkbarns. He had been present, I think, at the trial at Carlisle, and seldom mentioned the venerable judges charge to the jury, without shedding tears,—which had peculiar pathos, as flowing down features, carrying rather a sarcastic or almost a cynical expression.

This worthy gentleman's reputation for shrewd Scottish sense, knowledge of our national antiquities, and a racy humour peculiar to himself, must be still remembered. For myself, I have pride in recording that for many years we were, in Wordsworth's language,—

"A pair of friends, though I was young,
And 'George' was seventy-two."

W. S. ABBOTSFORD, AUG. 15, 1831.

APPENDIX TO INTRODUCTION.

[It has been suggested to the Author that it might be well to reprint here a detailed account of the public dinner alluded to in the foregoing Introduction, as given in the newspapers of the time; and the reader is accordingly presented with the following extract from the EDINBURGH WEEKLY JOURNAL for Wednesday, 28th February, 1827.]

THE THEATRICAL FUND DINNER.

Before proceeding with our account of this very interesting festival—for so it may be termed—it is our duty to present to our readers the following letter, which we have received from the President:—

TO THE EDITOR OF THE "EDINBURGH WEEKLY JOURNAL."

Sir,—I am extremely sorry I have not leisure to correct the copy you sent me of what I am stated to have said at the dinner for the Theatrical Fund. I am no orator, and upon such occasions as are alluded to, I say as well as I can what the time requires.

However, I hope your reporter has been more accurate in other instances than in mine. I have corrected one passage, in which I am made to speak with great impropriety and petulance, respecting the opinions of those who do not approve of dramatic entertainments. I have restored what I said, which was meant to be respectful, as every objection founded in conscience is, in my opinion, entitled to be so treated. Other errors I left as I found them, it being of little consequence whether I spoke sense or nonsense in what was merely intended for the purpose of the hour.

I am, sir,

Your obedient servant,

EDINBURGH, MONDAY. WALTER SCOTT.

The Theatrical Fund Dinner, which took place on Friday, in the Assembly Rooms, was conducted with admirable spirit. The Chairman, Sir WALTER SCOTT, among his other great qualifications, is well fitted to enliven such an entertainment. His manners are extremely easy, and his style of speaking simple and natural, yet full of vivacity and point; and he has the art, if it be art, of relaxing into a certain homeliness of manner, without losing one particle of his dignity. He thus takes off some of that solemn formality which belongs to such meetings, and, by his easy, and graceful familiarity, imparts to them somewhat of the pleasing character of a private entertainment. Near Sir W. Scott sat the Earl of Fife, Lord Meadowbank, Sir John Hope of Pinkie, Bart., Admiral Adam, Baron Clerk Rattray, Gilbert Innes, Esq., James Walker, Esq., Robert Dundas, Esq., Alexander Smith, Esq., etc.

The cloth being removed, "Non nobis, Domine," was sung by Messrs. Thorne, Swift, Collier, and Hartley, after which the following toasts were given from the chair:—

"The King"—all the honours.

"The Duke of Clarence and the Royal Family."

The CHAIRMAN, in proposing the next toast, which he wished to be drunk in solemn silence, said it was to the memory of a regretted-prince, whom we had lately lost. Every individual would at once conjecture to whom he alluded. He had no intention to dwell on his military merits. They had been told in the senate; they had been repeated in the cottage; and whenever a soldier was the theme, his name was never far distant. But it was chiefly in connection with the business of this meeting, which his late Royal Highness had condescended in a particular manner to patronize, that they were called on to drink his health. To that charity he had often sacrificed his time, and had given up the little leisure which he had from important business. He was always ready to attend on every occasion of this kind, and it was in that view that he proposed to drink to the memory of his late Royal Highness the Duke of York.—Drunk in solemn silence.

The CHAIRMAN then requested that gentlemen would fill a bumper as full as it would hold, while he would say only a few words. He was in the habit of hearing speeches, and he knew the feeling with which long ones were regarded. He was sure that it was perfectly unnecessary for him to enter into any vindication of the dramatic art, which they had come here to support. This, however, he considered to be the proper time and proper occasion for him to say a few words on that love of representation which was an innate feeling in human nature. It was the first amusement that the child had. It grew greater as he grew up; and even in the decline of life nothing amuses so much as when a common tale is told with appropriate personification. The first thing a child does is to ape his schoolmaster by flogging a chair. The assuming a character ourselves, or the seeing others assume an imaginary character, is an enjoyment natural to humanity. It was implanted in our very nature to take pleasure from such representations, at proper times and on proper occasions. In all ages the theatrical art had kept pace with the improvement of mankind, and with the progress of letters and the fine arts. As man has advanced from the ruder stages of society, the love of dramatic representations has increased, and all works of this nature have been improved in character and in structure. They had only to turn their eyes to the history of ancient Greece, although he did not pretend to be very deeply versed in its ancient drama. Its first tragic poet commanded a body of troops at the battle of Marathon. Sophocles and Euripides were men of rank in Athens when Athens was in its highest renown. They shook Athens with their discourses, as their theatrical works shook the theatre itself. If they turned to France in the time of Louis the Fourteenth—that era which is the classical history of that country—they would find that it was referred to by all Frenchmen as the golden age of the drama there. And also in England in the time of Queen Elizabeth the drama was at its highest pitch, when the nation began to mingle deeply and wisely in the general politics of Europe, not only not receiving laws from others, but giving laws to the world, and vindicating the rights of mankind. (Cheers.) There have been various times when the dramatic art subsequently fell into disrepute. Its professors have been stigmatized, and laws have been passed against them, less dishonourable to them than to the statesmen by whom they were proposed, and to the legislators by whom they were adopted. What were the times in which these laws were passed? Was it not when virtue was seldom inculcated as a moral duty that we were required to relinquish the most rational of all our amusements, when the clergy were enjoined celibacy, and when the laity were denied the right to read their Bibles? He thought that it must have been from a notion of penance that they erected the drama into an ideal place of profaneness, and spoke of the theatre as of the tents of sin. He did not mean to dispute that there were many excellent persons who thought differently from him, and he disclaimed the slightest idea of charging them with bigotry or hypocrisy on that account. He gave them full credit for their tender consciences, in making these objections, although they did not appear relevant to him. But to these persons, being, as he believed them, men of worth and piety, he was sure the purpose of this meeting would furnish some apology for an error, if there be any, in the opinions of those who attend. They would approve the gift, although they might differ in other points. Such might not approve of going to the theatre, but at least could not deny that they might give away from their superfluity what was required for the relief of the sick, the support of the aged, and the comfort of the afflicted. These were duties enjoined by our religion itself. (Loud cheers.)

The performers are in a particular manner entitled to the support or regard, when in old age or distress, of those who have partaken of the amusements of those places which they render an ornament to society. Their art was of a peculiarly delicate and precarious nature. They had to serve a long apprenticeship. It was very long before even the first-rate geniuses could acquire the mechanical knowledge of the stage business. They must languish long in obscurity before they can avail themselves of their natural talents; and after that they have but a short space of time, during which they are fortunate if they can provide the means of comfort in the decline of life. That comes late, and lasts but a short time; after which they are left dependent. Their limbs fail—their teeth are loosened—their voice is lost and they are left, after giving happiness to others, in a most disconsolate state. The public were liberal and generous to those deserving their protection. It was a sad thing to be dependent on the favour, or, he might say, in plain terms, on the caprice, of the public; and this more particularly for a class of persons of whom extreme prudence is not the character. There might be instances of opportunities being neglected. But let each gentleman tax himself, and consider the opportunities THEY had neglected, and the sums of money THEY had wasted; let every gentleman look into his own bosom, and say whether these were circumstances which would soften his own feelings, were he to be plunged into distress. He put it to every generous bosom—to every better feeling—to say what consolation was it to old age to be told that you might have made provision at a time which had been neglected—(loud cheers)—and to find it objected, that if you had pleased you might have been wealthy. He had hitherto been speaking of what, in theatrical language, was called STARS; but they were sometimes falling ones. There was another class of sufferers naturally and necessarily connected with the theatre, without whom it was impossible to go on. The sailors have a saying, Every man cannot be a boatswain. If there must be a great actor to act Hamlet, there must also be people to act Laertes, the King, Rosencrantz, and Guildenstern, otherwise a drama cannot go on. If even Garrick himself were to rise from the dead, he could not act Hamlet alone. There must be generals, colonels, commanding-officers, subalterns. But what are the private soldiers to do? Many have mistaken their own talents, and have been driven in early youth to try the stage, to which they are not competent. He would know what to say to the indifferent poet and to the bad artist. He would say that it was foolish, and he would recommend to the poet to become a scribe, and the artist to paint sign-posts. (Loud laughter.) But you could not send the player adrift; for if he cannot play Hamlet, he must play Guildenstern. Where there are many labourers, wages must be low and no man in such a situation can decently support a wife and family, and save something off his income for old age. What is this man to do in later life? Are you to cast him off like an old hinge, or a piece of useless machinery, which has done its work? To a person who had contributed to our amusement, this would be unkind, ungrateful, and unchristian. His wants are not of his own making, but arise from the natural sources of sickness and old age. It cannot be denied that there is one class of sufferers to whom no imprudence can be ascribed, except on first entering on the profession. After putting his hand to the dramatic plough, he cannot draw back, but must continue at it, and toil, till death release him from want, or charity, by its milder influence, steps in to render that want more tolerable. He had little more to say, except that he sincerely hoped that the collection to-day, from the number of respectable gentlemen present, would meet the views entertained by the patrons. He hoped it would do so. They should not be disheartened. Though they could not do a great deal, they might do something. They had this consolation, that everything they parted with from their superfluity would do some good. They would sleep the better themselves when they had been the means of giving sleep to others. It was ungrateful and unkind that those who had sacrificed their youth to our amusement should not receive the reward due to them, but should be reduced to hard fare in their old age. We cannot think of poor Falstaff going to bed without his cup of sack, or Macbeth fed on bones as marrowless as those of Banquo. (Loud cheers and laughter.) As he believed that they were all as fond of the dramatic art as he was in his younger days, he would propose that they should drink "The Theatrical Fund," with three times three.

Mr. MACKAY rose, on behalf of his brethren, to return their thanks for the toast just drunk. Many of the gentlemen present, he said, were perhaps not fully acquainted with the nature and intention of the institution, and it might not be amiss to enter into some explanation on the subject. With whomsoever the idea of a Theatrical Fund might have originated (and it had been disputed by the surviving relatives of two or three individuals), certain it was that the first legally constituted Theatrical Fund owed its origin to one of the brightest ornaments of the profession, the late David Garrick. That eminent actor conceived that, by a weekly subscription in the theatre, a fund might be raised among its members, from which a portion might be given to those of his less fortunate brethren, and thus an opportunity would be offered for prudence to provide what fortune had denied—a comfortable provision for the winter of life. With the welfare of his profession constantly at heart, the zeal with which he laboured to uphold its respectability, and to impress upon the minds or his brethren, not only the necessity, but the blessing of independence, the Fund became his peculiar care. He drew up a form of laws for its government, procured at his own expense the passing of an Act of Parliament for its confirmation, bequeathed to it a handsome legacy, and thus became the father of the Drury Lane Fund. So constant was his attachment to this infant establishment, that he chose to grace the close of the brightest theatrical life on record by the last display of his transcendent talent on the occasion of a benefit for this child of his adoption, which ever since has gone by the name of the Garrick Fund. In imitation of his noble example, funds had been established in several provincial theatres in England; but it remained for Mrs. Henry Siddons and Mr. William Murray to become the founders of the first Theatrical Fund in Scotland. (Cheers.) This Fund commenced under the most favourable auspices. It was liberally supported by the management, and highly patronized by the public. Notwithstanding, it fell short in the accomplishment of its intentions. What those intentions were, he (Mr. Mackay) need not recapitulate, but they failed; and he did not hesitate to confess that a want of energy on the part of the performers was the probable cause. A new set of Rules and Regulations were lately drawn up, submitted to and approved of at a general meeting of the members of the Theatre, and accordingly the Fund was remodelled on the 1st of January last. And here he thought he did but echo the feelings of his brethren, by publicly acknowledging the obligations they were under to the management for the aid given and the warm interest they had all along taken in the welfare of the Fund. (Cheers.) The nature and object of the profession had been so well treated of by the President that he would say nothing; but of the numerous offspring of science and genius that court precarious fame, the actor boasts the slenderest claim of all—the sport of fortune, the creatures of fashion, and the victims of caprice, they are seen, heard, and admired, but to be forgot. They leave no trace, no memorial of their existence—they "come like shadows, so depart." (Cheers.) Yet humble though their pretensions be, there was no profession, trade, or calling where such a combination of requisites, mental and bodily, were indispensable. In all others the principal may practise after he has been visited by the afflicting hand of Providence—some by the loss of limb, some of voice, and many, when the faculty of the mind is on the wane, may be assisted by dutiful children or devoted servants. Not so the actor, He must retain all he ever did possess, or sink dejected to a mournful home. (Applause.) Yet while they are toiling for ephemeral theatric fame, how very few ever possess the means of hoarding in their youth that which would give bread in old age! But now a brighter prospect dawned upon them, and to the success of this their infant establishment they looked with hope, as to a comfortable and peaceful home in their declining years. He concluded by tendering to the meeting, in the name of his brethren and sisters, their unfeigned thanks for their liberal support, and begged to propose "The Health of the Patrons of the Edinburgh Theatrical Fund." (Cheers.)

Lord MEADOWBANK said that, by desire of his Hon. Friend in the chair, and of his Noble Friend at his right hand, he begged leave to return thanks for the honour which had been conferred on the Patrons of this excellent institution. He could answer for himself—he could answer for them all—that they were deeply impressed with the meritorious objects which it has in view, and of their anxious wish to promote its interests. For himself, he hoped he might be permitted to say that he was rather surprised at finding his own name as one of the Patrons, associated with so many individuals of high rank and powerful influence. But it was an excuse for those who had placed him in a situation so honourable and so distinguished, that when this charity was instituted he happened to hold a high and responsible station under the Crown, when he might have been of use in assisting and promoting its objects. His Lordship much feared that he could have little expectation, situated as he now was, of doing either; but he could confidently assert that few things would give him greater gratification than being able to contribute to its prosperity and support. And indeed, when one recollects the pleasure which at all periods of life he has received from the exhibitions of the stage, and the exertions of the meritorious individuals for whose aid this Fund has been established, he must be divested both of gratitude and feeling who would not give his best endeavours to promote its welfare. And now, that he might in some measure repay the gratification which had been afforded himself, he would beg leave to propose a toast, the health of one of the Patrons, a great and distinguished individual, whose name must always stand by itself, and which, in an assembly such as this, or in any other assembly of Scotsmen, can never be received, not, he would say, with ordinary feelings of pleasure or of delight, but with those of rapture and enthusiasm. In doing so he felt that he stood in a somewhat new situation. Whoever had been called upon to propose the health of his Hon. Friend to whom he alluded, some time ago, would have found himself enabled, from the mystery in which certain matters were involved, to gratify himself and his auditors by allusions which found a responding chord in their own feelings, and to deal in the language, the sincere language, of panegyric, without intruding on the modesty of the great individual to whom he referred. But it was no longer possible, consistently with the respect to one's auditors, to use upon this subject terms either of mystification or of obscure or indirect allusion. The clouds have been dispelled; the DARKNESS VISIBLE has been cleared away; and the Great Unknown—the minstrel of our native land—the mighty magician who has rolled back the current of time, and conjured up before our living senses the men and the manners of days which have long passed away—stands revealed to the hearts and the eyes of his affectionate and admiring countrymen. If he himself were capable of imagining all that belonged to this mighty subject—were he even able to give utterance to all that, as a friend, as a man, and as a Scotsman, he must feel regarding it—yet knowing, as he well did, that this illustrious individual was not more distinguished for his towering talents than for those feelings which rendered such allusions ungrateful to himself, however sparingly introduced, he would, on that account, still refrain from doing that which would otherwise be no less pleasing to him than to his audience. But this his Lordship, hoped he would be allowed to say (his auditors would not pardon him were he to say less), we owe to him, as a people, a large and heavy debt of gratitude. He it is who has opened to foreigners the grand and characteristic beauties of our country. It is to him that we owe that our gallant ancestors and the struggles of our illustrious patriots—who fought and bled in order to obtain and secure that independence and that liberty we now enjoy—have obtained a fame no longer confined to the boundaries of a remote and comparatively obscure nation, and who has called down upon their struggles for glory and freedom the admiration of foreign countries. He it is who has conferred a new reputation on our national character, and bestowed on Scotland an imperishable name, were it only by her having given birth to himself. (Loud and rapturous applause.)

Sir WALTER SCOTT certainly did not think that, in coming here to-day, he would have the task of acknowledging, before three hundred gentlemen, a secret which, considering that it was communicated to more than twenty people, had been remarkably well kept. He was now before the bar of his country, and might be understood to be on trial before Lord Meadowbank as an offender; yet he was sure that every impartial jury would bring in a verdict of Not Proven. He did not now think it necessary to enter into the reasons of his long silence. Perhaps caprice might have a considerable share in it. He had now to say, however, that the merits of these works, if they had any, and their faults, were entirely imputable to himself. (Long and loud cheering.) He was afraid to think on what he had done. "Look on't again I dare not." He had thus far unbosomed himself and he knew that it would be reported to the public. He meant, then, seriously to state, that when he said he was the author, he was the total and undivided author. With the exception of quotations, there was not a single word that was not derived from himself, or suggested in the course of his reading. The wand was now broken, and the book buried. You will allow me further to say, with Prospero, it is your breath that has filled my sails, and to crave one single toast in the capacity of the author of these novels; and he would dedicate a bumper to the health of one who has represented some of those characters, of which he had endeavoured to give the skeleton, with a degree of liveliness which rendered him grateful. He would propose "The Health of his friend Bailie Nicol Jarvie"—(loud applause)—and he was sure that when the author of Waverley and Rob Roy drinks to Nicol Jarvie, it would be received with that degree of applause to which that gentleman has always been accustomed, and that they would take care that on the present occasion it should be PRODIGIOUS! (Long and vehement applause.)

Mr. MACKAY, who here spoke with great humour in the character of Bailie Jarvie.—My conscience! My worthy father the deacon could not have believed that his son could hae had sic a compliment paid to him by the Great Unknown!

Sir WALTER SCOTT.—The Small Known now, Mr. Bailie.

Mr. MACKAY.—He had been long identified with the Bailie, and he was vain of the cognomen which he had now worn for eight years; and he questioned if any of his brethren in the Council had given such universal satisfaction. (Loud laughter and applause.) Before he sat down, he begged to propose "The Lord Provost and the City of Edinburgh."

Sir WALTER SCOTT apologized for the absence of the Lord Provost, who had gone to London on public business.

Tune—"Within a mile of Edinburgh town."

Sir WALTER SCOTT gave "The Duke of Wellington and the army."

Glee—"How merrily we live."

"Lord Melville and the Navy, that fought till they left nobody to fight with, like an arch sportsman who clears all and goes after the game."

Mr. PAT. ROBERTSON.—They had heard this evening a toast, which had been received with intense delight, which will be published in every newspaper, and will be hailed with joy by all Europe. He had one toast assigned him which he had great pleasure in giving. He was sure that the stage had in all ages a great effect on the morals and manners of the people. It was very desirable that the stage should be well regulated; and there was no criterion by which its regulation could be better determined than by the moral character and personal respectability of the performers. He was not one of those stern moralists who objected to the theatre. The most fastidious moralist could not possibly apprehend any injury from the stage of Edinburgh, as it was presently managed, and so long as it was adorned by that illustrious individual, Mrs. Henry Siddons, whose public exhibitions were not more remarkable for feminine grace and delicacy than was her private character for every virtue which could be admired in domestic life. He would conclude with reciting a few words from Shakespeare, in a spirit not of contradiction to those stern moralists who disliked the theatre, but of meekness: "Good, my lord, will you see the players well bestowed? Do you hear, let them be well used, for they are the abstract and brief chronicles of the time." He then gave "Mrs. Henry Siddons, and success to the Theatre Royal of Edinburgh."

Mr. MURRAY.—Gentlemen, I rise to return thanks for the honour you have done Mrs. Siddons, in doing which I am somewhat difficulted, from the extreme delicacy which attends a brother's expatiating upon a sister's claims to honours publicly paid—(hear, hear)—yet, gentlemen, your kindness emboldens me to say that, were I to give utterance to all a brother's feelings, I should not exaggerate those claims. (Loud applause.) I therefore, gentlemen, thank you most cordially for the honour you have done her, and shall now request permission to make an observation on the establishment of the Edinburgh Theatrical Fund. Mr. Mackay has done Mrs. Henry Siddons and myself the honour to ascribe the establishment to us. But no, gentlemen, it owes its origin to a higher source—the publication of the novel of Rob Roy—the unprecedented success of the opera adapted from that popular production. (Hear, hear.) It was that success which relieved the Edinburgh Theatre from its difficulties, and enabled Mrs. Siddons to carry into effect the establishment of a fund she had long desired, but was prevented from effecting from the unsettled state of her theatrical concerns. I therefore hope that in future years, when the aged and infirm actor derives relief from this fund, he will, in the language of the gallant Highlander, "Cast his eye to good old Scotland, and not forget Rob Roy." (Loud applause.)

Sir WALTER SCOTT here stated that Mrs. Siddons wanted the means but not the will of beginning the Theatrical Fund. He here alluded to the great merits of Mr. Murray's management, and to his merits as an actor, which were of the first order, and of which every person who attends the Theatre must be sensible; and after alluding to the embarrassments with which the Theatre had been at one period threatened, he concluded by giving "The Health of Mr. Murray," which was drunk with three times three.

Mr. MURRAY.—Gentlemen, I wish I could believe that in any degree I merited the compliments with which it has pleased Sir Walter Scott to preface the proposal of my health, or the very flattering manner in which you have done me the honour to receive it. The approbation of such an assembly is most gratifying to me, and might encourage feelings of vanity, were not such feelings crushed by my conviction that no man holding the situation I have so long held in Edinburgh could have failed, placed in the peculiar circumstances in which I have been placed. Gentlemen, I shall not insult your good taste by eulogiums upon your judgment or kindly feeling, though to the first I owe any improvement I may have made as an actor, and certainly my success as a manager to the second. (Applause.) When, upon the death of my dear brother, the late Mr. Siddons, it was proposed that I should undertake the management of the Edinburgh Theatre, I confess I drew back, doubting my capability to free it from the load of debt and difficulty with which it was surrounded. In this state of anxiety, I solicited the advice of one who had ever honoured me with his kindest regard, and whose name no member of my profession can pronounce without feelings of the deepest respect and gratitude. I allude to the late Mr. John Kemble. (Great applause.) To him I applied, and with the repetition of his advice I shall cease to trespass upon your time—(hear, hear)—"My dear William, fear not. Integrity and assiduity must prove an overmatch for all difficulty; and though I approve your not indulging a vain confidence in your own ability, and viewing with respectful apprehension the judgment of the audience you have to act before, yet be assured that judgment will ever be tempered by the feeling that you are acting for the widow and the fatherless." (Loud applause.) Gentlemen, those words have never passed from my mind; and I feel convinced that you have pardoned my many errors, from the feeling that I was striving for the widow and the fatherless. (Long and enthusiastic applause followed Mr. Murray's address.)

Sir WALTER SCOTT gave "The Health of the Stewards."

Mr. VANDENHOFF.—Mr. President and Gentlemen, the honour conferred upon the Stewards, in the very flattering compliment you have just paid us, calls forth our warmest acknowledgments. In tendering you our thanks for the approbation you have been pleased to express of our humble exertions, I would beg leave to advert to the cause in which we have been engaged. Yet, surrounded as I am by the genius—the eloquence—of this enlightened city, I cannot but feel the presumption which ventures to address you on so interesting a subject. Accustomed to speak in the language of others, I feel quite at a loss for terms wherein to clothe the sentiments excited by the present occasion. (Applause.) The nature of the institution which has sought your fostering patronage, and the objects which it contemplates, have been fully explained to you. But, gentlemen, the relief which it proposes is not a gratuitous relief, but to be purchased by the individual contribution of its members towards the general good. This Fund lends no encouragement to idleness or improvidence, but it offers an opportunity to prudence in vigour and youth to make provision against the evening of life and its attendant infirmity. A period is fixed at which we admit the plea of age as an exemption from professional labour. It is painful to behold the veteran on the stage (compelled by necessity) contending against physical decay, mocking the joyousness of mirth with the feebleness of age, when the energies decline, when the memory fails! and "the big, manly voice, turning again towards childish treble, pipes and whistles in the sound." We would remove him from the mimic scene, where fiction constitutes the charm; we would not view old age caricaturing itself. (Applause.) But as our means may be found, in time of need, inadequate to the fulfilment of our wishes—fearful of raising expectations which we may be unable to gratify—desirous not "to keep the word of promise to the ear, and break it to the hope"—we have presumed to court the assistance of the friends of the drama to strengthen our infant institution. Our appeal has been successful beyond our most sanguine expectations. The distinguished patronage conferred on us by your presence on this occasion, and the substantial support which your benevolence has so liberally afforded to our institution, must impress every member of the Fund with the most grateful sentiments—sentiments which no language can express, no time obliterate. (Applause.) I will not trespass longer on your attention. I would the task of acknowledging our obligation had fallen into abler hands. (Hear, hear.) In the name of the Stewards, I most respectfully and cordially thank you for the honour you have done us, which greatly overpays our poor endeavours. (Applause.)

[This speech, though rather inadequately reported, was one of the best delivered on this occasion. That it was creditable to Mr. Vandenhoff's taste and feelings, the preceding sketch will show; but how much it was so, it does not show.]

Mr. J. CAY gave "Professor Wilson and the University of Edinburgh, of which he was one of the brightest ornaments."

Lord MEADOWBANK, after a suitable eulogium, gave "The Earl of Fife," which was drunk with three times three.

Earl FIFE expressed his high gratification at the honour conferred on him. He intimated his approbation of the institution, and his readiness to promote its success by every means in his power. He concluded with giving "The Health of the Company of Edinburgh."

Mr. JONES, on rising to return thanks, being received with considerable applause, said he was truly grateful for the kind encouragement he had experienced, but the novelty of the situation in which he now was renewed all the feelings he experienced when he first saw himself announced in the bills as a young gentleman, being his first appearance on any stage. (Laughter and applause.) Although in the presence of those whose indulgence had, in another sphere, so often shielded him from the penalties of inability, he was unable to execute the task which had so unexpectedly devolved upon him in behalf of his brethren and himself. He therefore begged the company to imagine all that grateful hearts could prompt the most eloquent to utter, and that would be a copy of their feelings. (Applause.) He begged to trespass another moment on their attention, for the purpose of expressing the thanks of the members of the Fund to the Gentlemen of the Edinburgh Professional Society of Musicians, who, finding that this meeting was appointed to take place on the same evening with their concert, had, in the handsomest manner, agreed to postpone it. Although it was his duty thus to preface the toast he had to propose, he was certain the meeting required no further inducement than the recollection of the pleasure the exertions of those gentlemen had often afforded them within those walls, to join heartily in drinking "Health and Prosperity to the Edinburgh Professional Society of Musicians." (Applause.)

Mr. PAT. ROBERTSON Proposed "The Health of Mr. Jeffrey," whose absence was owing to indisposition. The public was well aware that he was the most distinguished advocate at the bar. He was likewise distinguished for the kindness, frankness, and cordial manner in which he communicated with the junior members of the profession, to the esteem of whom his splendid talents would always entitle him.

Mr. J. MACONOCHIE gave "The Health of Mrs. Siddons, senior, the most distinguished ornament of the stage."

Sir W. SCOTT said that if anything could reconcile him to old age, it was the reflection that he had seen the rising as well as the setting sun of Mrs. Siddons. He remembered well their breakfasting near to the Theatre—waiting the whole day—the crushing at the doors at six o'clock—and their going in and counting their fingers till seven o'clock. But the very first step—the very first word which she uttered—was sufficient to overpay him for all his labours. The house was literally electrified; and it was only from witnessing the effects of her genius that he could guess to what a pitch theatrical excellence could be carried. Those young gentlemen who have only seen the setting sun of this distinguished performer, beautiful and serene as that was, must give us old fellows, who have seen its rise and its meridian, leave to hold our heads a little higher.

Mr. DUNDAS gave "The Memory of Home, the author of Douglas."

Mr. MACKAY here announced that the subscriptions for the night amounted to L280, and he expressed gratitude for this substantial proof of their kindness. [We are happy to state that subscriptions have since flowed in very liberally.]

Mr. MACKAY here entertained the company with a pathetic song.

Sir WALTER SCOTT apologized for having so long forgotten their native land. He would now give "Scotland, the land of Cakes." He would give every river, every loch, every hill, from Tweed to Johnnie Groat's house—every lass in her cottage and countess in her castle—and may her sons stand by her, as their fathers did before them; and he who would not drink a bumper to his toast, may he never drink whisky more!

Sir WALTER SCOTT here gave "Lord Meadowbank," who returned thanks.

Mr. H. G. BELL said that he should not have ventured to intrude himself upon the attention of the assembly, did he not feel confident that the toast he begged to have the honour to propose would make amends for the very imperfect manner in which he might express his sentiments regarding it. It had been said that, notwithstanding the mental supremacy of the present age—notwithstanding that the page of our history was studded with names destined also for the page of immortality—that the genius of Shakespeare was extinct, and the fountain of his inspiration dried up. It might be that these observations were unfortunately correct, or it might be that we were bewildered with a name, not disappointed of the reality; for though Shakespeare had brought a Hamlet, an Othello, and a Macbeth, an Ariel, a Juliet, and a Rosalind, upon the stage, were there not authors living who had brought as varied, as exquisitely painted, and as undying a range of characters into our hearts? The shape of the mere mould into which genius poured its golden treasures was surely a matter of little moment, let it be called a Tragedy, a Comedy, or a Waverley Novel. But even among the dramatic authors of the present day, he was unwilling to allow that there was a great and palpable decline from the glory of preceding ages, and his toast alone would bear him out in denying the truth of the proposition. After eulogizing the names of Baillie, Byron, Coleridge, Maturin, and others, he begged to have the honour of proposing "The Health of James Sheridan Knowles."

Sir WALTER SCOTT. Gentlemen, I crave a bumper all over. The last toast reminds me of a neglect of duty. Unaccustomed to a public duty of this kind, errors in conducting the ceremonial of it may be excused, and omissions pardoned. Perhaps I have made one or two omissions in the course of the evening for which I trust you will grant me your pardon and indulgence. One thing in particular I have omitted, and I would now wish to make amends for it by a libation of reverence and respect to the memory of SHAKESPEARE. He was a man of universal genius, and from a period soon after his own era to the present day he has been universally idolized. When I come to his honoured name, I am like the sick man who hung up his crutches at the shrine, and was obliged to confess that he did not walk better than before. It is indeed difficult, gentlemen, to compare him to any other individual. The only one to whom I call at all compare him is the wonderful Arabian dervise, who dived into the body of each, and in this way became familiar with the thoughts and secrets of their hearts. He was a man of obscure origin, and, as a player, limited in his acquirements; but he was born evidently with a universal genius. His eyes glanced at all the varied aspects of life, and his fancy portrayed with equal talents the king on the throne and the clown who crackles his chestnuts at a Christmas fire. Whatever note he takes, he strikes it just and true, and awakens a corresponding chord in our own bosoms, Gentlemen, I propose "The Memory of William Shakespeare."

Glee—"Lightly tread, 'tis hallowed ground."

After the glee, Sir WALTER rose and begged to propose as a toast the health of a lady, whose living merit is not a little honourable to Scotland. The toast (said he) is also flattering to the national vanity of a Scotchman, as the lady whom I intend to propose is a native of this country. From the public her works have met with the most favourable reception. One piece of hers, in particular, was often acted here of late years, and gave pleasure of no mean kind to many brilliant and fashionable audiences. In her private character she (he begged leave to say) is as remarkable as in a public sense she is for her genius. In short, he would in one word name—"Joanna Baillie."

This health being drunk, Mr. THORNE was called on for a song, and sung, with great taste and feeling, "The Anchor's Weighed."

W. MENZIES, Esq., Advocate, rose to propose the health of a gentleman for many years connected at intervals with the dramatic art in Scotland. Whether we look at the range of characters he performs, or at the capacity which he evinces in executing those which he undertakes, he is equally to be admired. In all his parts he is unrivalled. The individual to whom he alluded is (said he) well known to the gentlemen present, in the characters of Malvolio, Lord Ogleby, and the Green Man; and in addition to his other qualities, he merits, for his perfection in these characters, the grateful sense of this meeting. He would wish, in the first place, to drink his health as an actor. But he was not less estimable in domestic life, and as a private gentleman; and when he announced him as one whom the chairman had honoured with his friendship, he was sure that all present would cordially join him in drinking "The Health of Mr. Terry."

Mr. WILLIAM ALLAN, banker, said that he did not rise with the intention of making a speech. He merely wished to contribute in a few words to the mirth of the evening—an evening which certainly had not passed off without some blunders. It had been understood—at least he had learnt or supposed from the expressions of Mr. Pritchard—that it would be sufficient to put a paper, with the name of the contributor, into the box, and that the gentleman thus contributing would be called on for the money next morning. He, for his part, had committed a blunder but it might serve as a caution to those who may be present at the dinner of next year. He had merely put in his name, written on a slip of paper, without the money. But he would recommend that, as some of the gentlemen might be in the same situation, the box should be again sent round, and he was confident that they, as well as he, would redeem their error.

Sir WALTER SCOTT said that the meeting was somewhat in the situation of Mrs. Anne Page, who had L300 and possibilities. We have already got, said he, L280, but I should like, I confess, to have the L300. He would gratify himself by proposing the health of an honourable person, the Lord Chief Baron, whom England has sent to us, and connecting with it that of his "yokefellow on the bench," as Shakespeare says, Mr. Baron Clerk—The Court of Exchequer.

Mr. Baron CLERK regretted the absence of his learned brother. None, he was sure, could be more generous in his nature, or more ready to help a Scottish purpose.

Sir WALTER SCOTT,—There is one who ought to be remembered on this occasion. He is, indeed, well entitled to our grateful recollection—one, in short, to whom the drama in this city owes much. He succeeded, not without trouble, and perhaps at some considerable sacrifice, in establishing a theatre. The younger part of the company may not recollect the theatre to which I allude, but there are some who with me may remember by name a place called Carrubber's Close. There Allan Ramsay established his little theatre. His own pastoral was not fit for the stage, but it has its admirers in those who love the Doric language in which it is written; and it is not without merits of a very peculiar kind. But laying aside all considerations of his literary merit, Allan was a good, jovial, honest fellow, who could crack a bottle with the best. "The Memory of Allan Ramsay."

Mr. MURRAY, on being requested, sung "'Twas merry in the hall," and at the conclusion was greeted with repeated rounds of applause.

Mr. JONES.—One omission I conceive has been made. The cause of the Fund has been ably advocated, but it is still susceptible, in my opinion, of an additional charm—

"Without the smile from partial beauty won,
Oh, what were man?—a world without a sun!"

And there would not be a darker spot in poetry than would be the corner in Shakespeare Square, if, like its fellow, the Register Office, the Theatre were deserted by the ladies. They are, in fact, our most attractive stars. "The Patronesses of the Theatre, the Ladies of the City of Edinburgh." This toast I ask leave to drink with all the honours which conviviality can confer.

Mr. PATRICK ROBERTSON would be the last man willingly to introduce any topic calculated to interrupt the harmony of the evening; yet he felt himself treading upon ticklish ground when he approached the region of the Nor' Loch. He assured the company, however, that he was not about to enter on the subject of the Improvement Bill. They all knew that if the public were unanimous—if the consent of all parties were obtained—if the rights and interests of everybody were therein attended to, saved, reserved, respected, and excepted—if everybody agreed to it—and, finally, a most essential point, if nobody opposed it—then, and in that case, and provided also that due intimation were given, the bill in question might pass—would pass—or might, could, would, or should pass—all expenses being defrayed. (Laughter.) He was the advocate of neither champion, and would neither avail himself of the absence of the Right Hon. the Lord Provost, nor take advantage of the non-appearance of his friend, Mr. Cockburn. (Laughter.) But in the midst of these civic broils there had been elicited a ray of hope that, at some future period, in Bereford Park, or some other place, if all parties were consulted and satisfied, and if intimation were duly made at the kirk doors of all the parishes in Scotland, in terms of the statute in that behalf provided—the people of Edinburgh might by possibility get a new Theatre. (Cheers and laughter.) But wherever the belligerent powers might be pleased to set down this new Theatre, he was sure they all hoped to meet the Old Company in it. He should therefore propose "Better Accommodation to the Old Company in the new Theatre, site unknown."—Mr. Robertson's speech was most humorously given, and he sat down amidst loud cheers and laughter.

Sir WALTER SCOTT.—Wherever the new Theatre is built, I hope it will not be large. There are two errors which we commonly commit—the one arising from our pride, the other from our poverty. If there are twelve plans, it is odds but the largest, without any regard to comfort, or an eye to the probable expense, is adopted. There was the College projected on this scale, and undertaken in the same manner, and who shall see the end of it? It has been building all my life, and may probably last during the lives of my children, and my children's children. Let not the same prophetic hymn be sung when we commence a new Theatre, which was performed on the occasion of laying the foundation-stone of a certain edifice, "Behold the endless work begun." Playgoing folks should attend somewhat to convenience. The new Theatre should, in the first place, be such as may be finished in eighteen months or two years; and, in the second place, it should be one in which we can hear our old friends with comfort. It is better that a moderate-sized house should be crowded now and then, than to have a large theatre with benches continually empty, to the discouragement of the actors and the discomfort of the spectators. (Applause.) He then commented in flattering terms on the genius of

Mackenzie and his private worth, and concluded by proposing "The Health of Henry Mackenzie, Esq."

Immediately afterwards he said:—Gentlemen, it is now wearing late, and I shall request permission to retire. Like Partridge, I may say, "NON SUM QUALIS ERAM." At my time of day I can agree with Lord Ogilvie as to his rheumatism, and say, "There's a twinge." I hope, therefore, you will excuse me for leaving the chair.—The worthy Baronet then retired amidst long, loud, and rapturous cheering.

Mr. PATRICK ROBERTSON was then called to the chair by common acclamation.

Gentlemen, said Mr. Robertson, I take the liberty of asking you to fill a bumper to the very brim. There is not one of us who will not remember, while he lives, being present at this day's festival, and the declaration made this night by the gentleman who has just left the chair. That declaration has rent the veil from the features of the Great Unknown—a name which must now merge in the name of the Great Known. It will be henceforth coupled with the name of SCOTT, which will become familiar like a household word. We have heard the confession from his own immortal lips— (cheering)—and we cannot dwell with too much or too fervent praise on the merits of the greatest man whom Scotland has produced.

After which several other toasts were given, and Mr. Robertson left the room about half-past eleven. A few choice spirits, however, rallied round Captain Broadhead of the 7th Hussars, who was called to the chair, and the festivity was prolonged till an early hour on Saturday morning.

The band of the Theatre occupied the gallery, and that of the 7th Hussars the end of the room, opposite the chair, whose performances were greatly admired. It is but justice to Mr. Gibb to state that the dinner was very handsome (though slowly served in), and the wines good. The attention of the stewards was exemplary. Mr. Murray and Mr. Vandenhoff, with great good taste, attended on Sir Walter Scott's right and left, and we know that he has expressed himself much gratified by their anxious politeness and sedulity.

CHRONICLES OF THE CANONGATE—INTRODUCTORY.

CHAPTER I. MR. CHRYSTAL CROFTANGRY'S ACCOUNT OF HIMSELF.

Sic itur ad astra.

"This is the path to heaven." Such is the ancient motto attached to the armorial bearings of the Canongate, and which is inscribed, with greater or less propriety, upon all the public buildings, from the church to the pillory, in the ancient quarter of Edinburgh which bears, or rather once bore, the same relation to the Good Town that Westminster does to London, being still possessed of the palace of the sovereign, as it formerly was dignified by the residence of the principal nobility and gentry. I may therefore, with some propriety, put the same motto at the head of the literary undertaking by which I hope to illustrate the hitherto undistinguished name of Chrystal Croftangry.

The public may desire to know something of an author who pitches at such height his ambitious expectations. The gentle reader, therefore—for I am much of Captain Bobadil's humour, and could to no other extend myself so far—the GENTLE reader, then, will be pleased to understand that I am a a Scottish gentleman of the old school, with a fortune, temper, and person, rather the worse for wear. I have known the world for these forty years, having written myself man nearly since that period—and I do not think it is much mended. But this is an opinion which I keep to myself when I am among younger folk, for I recollect, in my youth, quizzing the Sexagenarians who carried back their ideas of a perfect state of society to the days of laced coats and triple ruffles, and some of them to the blood and blows of the Forty-five. Therefore I am cautious in exercising the right of censorship, which is supposed to be acquired by men arrived at, or approaching, the mysterious period of life, when the numbers of seven and nine multiplied into each other, form what sages have termed the Grand Climacteric.

Of the earlier part of my life it is only necessary to say, that I swept the boards of the Parliament-House with the skirts of my gown for the usual number of years during which young Lairds were in my time expected to keep term—got no fees—laughed, and made others laugh—drank claret at Bayle's, Fortune's, and Walker's—and ate oysters in the Covenant Close.

Becoming my own master, I flung my gown at the bar-keeper, and commenced gay man on my own account. In Edinburgh, I ran into all the expensive society which the place then afforded. When I went to my house in the shire of Lanark, I emulated to the utmost the expenses of men of large fortune, and had my hunters, my first-rate pointers, my game-cocks, and feeders. I can more easily forgive myself for these follies, than for others of a still more blamable kind, so indifferently cloaked over, that my poor mother thought herself obliged to leave my habitation, and betake herself to a small inconvenient jointure-house, which she occupied till her death. I think, however, I was not exclusively to blame in this separation, and I believe my mother afterwards condemned herself for being too hasty. Thank God, the adversity which destroyed the means of continuing my dissipation, restored me to the affections of my surviving parent.

My course of life could not last. I ran too fast to run long; and when I would have checked my career, I was perhaps too near the brink of the precipice. Some mishaps I prepared by my own folly, others came upon me unawares. I put my estate out to nurse to a fat man of business, who smothered the babe he should have brought back to me in health and strength, and, in dispute with this honest gentleman, I found, like a skilful general, that my position would be most judiciously assumed by taking it up near the Abbey of Holyrood. [See Note 1.—Holyrood.] It was then I first became acquainted with the quarter, which my little work will, I hope, render immortal, and grew familiar with those magnificent wilds, through which the Kings of Scotland once chased the dark-brown deer, but which were chiefly recommended to me in those days, by their being inaccessible to those metaphysical persons, whom the law of the neighbouring country terms John Doe and Richard Roe. In short, the precincts of the palace are now best known as being a place of refuge at any time from all pursuit for civil debt.

Dire was the strife betwixt my quondam doer and myself; during which my motions were circumscribed, like those of some conjured demon, within a circle, which, "beginning at the northern gate of the King's Park, thence running northways, is bounded on the left by the King's garden-wall, and the gutter, or kennel, in a line wherewith it crosses the High Street to the Watergate, and passing through the sewer, is bounded by the walls of the Tennis Court and Physic Gardens, etc. It then follows the wall of the churchyard, joins the north west wall of St Ann's Yards, and going east to the clackmill-house, turns southward to the turnstile in the King's Park wall, and includes the whole King's Park within the Sanctuary."

These limits, which I abridge from the accurate Maitland, once marked the Girth, or Asylum, belonging to the Abbey of Holyrood, and which, being still an appendage to the royal palace, has retained the privilege of an asylum for civil debt. One would think the space sufficiently extensive for a man to stretch his limbs in, as, besides a reasonable proportion of level ground (considering that the scene lies in Scotland), it includes within its precincts the mountain of Arthur's Seat and the rocks and pasture land called Salisbury Crags. But yet it is inexpressible how, after a certain time had elapsed, I used to long for Sunday, which permitted me to extend my walk without limitation. During the other six days of the week I felt a sickness of heart, which, but for the speedy approach of the hebdomadal day of liberty, I could hardly have endured. I experienced the impatience of a mastiff who tugs in vain to extend the limits which his chain permits.

Day after day I walked by the side of the kennel which divides the Sanctuary from the unprivileged part of the Canongate; and though the month was July, and the scene the old town of Edinburgh, I preferred it to the fresh air and verdant turf which I might have enjoyed in the King's Park, or to the cool and solemn gloom of the portico which surrounds the palace. To an indifferent person either side of the gutter would have seemed much the same, the houses equally mean, the children as ragged and dirty, the carmen as brutal—the whole forming the same picture of low life in a deserted and impoverished quarter of a large city. But to me the gutter or kennel was what the brook Kidron was to Shimei: death was denounced against him should he cross it, doubtless because it was known to his wisdom who pronounced the doom that, from the time the crossing the stream was debarred, the devoted man's desire to transgress the precept would become irresistible, and he would be sure to draw down on his head the penalty which he had already justly incurred by cursing the anointed of God. For my part, all Elysium seemed opening on the other side of the kennel; and I envied the little blackguards, who, stopping the current with their little dam-dykes of mud, had a right to stand on either side of the nasty puddle which best pleased them. I was so childish as even to make an occasional excursion across, were it only for a few yards, and felt the triumph of a schoolboy, who, trespassing in an orchard, hurries back again with a fluttering sensation of joy and terror, betwixt the pleasure of having executed his purpose and the fear of being taken or discovered.

I have sometimes asked myself what I should have done in case of actual imprisonment, since I could not bear without impatience a restriction which is comparatively a mere trifle; but I really could never answer the question to my own satisfaction. I have all my life hated those treacherous expedients called MEZZO-TERMINI, and it is possible with this disposition I might have endured more patiently an absolute privation of liberty than the more modified restrictions to which my residence in the Sanctuary at this period subjected me. If, however, the feelings I then experienced were to increase in intensity according to the difference between a jail and my actual condition, I must have hanged myself, or pined to death—there could have been no other alternative.

Amongst many companions who forgot and neglected me, of course, when my difficulties seemed to be inextricable, I had one true friend; and that friend was a barrister, who knew the laws of his country well, and tracing them up to the spirit of equity and justice in which they originate, had repeatedly prevented, by his benevolent and manly exertions, the triumphs of selfish cunning over simplicity and folly. He undertook my cause, with the assistance of a solicitor of a character similar to his own. My quondam doer had ensconced himself chin-deep among legal trenches, hornworks, and covered ways; but my two protectors shelled him out of his defences, and I was at length a free man, at liberty to go or stay wheresoever my mind listed.

    I left my lodgings as hastily as if it had been a pest-house. I did not even stop to receive some change that was due to me on settling with my landlady, and I saw the poor woman stand at her door looking after my precipitate flight, and shaking her head as she wrapped the silver which she was counting for me in a separate piece of paper, apart from the store in her own moleskin purse. An honest Highlandwoman was Janet MacEvoy, and deserved a greater remuneration, had I possessed the power of bestowing it. But my eagerness of delight was too extreme to pause for explanation with Janet. On I pushed through the groups of children, of whose sports I had been so often a lazy, lounging spectator. I sprung over the gutter as if it had been the fatal Styx, and I a ghost, which, eluding Pluto's authority, was making its escape from Limbo lake. My friend had difficulty to restrain me from running like a madman up the street; and in spite of his kindness and hospitality, which soothed me for a day or two, I was not quite happy until I found myself aboard of a Leith smack, and, standing down the Firth with a fair wind, might snap my fingers at the retreating outline of Arthur's Seat, to the vicinity of which I had been so long confined.

    It is not my purpose to trace my future progress through life. I had extricated myself, or rather had been freed by my friends, from the brambles and thickets of the law; but, as befell the sheep in the fable, a great part of my fleece was left behind me. Something remained, however: I was in the season for exertion, and, as my good mother used to say, there was always life for living folk. Stern necessity gave my manhood that prudence which my youth was a stranger to. I faced danger, I endured fatigue, I sought foreign climates, and proved that I belonged to the nation which is proverbially patient of labour and prodigal of life. Independence, like liberty to Virgil's shepherd, came late, but came at last, with no great affluence in its train, but bringing enough to support a decent appearance for the rest of my life, and to induce cousins to be civil, and gossips to say, "I wonder whom old Croft will make his heir? He must have picked up something, and I should not be surprised if it prove more than folk think of."

    My first impulse when I returned home was to rush to the house of my benefactor, the only man who had in my distress interested himself in my behalf. He was a snuff-taker, and it had been the pride of my heart to save the IPSA CORPORA of the first score of guineas I could hoard, and to have them converted into as tasteful a snuff-box as Rundell and Bridge could devise. This I had thrust for security into the breast of my waistcoat, while, impatient to transfer it to the person for whom it was destined, I hastened to his house in Brown Square. When the front of the house became visible a feeling of alarm checked me. I had been long absent from Scotland; my friend was some years older than I; he might have been called to the congregation of the just. I paused, and gazed on the house as if I had hoped to form some conjecture from the outward appearance concerning the state of the family within. I know not how it was, but the lower windows being all closed, and no one stirring, my sinister forebodings were rather strengthened. I regretted now that I had not made inquiry before I left the inn where I alighted from the mail-coach. But it was too late; so I hurried on, eager to know the best or the worst which I could learn.

    The brass-plate bearing my friend's name and designation was still on the door, and when it was opened the old domestic appeared a good deal older, I thought, than he ought naturally to have looked, considering the period of my absence. "Is Mr. Sommerville at home?" said I, pressing forward.

"Yes, sir," said John, placing himself in opposition to my entrance, "he is at home, but—"

"But he is not in," said I. "I remember your phrase of old, John. Come, I will step into his room, and leave a line for him."

John was obviously embarrassed by my familiarity. I was some one, he saw, whom he ought to recollect. At the same time it was evident he remembered nothing about me.

"Ay, sir, my master is in, and in his own room, but—"

I would not hear him out, but passed before him towards the well-known apartment. A young lady came out of the room a little disturbed, as it seemed, and said, "John, what is the matter?"

"A gentleman, Miss Nelly, that insists on seeing my master."

"A very old and deeply-indebted friend," said I, "that ventures to press myself on my much-respected benefactor on my return from abroad."

"Alas, sir," replied she, "my uncle would be happy to see you, but—"

At this moment something was heard within the apartment like the falling of a plate, or glass, and immediately after my friend's voice called angrily and eagerly for his niece. She entered the room hastily, and so did I. But it was to see a spectacle, compared with which that of my benefactor stretched on his bier would have been a happy one.

The easy-chair filled with cushions, the extended limbs swathed in flannel, the wide wrapping-gown and nightcap, showed illness; but the dimmed eye, once so replete with living fire—the blabber lip, whose dilation and compression used to give such character to his animated countenance—the stammering tongue, that once poured forth such floods of masculine eloquence, and had often swayed the opinion of the sages whom he addressed,—all these sad symptoms evinced that my friend was in the melancholy condition of those in whom the principle of animal life has unfortunately survived that of mental intelligence. He gazed a moment at me, but then seemed insensible of my presence, and went on—he, once the most courteous and well-bred—to babble unintelligible but violent reproaches against his niece and servant, because he himself had dropped a teacup in attempting to place it on a table at his elbow. His eyes caught a momentary fire from his irritation; but he struggled in vain for words to express himself adequately, as, looking from his servant to his niece, and then to the table, he laboured to explain that they had placed it (though it touched his chair) at too great a distance from him.

The young person, who had naturally a resigned Madonna-like expression of countenance, listened to his impatient chiding with the most humble submission, checked the servant, whose less delicate feelings would have entered on his justification, and gradually, by the sweet and soft tone of her voice, soothed to rest the spirit of causeless irritation.

She then cast a look towards me, which expressed, "You see all that remains of him whom you call friend." It seemed also to say, "Your longer presence here can only be distressing to us all."

"Forgive me, young lady," I said, as well as tears would permit; "I am a person deeply obliged to your uncle. My name is Croftangry."

"Lord! and that I should not hae minded ye, Maister Croftangry," said the servant. "Ay, I mind my master had muckle fash about your job. I hae heard him order in fresh candles as midnight chappit, and till't again. Indeed, ye had aye his gude word, Mr. Croftangry, for a' that folks said about you."

"Hold your tongue, John," said the lady, somewhat angrily; and then continued, addressing herself to me, "I am sure, sir, you must be sorry to see my uncle in this state. I know you are his friend. I have heard him mention your name, and wonder he never heard from you." A new cut this, and it went to my heart. But she continued, "I really do not know if it is right that any should—If my uncle should know you, which I scarce think possible, he would be much affected, and the doctor says that any agitation—But here comes Dr. — to give his own opinion."

Dr. — entered. I had left him a middle-aged man. He was now an elderly one; but still the same benevolent Samaritan, who went about doing good, and thought the blessings of the poor as good a recompense of his professional skill as the gold of the rich.

He looked at me with surprise, but the young lady said a word of introduction, and I, who was known to the doctor formerly, hastened to complete it. He recollected me perfectly, and intimated that he was well acquainted with the reasons I had for being deeply interested in the fate of his patient. He gave me a very melancholy account of my poor friend, drawing me for that purpose a little apart from the lady. "The light of life," he said, "was trembling in the socket; he scarcely expected it would ever leap up even into a momentary flash, but more was impossible." He then stepped towards his patient, and put some questions, to which the poor invalid, though he seemed to recognize the friendly and familiar voice, answered only in a faltering and uncertain manner.

The young lady, in her turn, had drawn back when the doctor approached his patient. "You see how it is with him," said the doctor, addressing me. "I have heard our poor friend, in one of the most eloquent of his pleadings, give a description of this very disease, which he compared to the tortures inflicted by Mezentius when he chained the dead to the living. The soul, he said, is imprisoned in its dungeon of flesh, and though retaining its natural and unalienable properties, can no more exert them than the captive enclosed within a prison-house can act as a free agent. Alas! to see HIM, who could so well describe what this malady was in others, a prey himself to its infirmities! I shall never forget the solemn tone of expression with which he summed up the incapacities of the paralytic—the deafened ear, the dimmed eye, the crippled limbs—in the noble words of Juvenal,—

"'Omni
Membrorum damno major, dementia, quae nec
Nomina servorum, nec vultum agnoscit amici.'"

As the physician repeated these lines, a flash of intelligence seemed to revive in the invalid's eye—sunk again—again struggled, and he spoke more intelligibly than before, and in the tone of one eager to say something which he felt would escape him unless said instantly. "A question of death-bed, a question of death-bed, doctor—a reduction EX CAPITE LECTI—Withering against Wilibus—about the MORBUS SONTICUS. I pleaded the cause for the pursuer—I, and—and—why, I shall forget my own name—I, and—he that was the wittiest and the best-humoured man living—"

The description enabled the doctor to fill up the blank, and the patient joyfully repeated the name suggested. "Ay, ay," he said, "just he—Harry—poor Harry—" The light in his eye died away, and he sunk back in his easy-chair.

"You have now seen more of our poor friend, Mr. Croftangry," said the physician, "than I dared venture to promise you; and now I must take my professional authority on me, and ask you to retire. Miss Sommerville will, I am sure, let you know if a moment should by any chance occur when her uncle can see you."

What could I do? I gave my card to the young lady, and taking my offering from my bosom—"if my poor friend," I said, with accents as broken almost as his own, "should ask where this came from, name me, and say from the most obliged and most grateful man alive. Say, the gold of which it is composed was saved by grains at a time, and was hoarded with as much avarice as ever was a miser's. To bring it here I have come a thousand miles; and now, alas, I find him thus!"

I laid the box on the table, and was retiring with a lingering step. The eye of the invalid was caught by it, as that of a child by a glittering toy, and with infantine impatience he faltered out inquiries of his niece. With gentle mildness she repeated again and again who I was, and why I came, etc. I was about to turn, and hasten from a scene so painful, when the physician laid his hand on my sleeve. "Stop," he said, "there is a change."

There was, indeed, and a marked one. A faint glow spread over his pallid features—they seemed to gain the look of intelligence which belongs to vitality—his eye once more kindled—his lip coloured—and drawing himself up out of the listless posture he had hitherto maintained, he rose without assistance. The doctor and the servant ran to give him their support. He waved them aside, and they were contented to place themselves in such a position behind as might ensure against accident, should his newly-acquired strength decay as suddenly as it had revived.

"My dear Croftangry," he said, in the tone of kindness of other days, "I am glad to see you returned. You find me but poorly; but my little niece here and Dr. — are very kind. God bless you, my dear friend! We shall not meet again till we meet in a better world."

I pressed his extended hand to my lips—I pressed it to my bosom—I would fain have flung myself on my knees; but the doctor, leaving the patient to the young lady and the servant, who wheeled forward his chair, and were replacing him in it, hurried me out of the room. "My dear sir," he said, "you ought to be satisfied; you have seen our poor invalid more like his former self than he has been for months, or than he may be perhaps again until all is over. The whole Faculty could not have assured such an interval. I must see whether anything can be derived from it to improve the general health. Pray, begone." The last argument hurried me from the spot, agitated by a crowd of feelings, all of them painful.

When I had overcome the shock of this great disappointment, I renewed gradually my acquaintance with one or two old companions, who, though of infinitely less interest to my feelings than my unfortunate friend, served to relieve the pressure of actual solitude, and who were not perhaps the less open to my advances that I was a bachelor somewhat stricken in years, newly arrived from foreign parts, and certainly independent, if not wealthy.

I was considered as a tolerable subject of speculation by some, and I could not be burdensome to any. I was therefore, according to the ordinary rule of Edinburgh hospitality, a welcome guest in several respectable families. But I found no one who could replace the loss I had sustained in my best friend and benefactor. I wanted something more than mere companionship could give me, and where was I to look for it? Among the scattered remnants of those that had been my gay friends of yore? Alas!

"Many a lad I loved was dead,
And many a lass grown old."

Besides, all community of ties between us had ceased to exist, and such of former friends as were still in the world held their life in a different tenor from what I did.

Some had become misers, and were as eager in saving sixpence as ever they had been in spending a guinea. Some had turned agriculturists; their talk was of oxen, and they were only fit companions for graziers. Some stuck to cards, and though no longer deep gamblers, rather played small game than sat out. This I particularly despised. The strong impulse of gaming, alas! I had felt in my time. It is as intense as it is criminal; but it produces excitation and interest, and I can conceive how it should become a passion with strong and powerful minds. But to dribble away life in exchanging bits of painted pasteboard round a green table for the piddling concern of a few shillings, can only be excused in folly or superannuation. It is like riding on a rocking-horse, where your utmost exertion never carries you a foot forward; it is a kind of mental treadmill, where you are perpetually climbing, but can never rise an inch. From these hints, my readers will perceive I am incapacitated for one of the pleasures of old age, which, though not mentioned by Cicero, is not the least frequent resource in the present day—the club-room, and the snug hand at whist.

To return to my old companions. Some frequented public assemblies, like the ghost of Beau Nash, or any other beau of half a century back, thrust aside by tittering youth, and pitied by those of their own age. In fine, some went into devotion, as the French term it, and others, I fear, went to the devil; a few found resources in science and letters; one or two turned philosophers in a small way, peeped into microscopes, and became familiar with the fashionable experiments of the day; some took to reading, and I was one of them.

Some grains of repulsion towards the society around me—some painful recollections of early faults and follies—some touch of displeasure with living mankind—inclined me rather to a study of antiquities, and particularly those of my own country. The reader, if I can prevail on myself to continue the present work, will probably be able to judge in the course of it whether I have made any useful progress in the study of the olden times.

I owed this turn of study, in part, to the conversation of my kind man of business, Mr. Fairscribe, whom I mentioned as having seconded the efforts of my invaluable friend in bringing the cause on which my liberty and the remnant of my property depended to a favourable decision. He had given me a most kind reception on my return. He was too much engaged in his profession for me to intrude on him often, and perhaps his mind was too much trammelled with its details to permit his being willingly withdrawn from them. In short, he was not a person of my poor friend Sommerville's expanded spirit, and rather a lawyer of the ordinary class of formalists; but a most able and excellent man. When my estate was sold! he retained some of the older title-deeds, arguing, from his own feelings, that they would be of more consequence to the heir of the old family than to the new purchaser. And when I returned to Edinburgh, and found him still in the exercise of the profession to which he was an honour, he sent to my lodgings the old family Bible, which lay always on my father's table, two or three other mouldy volumes, and a couple of sheepskin bags full of parchments and papers, whose appearance was by no means inviting.

The next time I shared Mr. Fairscribe's hospitable dinner, I failed not to return him due thanks for his kindness, which acknowledgment, indeed, I proportioned rather to the idea which I knew he entertained of the value of such things, than to the interest with which I myself regarded them. But the conversation turning on my family, who were old proprietors in the Upper Ward of Clydesdale, gradually excited some interest in my mind and when I retired to my solitary parlour, the first thing I did was to look for a pedigree or sort of history of the family or House of Croftangry, once of that Ilk, latterly of Glentanner. The discoveries which I made shall enrich the next chapter.

## CHAPTER II. IN WHICH MR. CROFTANGRY CONTINUES HIS STORY.

"What's property, dear Swift? I see it alter
From you to me, from me to Peter Walter."

"Croftangry—Croftandrew—Croftanridge—Croftandgrey for sa mony wise hath the name been spellit—is weel known to be ane house of grit antiquity; and it is said that King Milcolumb, or Malcolm, being the first of our Scottish princes quha removit across the Firth of Forth, did reside and occupy ane palace at Edinburgh, and had there ane valziant man, who did him man-service by keeping the croft, or corn-land, which was tilled for the convenience of the King's household, and was thence callit Croft-an-ri, that is to say, the King his croft; quhilk place, though now coverit with biggings, is to this day called Croftangry, and lyeth near to the royal palace. And whereas that some of those who bear this auld and honourable name may take scorn that it ariseth from the tilling of the ground, quhilk men account a slavish occupation, yet we ought to honour the pleugh and spade, seeing we all derive our being from our father Adam, whose lot it became to cultivate the earth, in respect of his fall and transgression.

"Also we have witness, as weel in holy writt as in profane history, of the honour in quhilk husbandrie was held of old, and how prophets have been taken from the pleugh, and great captains raised up to defend their ain countries, sic as Cincinnatus, and the like, who fought not the common enemy with the less valiancy that their alms had been exercised in halding the stilts of the pleugh, and their bellicose skill in driving of yauds and owsen.

"Likewise there are sindry honorable families, quhilk are now of our native Scottish nobility, and have clombe higher up the brae of preferment than what this house of Croftangry hath done, quhilk shame not to carry in their warlike shield and insignia of dignity the tools and implements the quhilk their first forefathers exercised in labouring the croft-rig, or, as the poet Virgilius calleth it eloquently, in subduing the soil, and no doubt this ancient house of Croftangry, while it continued to be called of that Ilk, produced many worshipful and famous patriots, of quhom I now praetermit the names; it being my purpose, if God shall spare me life for sic ane pious officium, or duty, to resume the first part of my narrative touching the house of Croftangry, when I can set down at length the evidents and historical witness anent the facts which I shall allege, seeing that words, when they are unsupported by proofs, are like seed sown on the naked rocks, or like an house biggit on the flitting and faithless sands."

Here I stopped to draw breath; for the style of my grandsire, the inditer of this goodly matter, was rather lengthy, as our American friends say. Indeed, I reserve the rest of the piece until I can obtain admission to the Bannatine Club, [This Club, of which the Author of Waverley has the honour to be President, was instituted in February 1823, for the purpose of printing and publishing works illustrative of the history, literature, and antiquities of Scotland. It continues to prosper, and has already rescued from oblivion many curious materials of Scottish history.] when I propose to throw off an edition, limited according to the rules of that erudite Society, with a facsimile of the manuscript, emblazonry of the family arms surrounded by their quartering, and a handsome disclamation of family pride, with HAEC NOS NOVIMUS ESSE NIHIL, or VIX EA NOSTRA VOCO.

In the meantime, to speak truth, I cannot but suspect that, though my worthy ancestor puffed vigorously to swell up the dignity of his family, we had never, in fact, risen above the rank of middling proprietors. The estate of Glentanner came to us by the intermarriage of my ancestor with Tib Sommeril, termed by the southrons Sommerville, a daughter of that noble house, but, I fear, on what my great-grandsire calls "the wrong side of the blanket." [The ancient Norman family of the Sommervilles came into this island with William the Conqueror, and established one branch in Gloucestershire, another in Scotland. After the lapse of seven hundred years, the remaining possessions of these two branches were united in the person of the late Lord Sommerville, on the death of his English kinsman, the well-known author of "The Chase."] Her husband, Gilbert, was killed fighting, as the INQUISITIO POST MORTEM has it, "SUB VEXILLO REGIS, APUD PRAELIUM JUXTA BRANXTON, LIE FLODDDEN-FIELD."

We had our share in other national misfortunes—were forfeited, like Sir John Colville of the Dale, for following our betters to the field of Langside; and in the contentious times of the last Stewarts we were severely fined for harbouring and resetting intercommuned ministers, and narrowly escaped giving a martyr to the Calendar of the Covenant, in the person of the father of our family historian. He "took the sheaf from the mare," however, as the MS. expresses it, and agreed to accept of the terms of pardon offered by Government, and sign the bond in evidence he would give no further ground of offence. My grandsire glosses over his father's backsliding as smoothly as he can, and comforts himself with ascribing his want of resolution to his unwillingness to wreck the ancient name and family, and to permit his lands and lineage to fall under a doom of forfeiture.

"And indeed," said the venerable compiler, "as, praised be God, we seldom meet in Scotland with these belly-gods and voluptuaries, whilk are unnatural enough to devour their patrimony bequeathed to them by their forbears in chambering and wantonness, so that they come, with the prodigal son, to the husks and the swine-trough; and as I have the less to dreid the existence of such unnatural Neroes in mine own family to devour the substance of their own house like brute beasts out of mere gluttonie and Epicurishnesse, so I need only warn mine descendants against over-hastily meddling with the mutations in state and in religion, which have been near-hand to the bringing this poor house of Croftangry to perdition, as we have shown more than once. And albeit I would not that my successors sat still altogether when called on by their duty to Kirk and King, yet I would have them wait till stronger and walthier men than themselves were up, so that either they may have the better chance of getting through the day, or, failing of that, the conquering party having some fatter quarry to live upon, may, like gorged hawks, spare the smaller game."

There was something in this conclusion which at first reading piqued me extremely, and I was so unnatural as to curse the whole concern, as poor, bald, pitiful trash, in which a silly old man was saying a great deal about nothing at all. Nay, my first impression was to thrust it into the fire, the rather that it reminded me, in no very flattering manner, of the loss of the family property, to which the compiler of the history was so much attached, in the very manner which he most severely reprobated. It even seemed to my aggrieved feelings that his unprescient gaze on futurity, in which he could not anticipate the folly of one of his descendants, who should throw away the whole inheritance in a few years of idle expense and folly, was meant as a personal incivility to myself, though written fifty or sixty years before I was born.

A little reflection made me ashamed or this feeling of impatience, and as I looked at the even, concise, yet tremulous hand in which the manuscript was written, I could not help thinking, according to an opinion I have heard seriously maintained, that something of a man's character may be conjectured from his handwriting. That neat but crowded and constrained small-hand argued a man of a good conscience, well-regulated passions, and, to use his own phrase, an upright walk in life; but it also indicated narrowness of spirit, inveterate prejudice, and hinted at some degree of intolerance, which, though not natural to the disposition, had arisen out of a limited education. The passages from Scripture and the classics, rather profusely than happily introduced, and written in a half-text character to mark their importance, illustrated that peculiar sort of pedantry which always considers the argument as gained if secured by a quotation. Then the flourished capital letters, which ornamented the commencement of each paragraph, and the names of his family and of his ancestors whenever these occurred in the page, do they not express forcibly the pride and sense of importance with which the author undertook and accomplished his task? I persuaded myself the whole was so complete a portrait of the man, that it would not have been a more undutiful act to have defaced his picture, or even to have disturbed his bones in his coffin, than to destroy his manuscript. I thought, for a moment, of presenting it to Mr. Fairscribe; but that confounded passage about the prodigal and swine-trough—I settled at last it was as well to lock it up in my own bureau, with the intention to look at it no more.

But I do not know how it was, that the subject began to sit nearer my heart than I was aware of, and I found myself repeatedly engaged in reading descriptions of farms which were no longer mine, and boundaries which marked the property of others. A love of the NATALE SOLUM, if Swift be right in translating these words, "family estate," began to awaken in my bosom—the recollections of my own youth adding little to it, save what was connected with field-sports. A career of pleasure is unfavourable for acquiring a taste for natural beauty, and still more so for forming associations of a sentimental kind, connecting us with the inanimate objects around us.

I had thought little about my estate while I possessed and was wasting it, unless as affording the rude materials out of which a certain inferior race of creatures, called tenants, were bound to produce (in a greater quantity than they actually did) a certain return called rent, which was destined to supply my expenses. This was my general view of the matter. Of particular places, I recollected that Garval Hill was a famous piece of rough upland pasture for rearing young colts, and teaching them to throw their feet; that Minion Burn had the finest yellow trout in the country; that Seggy-cleugh was unequalled for woodcocks; that Bengibbert Moors afforded excellent moorfowl-shooting; and that the clear, bubbling fountain called the Harper's Well was the best recipe in the world on the morning after a HARD-GO with my neighbour fox-hunters. Still, these ideas recalled, by degrees, pictures of which I had since learned to appreciate the merit—scenes of silent loneliness, where extensive moors, undulating into wild hills, were only disturbed by the whistle of the plover or the crow of the heathcock; wild ravines creeping up into mountains, filled with natural wood, and which, when traced downwards along the path formed by shepherds and nutters, were found gradually to enlarge and deepen, as each formed a channel to its own brook, sometimes bordered by steep banks of earth, often with the more romantic boundary of naked rocks or cliffs crested with oak, mountain ash, and hazel—all gratifying the eye the more that the scenery was, from the bare nature of the country around, totally unexpected.

I had recollections, too, of fair and fertile holms, or level plains, extending between the wooded banks and the bold stream of the Clyde, which, coloured like pure amber, or rather having the hue of the pebbles called Cairngorm, rushes over sheets of rock and beds of gravel, inspiring a species of awe from the few and faithless fords which it presents, and the frequency of fatal accidents, now diminished by the number of bridges. These alluvial holms were frequently bordered by triple and quadruple rows of large trees, which gracefully marked their boundary, and dipped their long arms into the foaming stream of the river. Other places I remembered, which had been described by the old huntsman as the lodge of tremendous wild-cats, or the spot where tradition stated the mighty stag to have been brought to bay, or where heroes, whose might was now as much forgotten, were said to have been slain by surprise, or in battle.

It is not to be supposed that these finished landscapes became visible before the eyes of my imagination, as the scenery of the stage is disclosed by the rising of the curtain. I have said that I had looked upon the country around me, during the hurried and dissipated period of my life, with the eyes, indeed, of my body, but without those of my understanding. It was piece by piece, as a child picks out its lesson, that I began to recollect the beauties of nature which had once surrounded me in the home of my forefathers. A natural taste for them must have lurked at the bottom of my heart, which awakened when I was in foreign countries, and becoming by degrees a favourite passion, gradually turned its eyes inwards, and ransacked the neglected stores which my memory had involuntarily recorded, and, when excited, exerted herself to collect and to complete.

I began now to regret more bitterly than ever the having fooled away my family property, the care and improvement of which I saw might have afforded an agreeable employment for my leisure, which only went to brood on past misfortunes, and increase useless repining. "Had but a single farm been reserved, however small," said I one day to Mr. Fairscribe, "I should have had a place I could call my home, and something that I could call business."

"It might have been managed," answered Fairscribe; "and for my part, I inclined to keep the mansion house, mains, and some of the old family acres together; but both Mr. —— and you were of opinion that the money would be more useful."

"True, true, my good friend," said I; "I was a fool then, and did not think I could incline to be Glentanner with L200 or L300 a year, instead of Glentanner with as many thousands. I was then a haughty, pettish, ignorant, dissipated, broken-down Scottish laird; and thinking my imaginary consequence altogether ruined, I cared not how soon, or how absolutely, I was rid of everything that recalled it to my own memory, or that of others."

"And now it is like you have changed your mind?" said Fairscribe. "Well, fortune is apt to circumduce the term upon us; but I think she may allow you to revise your condescendence."

"How do you mean, my good friend?"

"Nay," said Fairscribe, "there is ill luck in averring till one is sure of his facts. I will look back on a file of newspapers, and to-morrow you shall hear from me. Come, help yourself—I have seen you fill your glass higher."

"And shall see it again," said I, pouring out what remained of our bottle of claret; "the wine is capital, and so shall our toast be—'To your fireside, my good friend.' And now we shall go beg a Scots song without foreign graces from my little siren, Miss Katie."

The next day, accordingly, I received a parcel from Mr. Fairscribe with a newspaper enclosed, among the advertisements of which one was marked with a cross as requiring my attention. I read, to my surprise:—

"DESIRABLE ESTATE FOR SALE.

"By order of the Lords of Council and Session, will be exposed to sale in the New Sessions House of Edinburgh, on Wednesday, the 25th November, 18—, all and whole the lands and barony of Glentanner, now called Castle Treddles, lying in the Middle Ward of Clydesdale, and shire of Lanark, with the teinds, parsonage and vicarage, fishings in the Clyde, woods, mosses, moors, and pasturages," etc., etc.

The advertisement went on to set forth the advantages of the soil, situation, natural beauties, and capabilities of improvement, not forgetting its being a freehold estate, with the particular polypus capacity of being sliced up into two, three, or, with a little assistance, four freehold qualifications, and a hint that the county was likely to be eagerly contested between two great families. The upset price at which "the said lands and barony and others" were to be exposed was thirty years' purchase of the proven rental, which was about a fourth more than the property had fetched at the last sale. This, which was mentioned, I suppose, to show the improvable character of the land, would have given another some pain. But let me speak truth of myself in good as in evil—it pained not me. I was only angry that Fairscribe, who knew something generally of the extent of my funds, should have tantalized me by sending me information that my family property was in the market, since he must have known that the price was far out of my reach.

But a letter dropped from the parcel on the floor, which attracted my eye, and explained the riddle. A client of Mr. Fairscribe's, a moneyed man, thought of buying Glentanner, merely as an investment of money—it was even unlikely he would ever see it; and so the price of the whole being some thousand pounds beyond what cash he had on hand, this accommodating Dives would gladly take a partner in the sale for any detached farm, and would make no objection to its including the most desirable part of the estate in point of beauty, provided the price was made adequate. Mr. Fairscribe would take care I was not imposed on in the matter, and said in his card he believed, if I really wished to make such a purchase, I had better go out and look at the premises, advising me, at the same time, to keep a strict incognito—an advice somewhat superfluous, since I am naturally of a retired and reserved disposition.

## CHAPTER III. MR. CROFTANGRY, INTER ALIA, REVISITS GLENTANNER.

> Then sing of stage-coaches,
> And fear no reproaches
>   For riding in one;
> But daily be jogging,
> Whilst, whistling and flogging,
> Whilst, whistling and flogging,
> The coachman drives on.         FARQUHAR.

Disguised in a grey surtout which had seen service, a white castor on my head, and a stout Indian cane in my hand, the next week saw me on the top of a mail-coach driving to the westward.

I like mail-coaches, and I hate them. I like them for my convenience; but I detest them for setting the whole world a-gadding, instead of sitting quietly still minding their own business, and preserving the stamp of originality of character which nature or education may have impressed on them. Off they go, jingling against each other in the rattling vehicle till they have no more variety of stamp in them than so many smooth shillings—the same even in their Welsh wigs and greatcoats, each without more individuality than belongs to a partner of the company, as the waiter calls them, of the North Coach.

Worthy Mr. Piper, best of contractors who ever furnished four frampal jades for public use, I bless you when I set out on a journey myself; the neat coaches under your contract render the intercourse, from Johnnie Groat's House to Ladykirk and Cornhill Bridge, safe, pleasant, and cheap. But, Mr. Piper, you who are a shrewd arithmetician, did it never occur to you to calculate how many fools' heads, which might have produced an idea or two in the year, if suffered to remain in quiet, get effectually addled by jolting to and fro in these flying chariots of yours; how many decent countrymen become conceited bumpkins after a cattle-show dinner in the capital, which they could not have attended save for your means; how many decent country parsons return critics and spouters, by way of importing the newest taste from Edinburgh? And how will your conscience answer one day for carrying so many bonny lasses to barter modesty for conceit and levity at the metropolitan Vanity Fair?

Consider, too, the low rate to which you reduce human intellect. I do not believe your habitual customers have their ideas more enlarged than one of your coach-horses. They KNOWS the road, like the English postilion, and they know nothing besides. They date, like the carriers at Gadshill, from the death of Robin Ostler; [See Act II. Scene 1 of the First Part of Shakespeare's Henry IV.] the succession of guards forms a dynasty in their eyes; coachmen are their ministers of state; and an upset is to them a greater incident than a change of administration. Their only point of interest on the road is to save the time, and see whether the coach keeps the hour. This is surely a miserable degradation of human intellect. Take my advice, my good sir, and disinterestedly contrive that once or twice a quarter your most dexterous whip shall overturn a coachful of these superfluous travellers, IN TERROREM to those who, as Horace says, "delight in the dust raised by your chariots."

Your current and customary mail-coach passenger, too, gets abominably selfish, schemes successfully for the best seat, the freshest egg, the right cut of the sirloin. The mode of travelling is death to all the courtesies and kindnesses of life, and goes a great way to demoralize the character, and cause it to retrograde to barbarism. You allow us excellent dinners, but only twenty minutes to eat them. And what is the consequence? Bashful beauty sits on the one side of us, timid childhood on the other; respectable, yet somewhat feeble, old age is placed on our front; and all require those acts of politeness which ought to put every degree upon a level at the convivial board. But have we time— we the strong and active of the party—to perform the duties of the table to the more retired and bashful, to whom these little attentions are due? The lady should be pressed to her chicken, the old man helped to his favourite and tender slice, the child to his tart. But not a fraction of a minute have we to bestow on any other person than ourselves; and the PRUT-PRUT—TUT-TUT of the guard's discordant note summons us to the coach, the weaker party having gone without their dinner, and the able-bodied and active threatened with indigestion, from having swallowed victuals like a Lei'stershire clown bolting bacon.

On the memorable occasion I am speaking of I lost my breakfast, sheerly from obeying the commands of a respectable-looking old lady, who once required me to ring the bell, and another time to help the tea-kettle. I have some reason to think she was literally an OLD-STAGER, who laughed in her sleeve at my complaisance; so that I have sworn in my secret soul revenge upon her sex, and all such errant damsels of whatever age and degree whom I may encounter in my travels. I mean all this without the least ill-will to my friend the contractor, who, I think, has approached as near as any one is like to do towards accomplishing the modest wish cf the Amatus and Amata of the Peri Bathous,—

"Ye gods, annihilate but time and space,
   And make two lovers happy."

I intend to give Mr. P. his full revenge when I come to discuss the more recent enormity of steamboats; meanwhile, I shall only say of both these modes of conveyance, that—

"There is no living with them or without them."

I am, perhaps, more critical on the—mail-coach on this particular occasion, that I did not meet all the respect from the worshipful company in his Majesty's carriage that I think I was entitled to. I must say it for myself that I bear, in my own opinion at least, not a vulgar point about me. My face has seen service, but there is still a good set of teeth, an aquiline nose, and a quick, grey eye, set a little too deep under the eyebrow; and a cue of the kind once called military may serve to show that my civil occupations have been sometimes mixed with those of war. Nevertheless, two idle young fellows in the vehicle, or rather on the top of it, were so much amused with the deliberation which I used in ascending to the same place of eminence, that I thought I should have been obliged to pull them up a little. And I was in no good-humour at an unsuppressed laugh following my descent when set down at the angle, where a cross road, striking off from the main one, led me towards Glentanner, from which I was still nearly five miles distant.

It was an old-fashioned road, which, preferring ascents to sloughs, was led in a straight line over height and hollow, through moor and dale. Every object around me; as I passed them in succession, reminded me of old days, and at the same time formed the strongest contrast with them possible. Unattended, on foot, with a small bundle in my hand, deemed scarce sufficient good company for the two shabby-genteels with whom I had been lately perched on the top of a mail-coach, I did not seem to be the same person with the young prodigal, who lived with the noblest and gayest in the land, and who, thirty years before, would, in the same country, have, been on the back of a horse that had been victor for a plate, or smoking aloof in his travelling chaise-and-four. My sentiments were not less changed than my condition. I could quite well remember that my ruling sensation in the days of heady youth was a mere schoolboy's eagerness to get farthest forward in the race in which I had engaged; to drink as many bottles as —; to be thought as good a judge of a horse as —; to have the knowing cut of —'s jacket. These were thy gods, O Israel!

Now I was a mere looker-on; seldom an unmoved, and sometimes an angry spectator, but still a spectator only, of the pursuits of mankind. I felt how little my opinion was valued by those engaged in the busy turmoil, yet I exercised it with the profusion of an old lawyer retired from his profession, who thrusts himself into his neighbour's affairs, and gives advice where it is not wanted, merely under pretence of loving the crack of the whip.

I came amid these reflections to the brow of a hill, from which I expected to see Glentanner, a modest-looking yet comfortable house, its walls covered with the most productive fruit-trees in that part of the country, and screened from the most stormy quarters of the horizon by a deep and ancient wood, which overhung the neighbouring hill. The house was gone; a great part of the wood was felled; and instead of the gentlemanlike mansion, shrouded and embosomed among its old hereditary trees, stood Castle Treddles, a huge lumping four-square pile of freestone, as bare as my nail, except for a paltry edging of decayed and lingering exotics, with an impoverished lawn stretched before it, which, instead of boasting deep green tapestry, enamelled with daisies and with crowsfoot and cowslips, showed an extent of nakedness, raked, indeed, and levelled, but where the sown grasses had failed with drought, and the earth, retaining its natural complexion, seemed nearly as brown and bare as when it was newly dug up.

The house was a large fabric, which pretended to its name of Castle only from the front windows being finished in acute Gothic arches (being, by the way, the very reverse of the castellated style), and each angle graced with a turret about the size of a pepper-box. In every other respect it resembled a large town-house, which, like a fat burgess, had taken a walk to the country on a holiday, and climbed to the top of all eminence to look around it. The bright red colour of the freestone, the size of the building, the formality of its shape, and awkwardness of its position, harmonized as ill with the sweeping Clyde in front, and the bubbling brook which danced down on the right, as the fat civic form, with bushy wig, gold-headed cane, maroon-coloured coat, and mottled silk stockings, would have accorded with the wild and magnificent scenery of Corehouse Linn.

I went up to the house. It was in that state of desertion which is perhaps the most unpleasant to look on, for the place was going to decay without having been inhabited. There were about the mansion, though deserted, none of the slow mouldering touches of time, which communicate to buildings, as to the human frame, a sort of reverence, while depriving them of beauty and of strength. The disconcerted schemes of the Laird of Castle Treddles had resembled fruit that becomes decayed without ever having ripened. Some windows broken, others patched, others blocked up with deals, gave a disconsolate air to all around, and seemed to say, "There Vanity had purposed to fix her seat, but was anticipated by Poverty."

To the inside, after many a vain summons, I was at length admitted by an old labourer. The house contained every contrivance for luxury and accommodation. The kitchens were a model; and there were hot closets on the office staircase, that the dishes might not cool, as our Scottish phrase goes, between the kitchen and the hall. But instead of the genial smell of good cheer, these temples of Comus emitted the damp odour of sepulchral vaults, and the large cabinets of cast-iron looked like the cages of some feudal Bastille. The eating room and drawing-room, with an interior boudoir, were magnificent apartments, the ceiling was fretted and adorned with stucco-work, which already was broken in many places, and looked in others damp and mouldering; the wood panelling was shrunk and warped, and cracked; the doors, which had not been hung for more than two years, were, nevertheless, already swinging loose from their hinges. Desolation, in short, was where enjoyment had never been; and the want of all the usual means to preserve was fast performing the work of decay.

The story was a common one, and told in a few words. Mr. Treddles, senior, who bought the estate, was a cautious, money-making person. His son, still embarked in commercial speculations, desired at the same time to enjoy his opulence and to increase it. He incurred great expenses, amongst which this edifice was to benumbered. To support these he speculated boldly, and unfortunately; and thus the whole history is told, which may serve for more places than Glentanner.

Strange and various feelings ran through my bosom as I loitered in these deserted apartments, scarce hearing what my guide said to me about the size and destination of each room. The first sentiment, I am ashamed to say, was one of gratified spite. My patrician pride was pleased that the mechanic, who had not thought the house of the Croftangrys sufficiently good for him, had now experienced a fall in his turn. My next thought was as mean, though not so malicious. "I have had the better of this fellow," thought I. "If I lost the estate, I at least spent the price; and Mr. Treddles has lost his among paltry commercial engagements."

"Wretch!" said the secret voice within, "darest thou exult in thy shame? Recollect how thy youth and fortune was wasted in those years, and triumph not in the enjoyment of an existence which levelled thee with the beasts that perish. Bethink thee how this poor man's vanity gave at least bread to the labourer, peasant, and citizen; and his profuse expenditure, like water spilt on the ground, refreshed the lowly herbs and plants where it fell. But thou! Whom hast thou enriched during thy career of extravagance, save those brokers of the devil—vintners, panders, gamblers, and horse-jockeys?" The anguish produced by this self-reproof was so strong that I put my hand suddenly to my forehead, and was obliged to allege a sudden megrim to my attendant, in apology for the action, and a slight groan with which it was accompanied.

I then made an effort to turn my thoughts into a more philosophical current, and muttered half aloud, as a charm to lull any more painful thoughts to rest,—

"NUNC AGER UMBRENI SUB NOMINE, NUPER OFELLI
DICTUS ERIT NULLI PROPRIUS; SED CEDIT IN USUM
NUNC MIHI, NUNC ALII.  QUOCIRCA VIVITE FORTES,
FORTIAQUE ADVERSIS OPPONITE PECTORA REBUS."

[Horace Sat.II Lib.2. The meaning will be best conveyed to the English reader in Pope's imitation:—

"What's property, dear Swift? You see it alter
From you to me, from me to Peter Walter;
Or in a mortgage prove a lawyer's share;
Or in a jointure vanish from the heir.

*****    *****    *****    *****    *****    *****    *****

"Shades, that to Bacon could retreat afford,
Become the portion of a booby lord;
And Helmsley, once proud Buckingham's delight,
Slides to a scrivener and city knight.
Let lands and houses have what lords they will,
Let us be fix'd, and our own masters still."]

In my anxiety to fix the philosophical precept in my mind, I recited the last line aloud, which, joined to my previous agitation, I afterwards found became the cause of a report that a mad schoolmaster had come from Edinburgh, with the idea in his head of buying Castle Treddles.

As I saw my companion was desirous of getting rid of me, I asked where I was to find the person in whose hands were left the map of the estate, and other particulars connected with the sale. The agent who had this in possession, I was told, lived at the town of —, which I was informed, and indeed knew well, was distant five miles and a bittock, which may pass in a country where they are less lavish of their land for two or three more. Being somewhat afraid of the fatigue of walking so far, I inquired if a horse or any sort of carriage was to be had, and was answered in the negative.

"But," said my cicerone, "you may halt a blink till next morning at the Treddles Arms, a very decent house, scarce a mile off."

"A new house, I suppose?" replied I.

"No, it's a new public, but it's an auld house; it was aye the Leddy's jointure-house in the Croftangry folk's time. But Mr. Treddles has fitted it up for the convenience of the country, poor man, he was a public-spirited man when he had the means."

"Duntarkin a public-house!" I exclaimed.

"Ay!" said the fellow, surprised at my naming the place by its former title; "ye'll hae been in this country before, I'm thinking?"

"Long since," I replied. "And there is good accommodation at the what-d'ye-call-'em arms, and a civil landlord?" This I said by way of saying something, for the man stared very hard at me.

"Very decent accommodation. Ye'll no be for fashing wi' wine, I'm thinking; and there's walth o' porter, ale, and a drap gude whisky" (in an undertone)—"Fairntosh—if you call get on the lee-side of the gudewife—for there is nae gudeman. They ca' her Christie Steele."

I almost started at the sound. Christie Steele! Christie Steele was my mother's body-servant, her very right hand, and, between ourselves, something like a viceroy over her. I recollected her perfectly; and though she had in former times been no favourite of mine, her name now sounded in my ear like that of a friend, and was the first word I had heard somewhat in unison with the associations around me. I sallied from Castle Treddles, determined to make the best of my way to Duntarkin, and my cicerone hung by me for a little way, giving loose to his love of talking—an opportunity which, situated as he was, the seneschal of a deserted castle, was not likely to occur frequently.

"Some folk think," said my companion, "that Mr. Treddles might as weel have put my wife as Christie Steele into the Treddles Arms; for Christie had been aye in service, and never in the public line, and so it's like she is ganging back in the world, as I hear. Now, my wife had keepit a victualling office."

"That would have been an advantage, certainly," I replied.

"But I am no sure that I wad ha' looten Eppie take it, if they had put it in her offer."

"That's a different consideration."

"Ony way, I wadna ha' liked to have offended Mr. Treddles. He was a wee toustie when you rubbed him again the hair; but a kind, weel-meaning man."

I wanted to get rid of this species of chat, and finding myself near the entrance of a footpath which made a short cut to Duntarkin, I put half a crown into my guide's hand, bade him good-evening, and plunged into the woods.

"Hout, sir—fie, sir—no from the like of you. Stay, sir, ye wunna find the way that gate.—Odd's mercy, he maun ken the gate as weel as I do mysel'. Weel, I wad like to ken wha the child is."

Such were the last words of my guide's drowsy, uninteresting tone of voice and glad to be rid of him, I strode out stoutly, in despite of large stones, briers, and BAD STEPS, which abounded in the road I had chosen. In the interim, I tried as much as I could, with verses from Horace and Prior, and all who have lauded the mixture of literary with rural life, to call back the visions of last night and this morning, imagining myself settled in same detached farm of the estate of Glentanner,—

"Which sloping hills around enclose—
Where many a birch and brown oak grows,"

when I should have a cottage with a small library, a small cellar, a spare bed for a friend, and live more happy and more honoured than when I had the whole barony. But the sight of Castle Treddles had disturbed all my own castles in the air. The realities of the matter, like a stone plashed into a limpid fountain, had destroyed the reflection of the objects around, which, till this act of violence, lay slumbering on the crystal surface, and I tried in vain to re-establish the picture which had been so rudely broken. Well, then, I would try it another way. I would try to get Christie Steele out of her PUBLIC, since she was not striving in it, and she who had been my mother's governante should be mine. I knew all her faults, and I told her history over to myself.

She was grand-daughter, I believe—at least some relative—of the famous Covenanter of the name, whom Dean Swift's friend, Captain Creichton, shot on his own staircase in the times of the persecutions; [See Note 2.—Steele a Covenanter, shot by Captain Creichton.] and had perhaps derived from her native stock much both of its good and evil properties. No one could say of her that she was the life and spirit of the family, though in my mother's time she directed all family affairs. Her look was austere and gloomy, and when she was not displeased with you, you could only find it out by her silence. If there was cause for complaint, real or imaginary, Christie was loud enough. She loved my mother with the devoted attachment of a younger sister; but she was as jealous of her favour to any one else as if she had been the aged husband of a coquettish wife, and as severe in her reprehensions as an abbess over her nuns. The command which she exercised over her was that, I fear, of a strong and determined over a feeble and more nervous disposition and though it was used with rigour, yet, to the best of Christie Steele's belief, she was urging her mistress to her best and most becoming course, and would have died rather than have recommended any other. The attachment of this woman was limited to the family of Croftangry; for she had few relations, and a dissolute cousin, whom late in life she had taken as a husband, had long left her a widow.

To me she had ever a strong dislike. Even from my early childhood she was jealous, strange as it may seem, of my interest in my mother's affections. She saw my foibles and vices with abhorrence, and without a grain of allowance; nor did she pardon the weakness of maternal affection even when, by the death of two brothers, I came to be the only child of a widowed parent. At the time my disorderly conduct induced my mother to leave Glentanner, and retreat to her jointure-house, I always blamed Christie Steele for having influenced her resentment and prevented her from listening to my vows of amendment, which at times were real and serious, and might, perhaps, have accelerated that change of disposition which has since, I trust, taken place. But Christie regarded me as altogether a doomed and predestinated child of perdition, who was sure to hold on my course, and drag downwards whosoever might attempt to afford me support.

Still, though I knew such had been Christie's prejudices against me in other days, yet I thought enough of time had since passed away to destroy all of them. I knew that when, through the disorder of my affairs, my mother underwent some temporary inconvenience about money matters, Christie, as a thing of course, stood in the gap, and having sold a small inheritance which had descended to her, brought the purchase money to her mistress, with a sense of devotion as deep as that which inspired the Christians of the first age, when they sold all they had, and followed the apostles of the church. I therefore thought that we might, in old Scottish phrase, "let byganes be byganes," and begin upon a new account. Yet I resolved, like a skilful general, to reconnoitre a little before laying down any precise scheme of proceeding, and in the interim I determined to preserve my incognito.

## CHAPTER IV. MR. CROFTANGRY BIDS ADIEU TO CLYDESDALE.

Alas, how changed from what it once had been!
'Twas now degraded to a common inn.   GAY.

An hour's brisk walking, or thereabouts, placed me in front of Duntarkin, which had also, I found, undergone considerable alterations, though it had not been altogether demolished like the principal mansion. An inn-yard extended before the door of the decent little jointure-house, even amidst the remnants of the holly hedges which had screened the lady's garden. Then a broad, raw-looking, new-made road intruded itself up the little glen, instead of the old horseway, so seldom used that it was almost entirely covered with grass. It is a great enormity, of which gentlemen trustees on the highways are sometimes guilty, in adopting the breadth necessary for an avenue to the metropolis, where all that is required is an access to some sequestered and unpopulous district. I do not say anything of the expense—that the trustees and their constituents may settle as they please. But the destruction of silvan beauty is great when the breadth of the road is more than proportioned to the vale through which it runs, and lowers, of course, the consequence of any objects of wood or water, or broken and varied ground, which might otherwise attract notice and give pleasure. A bubbling runnel by the side of one of those modern Appian or Flaminian highways is but like a kennel; the little hill is diminished to a hillock—the romantic hillock to a molehill, almost too small for sight.

Such an enormity, however, had destroyed the quiet loneliness of Duntarkin, and intruded its breadth of dust and gravel, and its associations of pochays and mail-coaches, upon one of the most sequestered spots in the Middle Ward of Clydesdale. The house was old and dilapidated, and looked sorry for itself, as if sensible of a derogation; but the sign was strong and new, and brightly painted, displaying a heraldic shield (three shuttles in a field diapre), a web partly unfolded for crest, and two stout giants for supporters, each one holding a weaver's beam proper. To have displayed this monstrous emblem on the front of the house might have hazarded bringing down the wall, but for certain would have blocked up one or two windows. It was therefore established independent of the mansion, being displayed in an iron framework, and suspended upon two posts, with as much wood and iron about it as would have built a brig; and there it hung, creaking, groaning, and screaming in every blast of wind, and frightening for five miles' distance, for aught I know, the nests of thrushes and linnets, the ancient denizens of the little glen.

When I entered the place I was received by Christie Steele herself, who seemed uncertain whether to drop me in the kitchen, or usher me into a separate apartment, as I called for tea, with something rather more substantial than bread and butter, and spoke of supping and sleeping, Christie at last inducted me into the room where she herself had been sitting, probably the only one which had a fire, though the month was October. This answered my plan; and as she was about to remove her spinning-wheel, I begged she would have the goodness to remain and make my tea, adding that I liked the sound of the wheel, and desired not to disturb her housewife thrift in the least.

"I dinna ken, sir," she replied, in a dry, REVECHE tone, which carried me back twenty years, "I am nane of thae heartsome landleddies that can tell country cracks, and make themsel's agreeable, and I was ganging to put on a fire for you in the Red Room; but if it is your will to stay here, he that pays the lawing maun choose the lodging."

I endeavoured to engage her in conversation; but though she answered, with a kind of stiff civility, I could get her into no freedom of discourse, and she began to look at her wheel and at the door more than once, as if she meditated a retreat. I was obliged, therefore, to proceed to some special questions; that might have interest for a person whose ideas were probably of a very bounded description.

I looked round the apartment, being the same in which I had last seen my poor mother. The author of the family history, formerly mentioned, had taken great credit to himself for the improvements he had made in this same jointure-house of Duntarkin, and how, upon his marriage, when his mother took possession of the same as her jointure-house, "to his great charges and expenses he caused box the walls of the great parlour" (in which I was now sitting), "empanel the same, and plaster the roof, finishing the apartment with ane concave chimney, and decorating the same with pictures, and a barometer and thermometer." And in particular, which his good mother used to say she prized above all the rest, he had caused his own portraiture be limned over the mantlepiece by a skilful hand. And, in good faith, there he remained still, having much the visage which I was disposed to ascribe to him on the evidence of his handwriting,—grim and austere, yet not without a cast of shrewdness and determination; in armour, though he never wore it, I fancy; one hand on an open book, and one resting on the hilt of his sword, though I dare say his head never ached with reading, nor his limbs with fencing.

"That picture is painted on the wood, madam," said I.

"Ay, sir, or it's like it would not have been left there; they look a' they could."

"Mr. Treddles's creditors, you mean?" said I.

"Na," replied she dryly, "the creditors of another family, that sweepit cleaner than this poor man's, because I fancy there was less to gather."

"An older family, perhaps, and probably more remembered and regretted than later possessors?"

Christie here settled herself in her seat, and pulled her wheel towards her. I had given her something interesting for her thoughts to dwell upon, and her wheel was a mechanical accompaniment on such occasions, the revolutions of which assisted her in the explanation of her ideas.

"Mair regretted—mair missed? I liked ane of the auld family very weel, but I winna say that for them a'. How should they be mair missed than the Treddleses? The cotton mill was such a thing for the country! The mair bairns a cottar body had the better; they would make their awn keep frae the time they were five years auld, and a widow wi' three or four bairns was a wealthy woman in the time of the Treddleses."

"But the health of these poor children, my good friend—their education and religious instruction—"

"For health," said Christie, looking gloomily at me, "ye maun ken little of the warld, sir, if ye dinna ken that the health of the poor man's body, as well as his youth and his strength, are all at the command of the rich man's purse. There never was a trade so unhealthy yet but men would fight to get wark at it for twa pennies a day aboon the common wage. But the bairns were reasonably weel cared for in the way of air and exercise, and a very responsible youth heard them their Carritch, and gied them lessons in Reediemadeasy ["Reading made Easy," usually so pronounced in Scotland.] Now, what did they ever get before? Maybe on a winter day they wad be called out to beat the wood for cocks or siclike; and then the starving weans would maybe get a bite of broken bread, and maybe no, just as the butler was in humour—that was a' they got."

"They were not, then, a very kind family to the poor, these old possessors?" said I, somewhat bitterly; for I had expected to hear my ancestors' praises recorded, though I certainly despaired of being regaled with my own.

"They werena ill to them, sir, and that is aye something. They were just decent bien bodies; ony poor creature that had face to beg got an awmous, and welcome—they that were shamefaced gaed by, and twice as welcome. But they keepit an honest walk before God and man, the Croftangrys, and, as I said before, if they did little good, they did as little ill. They lifted their rents, and spent them; called in their kain and ate them; gaed to the kirk of a Sunday; bowed civilly if folk took aff their bannets as they gaed by, and lookit as black as sin at them that keepit them on."

"These are their arms that you have on the sign?"

"What! on the painted board that is skirling and groaning at the door? Na, these are Mr. Treddles's arms though they look as like legs as arms. Ill pleased I was at the fule thing, that cost as muckle as would hae repaired the house from the wa' stane to the rigging-tree. But if I am to bide here, I'll hae a decent board wi' a punch bowl on it."

"Is there a doubt of your staying here, Mrs. Steele?"

"Dinna Mistress me," said the cross old woman, whose fingers were now plying their thrift in a manner which indicated nervous irritation; "there was nae luck in the land since Luckie turned Mistress, and Mistress my Leddy. And as for staying here, if it concerns you to ken, I may stay if I can pay a hundred pund sterling for the lease, and I may flit if I canna, and so gude e'en to you, Christie,"—and round went the wheel with much activity.

"And you like the trade of keeping a public-house?"

"I can scarce say that," she replied. "But worthy Mr. Prendergast is clear of its lawfulness; and I hae gotten used to it, and made a decent living, though I never make out a fause reckoning, or give ony ane the means to disorder reason in my house."

"Indeed!" said I; "in that case, there is no wonder you have not made up the hundred pounds to purchase the lease."

"How do you ken," said she sharply, "that I might not have had a hundred punds of my ain fee? If I have it not, I am sure it is my ain faut. And I wunna ca' it faut neither, for it gaed to her wha was weel entitled to a' my service." Again she pulled stoutly at the flax, and the wheel went smartly round.

"This old gentleman," said I, fixing my eye on the painted panel, "seems to have had HIS arms painted as well as Mr. Treddles—that is, if that painting in the corner be a scutcheon."

"Ay, ay—cushion, just sae. They maun a' hae their cushions—there's sma' gentry without that—and so the arms, as they ca' them, of the house of Glentanner may be seen on an auld stane in the west end of the house. But to do them justice; they didna propale sae muckle about them as poor Mr. Treddles did—it's like they were better used to them."

"Very likely. Are there any of the old family in life, goodwife?"

"No," she replied; then added; after a moment's hesitation, "Not that I know of"—and the wheel, which had intermitted, began again to revolve.

"Gone abroad, perhaps?" I suggested.

She now looked up, and faced me. "No, sir. There were three sons of the last laird of Glentanner, as he was then called. John and William were hopeful young gentlemen, but they died early—one of a decline brought on by the mizzles, the other lost his life in a fever. It would hae been lucky for mony ane that Chrystal had gane the same gate."

"Oh, he must have been the young spendthrift that sold the property? Well, but you should you have such an ill-will against him; remember necessity has no law. And then, goodwife, he was not more culpable than Mr. Treddles, whom you are so sorry for."

"I wish I could think sae, sir, for his mother's sake. But Mr. Treddles was in trade, and though he had no preceese right to do so, yet there was some warrant for a man being expensive that imagined he was making a mint of money. But this unhappy lad devoured his patrimony, when he kenned that he was living like a ratten in a Dunlap cheese, and diminishing his means at a' hands. I canna bide to think on't." With this she broke out into a snatch of a ballad, but little of mirth was there either in the tone or the expression:—

"For he did spend, and make an end
Of gear that his forefathers wan;
Of land and ware he made him bare,

So speak nae mair of the auld gudeman."

"Come, dame," said I, "it is a long lane that has no turning. I will not keep from you that I have heard something of this poor fellow, Chrystal Croftangry. He has sown his wild oats, as they say, and has settled into a steady, respectable man."

"And wha tell'd ye that tidings?" said she, looking sharply at me.

"Not, perhaps, the best judge in the world of his character, for it was himself, dame."

"And if he tell'd you truth, it was a virtue he did not aye use to practise," said Christie.

"The devil!" said I, considerably nettled; "all the world held him to be a man of honour."

"Ay, ay! he would hae shot onybody wi' his pistols and his guns that had evened him to be a liar. But if he promised to pay an honest tradesman the next term-day, did he keep his word then? And if he promised a puir, silly lass to make gude her shame, did he speak truth then? And what is that but being a liar, and a black-hearted, deceitful liar to boot?"

My indignation was rising, but I strove to suppress it; indeed, I should only have afforded my tormentor a triumph by an angry reply. I partly suspected she began to recognize me, yet she testified so little emotion that I could not think my suspicion well founded. I went on, therefore, to say, in a tone as indifferent as I could command, "Well, goodwife, I see you will believe no good of this Chrystal of yours, till he comes back and buys a good farm on the estate, and makes you his housekeeper."

The old woman dropped her thread, folded her hands, as she looked up to heaven with a face of apprehension. "The Lord," she exclaimed, "forbid! The Lord in His mercy forbid! O sir! if you really know this unlucky man, persuade him to settle where folk ken the good that you say he has come to, and dinna ken the evil of his former days. He used to be proud enough—O dinna let him come here, even for his own sake. He used once to have some pride."

Here she once more drew the wheel close to her, and began to pull at the flax with both hands. "Dinna let him come here, to be looked down upon by ony that may be left of his auld reiving companions, and to see the decent folk that he looked over his nose at look over their noses at him, baith at kirk and market. Dinna let him come to his ain country, to be made a tale about when ony neighbour points him out to another, and tells what he is, and what he was, and how he wrecked a dainty estate, and brought harlots to the door-cheek of his father's house, till he made it nae residence for his mother; and how it had been foretauld by a servant of his ain house that he was a ne'er-do-weel and a child of perdition, and how her words were made good, and—"

"Stop there, goodwife, if you please," said I; "you have said as much as I can well remember, and more than it may be safe to repeat. I can use a great deal of freedom with the gentleman we speak of; but I think, were any other person to carry him half of your message, I would scarce ensure his personal safety. And now, as I see the night is settled to be a fine one, I will walk on to —, where I must meet a coach to-morrow as it passes to Edinburgh."

So saying, I paid my moderate reckoning, and took my leave, without being able to discover whether the prejudiced and hard-hearted old woman did, or did not, suspect the identity of her guest with the Chrystal Croftangry against whom she harboured so much dislike.

The night was fine and frosty, though, when I pretended to see what its character was, it might have rained like the deluge. I only made the excuse to escape from old Christie Steele. The horses which run races in the Corso at Rome without any riders, in order to stimulate their exertion, carry each his own spurs namely, small balls of steel, with sharp, projecting spikes, which are attached to loose straps of leather, and, flying about in the violence of the agitation, keep the horse to his speed by pricking him as they strike against his flanks. The old woman's reproaches had the same effect on me, and urged me to a rapid pace, as if it had been possible to escape from my own recollections. In the best days of my life, when I won one or two hard walking matches, I doubt if I ever walked so fast as I did betwixt the Treddles Arms and the borough town for which I was bound. Though the night was cold, I was warm enough by the time I got to my inn; and it required a refreshing draught of porter, with half an hour's repose, ere I could determine to give no further thought to Christie and her opinions than those of any other vulgar, prejudiced old woman. I resolved at last to treat the thing EN BAGATELLE, and calling for writing materials, I folded up a cheque for L100, with these lines on the envelope:—

"Chrystal, the ne'er-do-weel,
Child destined to the deil,
Sends this to Christie Steele."

And I was so much pleased with this new mode of viewing the subject, that I regretted the lateness of the hour prevented my finding a person to carry the letter express to its destination.

"But with the morning cool reflection came."

I considered that the money, and probably more, was actually due by me on my mother's account to Christie, who had lent it in a moment of great necessity, and that the returning it in a light or ludicrous manner was not unlikely to prevent so touchy and punctilious a person from accepting a debt which was most justly her due, and which it became me particularly to see satisfied. Sacrificing, then, my triad with little regret (for it looked better by candlelight, and through the medium of a pot of porter, than it did by daylight, and with bohea for a menstruum), I determined to employ Mr. Fairscribe's mediation in buying up the lease of the little inn, and conferring it upon Christie in the way which should make it most acceptable to her feelings. It is only necessary to add that my plan succeeded, and that Widow Steele even yet keeps the Treddles Arms. Do not say, therefore, that I have been disingenuous with you, reader; since, if I have not told all the ill of myself I might have done, I have indicated to you a person able and willing to supply the blank, by relating all my delinquencies as well as my misfortunes.

In the meantime I totally abandoned the idea of redeeming any part of my paternal property, and resolved to take Christie Steele's advice, as young Norval does Glenalvon's, "although it sounded harshly."

## CHAPTER V. MR. CROFTANGRY SETTLES IN THE CANONGATE.

If you will know my house,
'Tis at the tuft of olives here hard by.   AS YOU LIKE IT.

By a revolution of humour which I am unable to account for, I changed my mind entirely on my plans of life, in consequence of the disappointment, the history of which fills the last chapter. I began to discover that the country would not at all suit me; for I had relinquished field-sports, and felt no inclination whatever to farming, the ordinary vocation of country gentlemen. Besides that, I had no talent for assisting either candidate in case of an expected election, and saw no amusement in the duties of a road trustee, a commissioner of supply, or even in the magisterial functions of the bench. I had begun to take some taste for reading; and a domiciliation in the country must remove me from the use of books, excepting the small subscription library, in which the very book which you want is uniformly sure to be engaged.

I resolved, therefore, to make the Scottish metropolis my regular resting-place, reserving to myself to take occasionally those excursions which, spite of all I have said against mail-coaches, Mr. Piper has rendered so easy. Friend of our life and of our leisure, he secures by dispatch against loss of time, and by the best of coaches, cattle, and steadiest of drivers, against hazard of limb, and wafts us, as well as our letters, from Edinburgh to Cape Wrath in the penning of a paragraph.

When my mind was quite made up to make Auld Reekie my headquarters, reserving the privilege of EXPLORING in all directions, I began to explore in good earnest for the purpose of discovering a suitable habitation. "And whare trew ye I gaed?" as Sir Pertinax says. Not to George's Square—nor to Charlotte Square—nor to the old New Town—nor to the new New Town—nor to the Calton Hill. I went to the Canongate, and to the very portion of the Canongate in which I had formerly been immured, like the errant knight, prisoner in some enchanted castle, where spells have made the ambient air impervious to the unhappy captive, although the organs of sight encountered no obstacle to his free passage.

Why I should have thought of pitching my tent here I cannot tell. Perhaps it was to enjoy the pleasures of freedom where I had so long endured the bitterness of restraint, on the principle of the officer who, after he had retired from the army, ordered his servant to continue to call him at the hour or parade, simply that he might have the pleasure of saying, "D—n the parade!" and turning to the other side to enjoy his slumbers. Or perhaps I expected to find in the vicinity some little old-fashioned house, having somewhat of the RUS IN URBE which I was ambitious of enjoying. Enough: I went, as aforesaid, to the Canongate.

I stood by the kennel, of which I have formerly spoken, and, my mind being at ease, my bodily organs were more delicate. I was more sensible than heretofore, that, like the trade of Pompey in MEASURE FOR MEASURE,—it did in some sort—pah an ounce of civet, good apothecary! Turning from thence, my steps naturally directed themselves to my own humble apartment, where my little Highland landlady, as dapper and as tight as ever, (for old women wear a hundred times better than the hard-wrought seniors of the masculine sex), stood at the door, TEEDLING to herself a Highland song as she shook a table napkin over the fore-stair, and then proceeded to fold it up neatly for future service.

"How do you, Janet?"

"Thank ye, good sir," answered my old friend, without looking at me; "but ye might as weel say Mrs. MacEvoy, for she is na a'body's Shanet—umph."

"You must be MY Janet, though, for all that. Have you forgot me? Do you not remember Chrystal Croftangry?"

The light, kind-hearted creature threw her napkin into the open door, skipped down the stair like a fairy, three steps at once, seized me by the hands—both hands—jumped up, and actually kissed me. I was a little ashamed; but what swain, of somewhere inclining to sixty could resist the advances of a fair contemporary? So we allowed the full degree of kindness to the meeting—HONI SOIT QUI MAL Y PENSE—and then Janet entered instantly upon business. "An ye'll gae in, man, and see your auld lodgings, nae doubt and Shanet will pay ye the fifteen shillings of change that ye ran away without, and without bidding Shanet good day. But never mind" (nodding good-humouredly), "Shanet saw you were carried for the time."

By this time we were in my old quarters, and Janet, with her bottle of cordial in one hand and the glass in the other, had forced on me a dram of usquebaugh, distilled with saffron and other herbs, after some old-fashioned Highland receipt. Then was unfolded, out of many a little scrap of paper, the reserved sum of fifteen shillings, which Janet had treasured for twenty years and upwards.

"Here they are," she said, in honest triumph, "just the same I was holding out to ye when ye ran as if ye had been fey. Shanet has had siller, and Shanet has wanted siller, mony a time since that. And the gauger has come, and the factor has come, and the butcher and baker—Cot bless us just like to tear poor auld Shanet to pieces; but she took good care of Mr. Croftangry's fifteen shillings."

"But what if I had never come back, Janet?"

"Och, if Shanet had heard you were dead, she would hae gien it to the poor of the chapel, to pray for Mr. Croftangry," said Janet, crossing herself, for she was a Catholic, "You maybe do not think it would do you cood, but the blessing of the poor can never do no harm."

I agreed heartily in Janet's conclusion; and as to have desired her to consider the hoard as her own property would have been an indelicate return to her for the uprightness of her conduct, I requested her to dispose of it as she had proposed to do in the event of my death—that is, if she knew any poor people of merit to whom it might be useful.

"Ower mony of them," raising the corner of her checked apron to her eyes—"e'en ower mony of them, Mr. Croftangry. Och, ay. 'There is the puir Highland creatures frae Glenshee, that cam down for the harvest, and are lying wi' the fever—five shillings to them; and half a crown to Bessie MacEvoy, whose coodman, puir creature, died of the frost, being a shairman, for a' the whisky he could drink to keep it out o' his stamoch; and—"

But she suddenly interrupted the bead-roll of her proposed charities, and assuming a very sage look, and primming up her little chattering mouth, she went on in a different tone—"But och, Mr. Croftangry, bethink ye whether ye will not need a' this siller yoursel', and maybe look back and think lang for ha'en kiven it away, whilk is a creat sin to forthink a wark o' charity, and also is unlucky, and moreover is not the thought of a shentleman's son like yoursel', dear. And I say this, that ye may think a bit, for your mother's son kens that ye are no so careful as you should be of the gear, and I hae tauld ye of it before, jewel."

I assured her I could easily spare the money, without risk of future repentance; and she went on to infer that in such a case "Mr. Croftangry had grown a rich man in foreign parts, and was free of his troubles with messengers and sheriff-officers, and siclike scum of the earth, and Shanet MacEvoy's mother's daughter be a blithe woman to hear it. But if Mr. Croftangry was in trouble, there was his room, and his ped, and Shanet to wait on him, and tak payment when it was quite convenient."

I explained to Janet my situation, in which she expressed unqualified delight. I then proceeded to inquire into her own circumstances, and though she spoke cheerfully and contentedly, I could see they were precarious. I had paid more than was due; other lodgers fell into an opposite error, and forgot to pay Janet at all. Then, Janet being ignorant of all indirect modes of screwing money out of her lodgers, others in the same line of life, who were sharper than the poor, simple Highland woman, were enabled to let their apartments cheaper in appearance, though the inmates usually found them twice as dear in the long run.

As I had already destined my old landlady to be my house-keeper and governante, knowing her honesty, good-nature, and, although a Scotchwoman, her cleanliness and excellent temper (saving the short and hasty expressions of anger which Highlanders call a FUFF), I now proposed the plan to her in such a way as was likely to make it most acceptable. Very acceptable as the proposal was, as I could plainly see, Janet, however, took a day to consider upon it; and her reflections against our next meeting had suggested only one objection, which was singular enough.

"My honour," so she now termed me, "would pe for biding in some fine street apout the town. Now Shanet wad ill like to live in a place where polish, and sheriffs, and bailiffs, and sie thieves and trash of the world, could tak puir shentlemen by the throat, just because they wanted a wheen dollars in the sporran. She had lived in the bonny glen of Tomanthoulick. Cot, an ony of the vermint had come there, her father wad hae wared a shot on them, and he could hit a buck within as many measured yards as e'er a man of his clan, And the place here was so quiet frae them, they durst na put their nose ower the gutter. Shanet owed nobody a bodle, but she couldna pide to see honest folk and pretty shentlemen forced away to prison whether they would or no; and then, if Shanet was to lay her tangs ower ane of the ragamuffins' heads, it would be, maybe, that the law would gi'ed a hard name."

One thing I have learned in life—never to speak sense when nonsense will answer the purpose as well. I should have had great difficulty to convince this practical and disinterested admirer and vindicator of liberty, that arrests seldom or never were to be seen in the streets of Edinburgh; and to satisfy her of their justice and necessity would have been as difficult as to convert her to the Protestant faith. I therefore assured her my intention, if I could get a suitable habitation, was to remain in the quarter where she at present dwelt. Janet gave three skips on the floor, and uttered as many short, shrill yells of joy. Yet doubt almost instantly returned, and she insisted on knowing what possible reason I could have for making my residence where few lived, save those whose misfortunes drove them thither. It occurred to me to answer her by recounting the legend of the rise of my family, and of our deriving our name from a particular place near Holyrood Palace. This, which would have appeared to most people a very absurd reason for choosing a residence, was entirely satisfactory to Janet MacEvoy.

"Och, nae doubt! if it was the land of her fathers, there was nae mair to be said. Put it was queer that her family estate should just lie at the town tail, and covered with houses, where the King's cows—Cot bless them, hide and horn—used to craze upon. It was strange changes." She mused a little, and then added: "Put it is something better wi' Croftangry when the changes is frae the field to the habited place, and not from the place of habitation to the desert; for Shanet, her nainsell, kent a glen where there were men as weel as there may be in Croftangry, and if there werena altogether sae mony of them, they were as good men in their tartan as the others in their broadcloth. And there were houses, too; and if they were not biggit with stane and lime, and lofted like the houses at Croftangry, yet they served the purpose of them that lived there, and mony a braw bonnet, and mony a silk snood and comely white curch, would come out to gang to kirk or chapel on the Lord's day, and little bairns toddling after. And now—Och, Och, Ohellany, Ohonari! the glen is desolate, and the braw snoods and bonnets are gane, and the Saxon's house stands dull and lonely, like the single bare-breasted rock that the falcon builds on—the falcon that drives the heath-bird frae the glen."

Janet, like many Highlanders, was full of imagination, and, when melancholy themes came upon her, expressed herself almost poetically, owing to the genius of the Celtic language in which she thought, and in which, doubtless, she would have spoken, had I understood Gaelic. In two minutes the shade of gloom and regret had passed from her good-humoured features, and she was again the little, busy, prating, important old woman, undisputed owner of one flat of a small tenement in the Abbey Yard, and about to be promoted to be housekeeper to an elderly bachelor gentleman, Chrystal Croftangry, Esq.

It was not long before Janet's local researches found out exactly the sort of place I wanted, and there we settled. Janet was afraid I would not be satisfied, because it is not exactly part of Croftangry; but I stopped her doubts by assuring her it had been part and pendicle thereof in my forefather' time, which passed very well.

I do not intend to possess any one with an exact knowledge of my lodging; though, as Bobadil says, "I care not who knows it, since the cabin is convenient." But I may state in general, that it is a house "within itself," or, according to a newer phraseology in advertisements, SELF-CONTAINED, has a garden of near half an acre, and a patch of ground with trees in front. It boasts five rooms and servants' apartments—looks in front upon the palace, and from behind towards the hill and crags of the King's Park. Fortunately, the place had a name, which, with a little improvement, served to countenance the legend which I had imposed on Janet, and would not, perhaps have been sorry if I had been able to impose on myself. It was called Littlecroft; we have dubbed it Little Croftangry, and the men of letters belonging to the Post Office have sanctioned the change, and deliver letters so addressed. Thus I am to all intents and purposes Chrystal Croftangry of that Ilk.

My establishment consists of Janet, an under maid-servant, and a Highland wench for Janet to exercise her Gaelic upon, with a handy lad who can lay the cloth, and take care, besides, of a pony, on which I find my way to Portobello sands, especially when the cavalry have a drill; for, like an old fool as I am, I have not altogether become indifferent to the tramp of horses and the flash of weapons, of which, though no professional soldier, it has been my fate to see something in my youth. For wet mornings I have my book; is it fine weather? I visit, or I wander on the Crags, as the humour dictates. My dinner is indeed solitary, yet not quite so neither; for though Andrew waits, Janet—or, as she is to all the world but her master and certain old Highland gossips, Mrs. MacEvoy—attends, bustles about, and desires to see everything is in first-rate order, and to tell me, Cot pless us, the wonderful news of the palace for the day. When the cloth is removed, and I light my cigar, and begin to husband a pint of port, or a glass of old whisky and water, it is the rule of the house that Janet takes a chair at some distance, and nods or works her stocking, as she may be disposed—ready to speak, if I am in the talking humour, and sitting quiet as a mouse if I am rather inclined to study a book or the newspaper. At six precisely she makes my tea, and leaves me to drink it; and then occurs an interval of time which most old bachelors find heavy on their hands. The theatre is a good occasional resource, especially if Will Murray acts, or a bright star of eminence shines forth; but it is distant, and so are one or two public societies to which I belong. Besides, these evening walks are all incompatible with the elbow-chair feeling, which desires some employment that may divert the mind without fatiguing the body.

Under the influence of these impressions, I have sometimes thought of this literary undertaking. I must have been the Bonassus himself to have mistaken myself for a genius; yet I have leisure and reflections like my neighbours. I am a borderer, also, between two generations, and can point out more, perhaps, than others of those fading traces of antiquity which are daily vanishing; and I know many a modern instance and many an old tradition, and therefore I ask—

> "What ails me, I may not as well as they
> Rake up some threadbare tales, that mouldering lay
> In chimney corners, wont by Christmas fires
> To read and rock to sleep our ancient sires?
> No man his threshold better knows, than I
> Brute's first arrival and first victory,
> Saint George's sorrel and his cross of blood,
> Arthur's round board and Caledonian wood."

No shop is so easily set up as an antiquary's. Like those of the lowest order of pawnbrokers, a commodity of rusty iron, a bay or two of hobnails, a few odd shoe-buckles, cashiered kail-pots, and fire-irons declared incapable of service, are quite sufficient to set him up. If he add a sheaf or two of penny ballads and broadsides, he is a great man—an extensive trader. And then, like the pawnbrokers aforesaid, if the author understands a little legerdemain, he may, by dint of a little picking and stealing, make the inside of his shop a great deal richer than the out, and be able to show you things which cause those who do not understand the antiquarian trick of clean conveyance to wonder how the devil he came by them.

It may be said that antiquarian articles interest but few customers, and that we may bawl ourselves as rusty as the wares we deal in without any one asking; the price of our merchandise. But I do not rest my hopes upon this department of my labours only. I propose also to have a corresponding shop for Sentiment, and Dialogues, and Disquisition, which may captivate the fancy of those who have no relish, as the established phrase goes, for pure antiquity—a sort of greengrocer's stall erected in front of my ironmongery wares, garlanding the rusty memorials of ancient times with cresses, cabbages, leeks, and water purpy.

As I have some idea that I am writing too well to be understood, I humble myself to ordinary language, and aver, with becoming modesty, that I do think myself capable of sustaining a publication of a miscellaneous nature, as like to the Spectator or the Guardian, the Mirror or the Lounger, as my poor abilities may be able to accomplish. Not that I have any purpose of imitating Johnson, whose general learning and power of expression I do not deny, but many of whose Ramblers are little better than a sort of pageant, where trite and obvious maxims are made to swagger in lofty and mystic language, and get some credit only because they are not easily understood. There are some of the great moralist's papers which I cannot peruse without thinking on a second-rate masquerade, where the best-known and least-esteemed characters in town march in as heroes, and sultans, and so forth, and, by dint of tawdry dresses, get some consideration until they are found out. It is not, however, prudent to commence with throwing stones, just when I am striking out windows of my own.

I think even the local situation of Little Croftangry may be considered as favourable to my undertaking. A nobler contrast there can hardly exist than that of the huge city, dark with the smoke of ages, and groaning with the various sounds of active industry or idle revel, and the lofty and craggy hill, silent and solitary as the grave—one exhibiting the full tide of existence, pressing and precipitating itself forward with the force of an inundation; the other resembling some time-worn anchorite, whose life passes as silent and unobserved as the slender rill which escapes unheard, and scarce seen, from the fountain of his patron saint. The city resembles the busy temple, where the modern Comus and Mammon hold their court, and thousands sacrifice ease, independence, and virtue itself at their shrine; the misty and lonely mountain seems as a throne to the majestic but terrible Genius of feudal times, when the same divinities dispensed coronets and domains to those who had heads to devise and arms to execute bold enterprises.

I have, as it were, the two extremities of the moral world at my threshold. From the front door a few minutes' walk brings me into the heart of a wealthy and populous city; as many paces from my opposite entrance place me in a solitude as complete as Zimmerman could have desired. Surely, with such aids to my imagination, I may write better than if I were in a lodging in the New Town or a garret in the old. As the Spaniard says, "VIAMOS—CARACCO!"

I have not chosen to publish periodically, my reason for which was twofold. In the first place, I don't like to be hurried, and have had enough of duns in an early part of my life to make me reluctant to hear of or see one, even in the less awful shape of a printer's devil. But, secondly, a periodical paper is not easily extended in circulation beyond the quarter in which it is published. This work, if published in fugitive numbers, would scarce, without a high pressure on the part of the bookseller, be raised above the Netherbow, and never could be expected to ascend to the level of Princes Street. Now, I am ambitious that my compositions, though having their origin in this Valley of Holyrood, should not only be extended into those exalted regions I have mentioned, but also that they should cross the Forth, astonish the long town of Kirkcaldy, enchant the skippers and colliers of the East of Fife, venture even into the classic arcades of St. Andrews, and travel as much farther to the north as the breath of applause will carry their sails. As for a southward direction, it is not to be hoped for in my fondest dreams. I am informed that Scottish literature, like Scottish whisky, will be presently laid under a prohibitory duty. But enough of this. If any reader is dull enough not to comprehend the advantages which, in point of circulation, a compact book has over a collection of fugitive numbers, let him try the range of a gun loaded with hail-shot against that of the same piece charged with an equal weight of lead consolidated in a single bullet.

Besides, it was of less consequence that I should have published periodically, since I did not mean to solicit or accept of the contributions of friends, or the criticisms of those who may be less kindly disposed. Notwithstanding the excellent examples which might be quoted, I will establish no begging-box, either under the name of a lion's head or an ass's. What is good or ill shall be mine own, or the contribution of friends to whom I may have private access. Many of my voluntary assistants might be cleverer than myself, and then I should have a brilliant article appear among my chiller effusions, like a patch of lace on a Scottish cloak of Galashiels grey. Some might be worse, and then I must reject them, to the injury of the feelings of the writer, or else insert them, to make my own darkness yet more opaque and palpable. "Let every herring," says our old-fashioned proverb, "hang by his own head."

One person, however, I may distinguish, as she is now no more, who, living to the utmost term of human life, honoured me with a great share of her friendship—as, indeed, we were blood-relatives in the Scottish sense—Heaven knows how many degrees removed—and friends in the sense of Old England. I mean the late excellent and regretted Mrs. Bethune Baliol. But as I design this admirable picture of the olden time for a principal character in my work, I will only say here that she knew and approved of my present purpose; and though she declined to contribute to it while she lived, from a sense of dignified retirement, which she thought became her age, sex, and condition in life, she left me some materials for carrying on my proposed work which I coveted when I heard her detail them in conversation, and which now, when I have their substance in her own handwriting, I account far more valuable than anything I have myself to offer. I hope the mentioning her name in conjunction with my own will give no offence to any of her numerous friends, as it was her own express pleasure that I should employ the manuscripts which she did me the honour to bequeath me in the manner in which I have now used them. It must be added, however, that in most cases I have disguised names, and in some have added shading and colouring to bring out the narrative.

Much of my materials, besides these, are derived from friends, living or dead. The accuracy of some of these may be doubtful, in which case I shall be happy to receive, from sufficient authority, the correction of the errors which must creep into traditional documents. The object of the whole publication is to throw some light on the manners of Scotland as they were, and to contrast them occasionally with those of the present day. My own opinions are in favour of our own times in many respects, but not in so far as affords means for exercising the imagination or exciting the interest which attaches to other times. I am glad to be a writer or a reader in 1826, but I would be most interested in reading or relating what happened from half a century to a century before. We have the best of it. Scenes in which our ancestors thought deeply, acted fiercely, and died desperately, are to us tales to divert the tedium of a winter's evening, when we are engaged to no party, or beguile a summer's morning, when it is too scorching to ride or walk.

Yet I do not mean that my essays and narratives should be limited to Scotland. I pledge myself to no particular line of subjects, but, on the contrary, say with Burns—

"Perhaps it may turn out a sang,
Perhaps turn out a sermon."

I have only to add, by way of postscript to these preliminary chapters, that I have had recourse to Moliere's recipe, and read my manuscript over to my old woman, Janet MacEvoy.

The dignity of being consulted delighted Janet; and Wilkie, or Allan, would have made a capital sketch of her, as she sat upright in her chair, instead of her ordinary lounging posture, knitting her stocking systematically, as if she meant every twist of her thread and inclination of the wires to bear burden to the cadence of my voice. I am afraid, too, that I myself felt more delight than I ought to have done in my own composition, and read a little more oratorically than I should have ventured to do before an auditor of whose applause I was not so secure. And the result did not entirely encourage my plan of censorship. Janet did indeed seriously incline to the account of my previous life, and bestowed some Highland maledictions, more emphatic than courteous, on Christie Steele's reception of a "shentlemans in distress," and of her own mistress's house too. I omitted for certain reasons, or greatly abridged, what related to her-self. But when I came to treat of my general views in publication, I saw poor Janet was entirely thrown out, though, like a jaded hunter, panting, puffing, and short of wind, she endeavoured at least to keep up with the chase. Or, rather, her perplexity made her look all the while like a deaf person ashamed of his infirmity, who does not understand a word you are saying, yet desires you to believe that he does understand you, and who is extremely jealous that you suspect his incapacity. When she saw that some remark was necessary, she resembled exactly in her criticism the devotee who pitched on the "sweet word Mesopotamia" as the most edifying note which she could bring away from a sermon. She indeed hastened to bestow general praise on what she said was all "very fine;" but chiefly dwelt on what I, had said about Mr. Timmerman, as she was pleased to call the German philosopher, and supposed he must be of the same descent with the Highland clan of M'Intyre, which signifies Son of the Carpenter. "And a fery honourable name too—Shanet's own mither was a M'Intyre."

In short, it was plain the latter part of my introduction was altogether lost on poor Janet; and so, to have acted up to Moliere's system, I should have cancelled the whole, and written it anew. But I do not know how it is. I retained, I suppose, some tolerable opinion of my own composition, though Janet did not comprehend it, and felt loath to retrench those Delilahs of the imagination, as Dryden calls them, the tropes and figures of which are caviar to the multitude. Besides, I hate rewriting as much as Falstaff did paying back—it is a double labour. So I determined with myself to consult Janet, in future, only on such things as were within the limits of her comprehension, and hazard my arguments and my rhetoric on the public without her imprimatur. I am pretty sure she will "applaud it done." and in such narratives as come within her range of thought and feeling I shall, as I first intended, take the benefit of her unsophisticated judgment, and attend to it deferentially—that is, when it happens not to be in peculiar opposition to my own; for, after all, I say with Almanzor,—

"Know that I alone am king of me."

The reader has now my who and my whereabout, the purpose of the work, and the circumstances under which it is undertaken. He has also a specimen of the author's talents, and may judge for himself, and proceed, or send back the volume to the bookseller, as his own taste shall determine.

## CHAPTER VI. MR. CROFTANGRY'S ACCOUNT OF MRS. BETHUNE BALIOL.

The moon, were she earthly, no nobler.   CORIOLANUS.

When we set out on the jolly voyage of life, what a brave fleet there is around us, as, stretching our finest canvas to the breeze, all "shipshape and Bristol fashion," pennons flying, music playing, cheering each other as we pass, we are rather amused than alarmed when some awkward comrade goes right ashore for want of pilotage! Alas! when the voyage is well spent, and we look about us, toil-worn mariners, how few of our ancient consorts still remain in sight; and they, how torn and wasted, and, like ourselves, struggling to keep as long as possible off the fatal shore, against which we are all finally drifting!

I felt this very trite but melancholy truth in all its force the other day, when a packet with a black seal arrived, containing a letter addressed to me by my late excellent friend Mrs. Martha Bethune Baliol, and marked with the fatal indorsation, "To be delivered according to address, after I shall be no more." A letter from her executors accompanied the packet, mentioning that they had found in her will a bequest to me of a painting of some value, which she stated would just fit the space above my cupboard, and fifty guineas to buy a ring. And thus I separated, with all the kindness which we had maintained for many years, from a friend, who, though old enough to have been the companion of my mother, was yet, in gaiety of spirits and admirable sweetness of temper, capable of being agreeable, and even animating society, for those who write themselves in the vaward of youth, an advantage which I have lost for these five-and-thirty years. The contents of the packet I had no difficulty in guessing, and have partly hinted at them in the last chapter. But to instruct the reader in the particulars, and at the same time to indulge myself with recalling the virtues and agreeable qualities of my late friend, I will give a short sketch of her manners and habits.

Mrs. Martha Bethune Baliol was a person of quality and fortune, as these are esteemed in Scotland. Her family was ancient, and her connections honourable. She was not fond of specially indicating her exact age, but her juvenile recollections stretched backwards till before the eventful year 1745, and she remembered the Highland clans being in possession of the Scottish capital, though probably only as an indistinct vision. Her fortune, independent by her father's bequest, was rendered opulent by the death of more than one brave brother, who fell successively in the service of their country, so that the family estates became vested in the only surviving child of the ancient house of Bethune Baliol. My intimacy was formed with the excellent lady after this event, and when she was already something advanced in age.

She inhabited, when in Edinburgh, where she regularly spent the winter season, one of those old hotels which, till of late, were to be found in the neighbourhood of the Canongate and of the Palace of Holyrood House, and which, separated from the street, now dirty and vulgar, by paved courts and gardens of some extent, made amends for an indifferent access, by showing something of aristocratic state and seclusion when you were once admitted within their precincts. They have pulled her house down; for, indeed, betwixt building and burning, every ancient monument of the Scottish capital is now likely to be utterly demolished. I pause on the recollections of the place, however; and since nature has denied a pencil when she placed a pen in my hand, I will endeavour to make words answer the purpose of delineation.

Baliol's Lodging, so was the mansion named, reared its high stack of chimneys, among which were seen a turret or two, and one of those small projecting platforms called bartizans, above the mean and modern buildings which line the south side of the Canongate, towards the lower end of that street, and not distant from the Palace. A PORTE COCHERE, having a wicket for foot passengers, was, upon due occasion, unfolded by a lame old man, tall, grave, and thin, who tenanted a hovel beside the gate, and acted as porter. To this office he had been promoted by my friend's charitable feelings for an old soldier, and partly by an idea that his head, which was a very fine one, bore some resemblance to that of Garrick in the character of Lusignan. He was a man saturnine, silent, and slow in his proceedings, and would never open the PORTE COCHERE to a hackney coach, indicating the wicket with his finger as the proper passage for all who came in that obscure vehicle, which was not permitted to degrade with its ticketed presence the dignity of Baliol's Lodging. I do not think this peculiarity would have met with his lady's approbation, any more than the occasional partiality of Lusignan, or, as mortals called him, Archie Macready, to a dram. But Mrs. Martha Bethune Baliol, conscious that, in case of conviction, she could never have prevailed upon herself to dethrone the King of Palestine from the stone bench on which he sat for hours knitting his stocking, refused, by accrediting the intelligence, even to put him upon his trial, well judging that he would observe more wholesome caution if he conceived his character unsuspected, than if he were detected, and suffered to pass unpunished. For after all, she said, it would be cruel to dismiss an old Highland soldier for a peccadillo so appropriate to his country and profession.

The stately gate for carriages, or the humble accommodation for foot-passengers, admitted into a narrow and short passage running between two rows of lime-trees, whose green foliage during the spring contrasted strangely with the swart complexion of the two walls by the side of which they grew. This access led to the front of the house, which was formed by two gable ends, notched, and having their windows adorned with heavy architectural ornaments. They joined each other at right angles; and a half circular tower, which contained the entrance and the staircase, occupied the point of junction, and rounded the acute angle. One of other two sides of the little court, in which there was just sufficient room to turn a carriage, was occupied by some low buildings answering the purpose of offices; the other, by a parapet surrounded by a highly-ornamented iron railing, twined round with honeysuckle and other parasitical shrubs, which permitted the eye to peep into a pretty suburban garden, extending down to the road called the South Back of the Canongate, and boasting a number of old trees, many flowers, and even some fruit. We must not forget to state that the extreme cleanliness of the courtyard was such as intimated that mop and pail had done their utmost in that favoured spot to atone for the general dirt and dinginess of the quarter where the premises were situated.

Over the doorway were the arms of Bethune and Baliol, with various other devices, carved in stone. The door itself was studded with iron nails, and formed of black oak; an iron rasp, as it was called, was placed on it, instead of a knocker, for the purpose of summoning the attendants. [See Note 3.—Iron Rasp.] He who usually appeared at the summons was a smart lad, in a handsome livery, the son of Mrs. Martha's gardener at Mount Baliol. Now and then a servant girl, nicely but plainly dressed, and fully accoutred with stockings and shoes, would perform this duty; and twice or thrice I remember being admitted by Beauffet himself, whose exterior looked as much like that of a clergyman of rank as the butler of a gentleman's family. He had been valet-de-chambre to the last Sir Richard Bethune Baliol, and was, a person highly trusted by the present lady. A full stand, as it is called in Scotland, of garments of a dark colour, gold buckles in his shoes and at the knees of his breeches, with his hair regularly dressed and powdered, announced him to be a domestic of trust and importance. His mistress used to say of him,—

"He is sad and civil,
And suits well for a servant with my fortunes."

As no one can escape scandal, some said that Beauffet made a rather better thing of the place than the modesty of his old-fashioned wages would, unassisted, have amounted to. But the man was always very civil to me. He had been long in the family, had enjoyed legacies, and lain by a something of his own, upon which he now enjoys ease with dignity, in as far as his newly-married wife, Tibbie Shortacres, will permit him.

The Lodging—dearest reader, if you are tired, pray pass over the next four or five pages—was not by any means so large as its external appearance led people to conjecture. The interior accommodation was much cut up by cross walls and long passages, and that neglect of economizing space which characterizes old Scottish architecture. But there was far more room than my old friend required, even when she had, as was often the case, four or five young cousins under her protection; and I believe much of the house was unoccupied. Mrs. Bethune Baliol never, in my presence, showed herself so much offended as once with a meddling person who advised her to have the windows of these supernumerary apartments built up to save the tax. She said in ire that, while she lived, the light of God should visit the house of her fathers; and while she had a penny, king and country should have their due. Indeed, she was punctiliously loyal, even in that most staggering test of loyalty, the payment of imposts. Mr. Beauffet told me he was ordered to offer a glass of wine to the person who collected the income tax, and that the poor man was so overcome by a reception so unwontedly generous, that he had well-nigh fainted on the spot.

You entered by a matted anteroom into the eating-parlour, filled with old-fashioned furniture, and hung with family portraits, which, excepting one of Sir Bernard Bethune, in James the Sixth's time, said to be by Jameson, were exceedingly frightful. A saloon, as it was called, a long, narrow chamber, led out of the dining-parlour, and served for a drawing-room. It was a pleasant apartment, looking out upon the south flank of

Holyrood House, the gigantic slope of Arthur's Seat, and the girdle of lofty rocks called Salisbury Crags; objects so rudely wild, that the mind can hardly conceive them to exist in the vicinage of a populous metropolis. [The Rev. Mr. Bowles derives the name of these crags, as of the Episcopal city in the west of England, from the same root, both, in his opinion, which he very ably defends and illustrates, having been the sites of Druidical temples.] The paintings of the saloon came from abroad, and had some of them much merit. To see the best of them, however, you must be admitted into the very PENETRALIA of the temple, and allowed to draw the tapestry at the upper end of the saloon, and enter Mrs. Martha's own special dressing-room. This was a charming apartment, of which it would be difficult to describe the form, it had so many recesses which were filled up with shelves of ebony and cabinets of japan and ormolu—some for holding books, of which Mrs. Martha had an admirable collection, some for a display of ornamental china, others for shells and similar curiosities. In a little niche, half screened by a curtain of crimson silk, was disposed a suit of tilting armour of bright steel inlaid with silver, which had been worn on some memorable occasion by Sir Bernard Bethune, already mentioned; while over the canopy of the niche hung the broadsword with which her father had attempted to change the fortunes of Britain in 1715, and the spontoon which her elder brother bore when he was leading on a company of the Black Watch at Fontenoy. [The well-known original designation of the gallant 42nd Regiment. Being the first corps raised for the royal service in the Highlands, and allowed to retain their national garb, they were thus named from the contrast which their dark tartans furnished to the scarlet and white of the other regiments.]

There were some Italian and Flemish pictures of admitted authenticity, a few genuine bronzes, and other objects of curiosity, which her brothers or herself had picked up while abroad. In short, it was a place where the idle were tempted to become studious, the studious to grow idle where the grave might find matter to make them gay, and the gay subjects for gravity.

That it might maintain some title to its name, I must not forget to say that the lady's dressing-room exhibited a superb mirror, framed in silver filigree work; a beautiful toilette, the cover of which was of Flanders lace; and a set of boxes corresponding in materials and work to the frame of the mirror.

This dressing apparatus, however, was mere matter of parade. Mrs. Martha Bethune Baliol always went through the actual duties of the toilette in an inner apartment, which corresponded with her sleeping-room by a small detached staircase. There were, I believe, more than one of those TURNPIKE STAIRS, as they were called, about the house, by which the public rooms, all of which entered through each other, were accommodated with separate and independent modes of access. In the little boudoir we have described, Mrs. Martha Baliol had her choicest meetings. She kept early hours; and if you went in the morning, you must not reckon that space of day as extending beyond three o'clock, or four at the utmost. These vigilant habits were attended with some restraint on her visitors, but they were indemnified by your always finding the best society and the best information which were to be had for the day in the Scottish capital. Without at all affecting the blue stocking, she liked books. They amused her; and if the authors were persons of character, she thought she owed them a debt of civility, which she loved to discharge by personal kindness. When she gave a dinner to a small party, which she did now and then, she had the good nature to look for, and the good luck to discover, what sort of people suited each other best, and chose her company as Duke Theseus did his hounds,—

"Matched in mouth like bells,

Each under each,"
[Shakespeare's Midsummer Night's Dream, Act IV. Sc. I.]

so that every guest could take his part in the cry, instead of one mighty Tom of a fellow, like Dr. Johnson, silencing all besides by the tremendous depth of his diapason. On such occasions she afforded CHERE EXQUISE; and every now and then there was some dish of French, or even Scottish derivation, which, as well as the numerous assortment of VINS EXTRAORDINAIRES produced by Mr. Beauffet, gave a sort of antique and foreign air to the entertainment, which rendered it more interesting.

It was a great thing to be asked to such parties; and not less so to be invited to the early CONVERSAZIONE, which, in spite of fashion, by dint of the best coffee, the finest tea, and CHASSE CAFE that would have called the dead to life, she contrived now and then to assemble in her saloon already mentioned, at the unnatural hour of eight in the evening. At such time the cheerful old lady seemed to enjoy herself so much in the happiness of her guests that they exerted themselves in turn to prolong her amusement and their own; and a certain charm was excited around, seldom to be met with in parties of pleasure, and which was founded on the general desire of every one present to contribute something to the common amusement.

But although it was a great privilege to be admitted to wait on my excellent friend in the morning, or be invited to her dinner or evening parties, I prized still higher the right which I had acquired, by old acquaintance, of visiting Baliol's Lodging upon the chance of finding its venerable inhabitant preparing for tea, just about six o'clock in the evening. It was only to two or three old friends that she permitted this freedom; nor was this sort of chance-party ever allowed to extend itself beyond five in number. The answer to those who came later announced that the company was filled up for the evening, which had the double effect of making those who waited on Mrs. Bethune Baliol in this unceremonious manner punctual in observing her hour, and of adding the zest of a little difficulty to the enjoyment of the party.

It more frequently happened that only one or two persons partook of this refreshment on the same evening; or, supposing the case of a single gentleman, Mrs. Martha, though she did not hesitate to admit him to her boudoir, after the privilege of the French and the old Scottish school, took care, as she used to say, to prescribe all possible propriety, by commanding the attendance of her principal female attendant, Mrs. Alice Lambskin, who might, from the gravity and dignity of her appearance, have sufficed to matronize a whole boarding-school, instead of one maiden lady of eighty and upwards. As the weather permitted, Mrs. Alice sat duly remote from the company in a FAUTEUIL behind the projecting chimney-piece, or in the embrasure of a window, and prosecuted in Carthusian silence, with indefatigable zeal, a piece of embroidery, which seemed no bad emblem of eternity.

But I have neglected all this while to introduce my friend herself to the reader—at least so far as words can convey the peculiarities by which her appearance and conversation were distinguished.

A little woman, with ordinary features and an ordinary form, and hair which in youth had no decided colour, we may believe Mrs. Martha when she said of herself that she was never remarkable for personal charms; a modest admission, which was readily confirmed by certain old ladies, her contemporaries, who, whatever might have been the youthful advantages which they more than hinted had been formerly their own share, were now in personal appearance, as well as in everything else, far inferior to my accomplished friend. Mrs. Martha's features had been of a kind which might be said to wear well; their irregularity was now of little consequence, animated, as they were, by the vivacity of her conversation. Her teeth were excellent, and her eyes, although inclining to grey, were lively, laughing, and undimmed by time. A slight shade of complexion, more brilliant than her years promised, subjected my friend amongst strangers to the suspicion of having stretched her foreign habits as far as the prudent touch of the rouge. But it was a calumny; for when telling or listening to an interesting and affecting story, I have seen her colour come and go as if it played on the cheek of eighteen.

Her hair, whatever its former deficiencies was now the most beautiful white that time could bleach, and was disposed with some degree of pretension, though in the simplest manner possible, so as to appear neatly smoothed under a cap of Flanders lace, of an old-fashioned but, as I thought, of a very handsome form, which undoubtedly has a name, and I would endeavour to recur to it, if I thought it would make my description a bit more intelligible. I think I have heard her say these favourite caps had been her mother's, and had come in fashion with a peculiar kind of wig used by the gentlemen about the time of the battle of Ramillies. The rest of her dress was always rather costly and distinguished, especially in the evening. A silk or satin gown of some colour becoming her age, and of a form which, though complying to a certain degree with the present fashion, had always a reference to some more distant period, was garnished with triple ruffles. Her shoes had diamond buckles, and were raised a little at heel, an advantage which, possessed in her youth, she alleged her size would not permit her to forego in her old age. She always wore rings, bracelets, and other ornaments of value, either for the materials or the workmanship; nay, perhaps she was a little profuse in this species of display. But she wore them as subordinate matters, to which the habits of being constantly in high life rendered her indifferent; she wore them because her rank required it, and thought no more of them as articles of finery than a gentleman dressed for dinner thinks of his clean linen and well-brushed coat, the consciousness of which embarrasses the rustic beau on a Sunday.

Now and then, however, if a gem or ornament chanced to be noticed for its beauty or singularity, the observation usually led the way to an entertaining account of the manner in which it had been acquired, or the person from whom it had descended to its present possessor. On such and similar occasions my old friend spoke willingly, which is not uncommon; but she also, which is more rare, spoke remarkably well, and had in her little narratives concerning foreign parts or former days, which formed an interesting part of her conversation, the singular art of dismissing all the usual protracted tautology respecting time, place, and circumstances which is apt to settle like a mist upon the cold and languid tales of age, and at the same time of bringing forward, dwelling upon, and illustrating those incidents and characters which give point and interest to the story.

She had, as we have hinted, travelled a good deal in foreign countries; for a brother, to whom she was much attached, had been sent upon various missions of national importance to the Continent, and she had more than once embraced the opportunity of accompanying him. This furnished a great addition to the information which she could supply, especially during the last war, when the Continent was for so many years hermetically sealed against the English nation. But, besides, Mrs. Bethune Baliol visited different countries, not in the modern fashion, when English travel in caravans together, and see in France and Italy little besides the same society which they might have enjoyed at home. On the contrary, she mingled when abroad with the natives of those countries she visited, and enjoyed at once the advantage of their society, and the pleasure of comparing it with that of Britain.

In the course of her becoming habituated with foreign manners, Mrs. Bethune Baliol had, perhaps, acquired some slight tincture of them herself. Yet I was always persuaded that the peculiar vivacity of look and manner—the pointed and appropriate action with which she accompanied what she said—the use of the gold and gemmed TABATIERE, or rather, I should say, BONBONNIERE (for she took no snuff, and the little box contained only a few pieces of candled angelica, or some such ladylike sweetmeat), were of real old-fashioned Scottish growth, and such as might have graced the tea-table of Susannah, Countess of Eglinton, the patroness of Allan Ramsay [See Note 4.—Countess of Eglinton.], or of the Hon. Mrs. Colonel Ogilvy, who was another mirror by whom the Maidens of Auld Reekie were required to dress themselves. Although well acquainted with the customs of other countries, her manners had been chiefly formed in her own, at a time when great folk lived within little space and when the distinguished names of the highest society gave to Edinburgh the ECLAT which we now endeavour to derive from the unbounded expense and extended circle of our pleasures.

I was more confirmed in this opinion by the peculiarity of the dialect which Mrs. Baliol used. It was Scottish—decidedly Scottish—often containing phrases and words little used in the present day. But then her tone and mode of pronunciation were as different from the usual accent of the ordinary Scotch PATOIS, as the accent of St. James's is from that of Billingsgate. The vowels were not pronounced much broader than in the Italian language, and there was none of the disagreeable drawl which is so offensive to southern ears. In short, it seemed to be the Scottish as spoken by the ancient Court of Scotland, to which no idea of vulgarity could be attached; and the lively manners and gestures with which it was accompanied were so completely in accord with the sound of the voice and the style of talking, that I cannot assign them a different origin. In long derivation, perhaps the manner of the Scottish court might have been originally formed on that of France, to which it had certainly some affinity; but I will live and die in the belief that those of Mrs. Baliol, as pleasing as they were peculiar, came to her by direct descent from the high dames who anciently adorned with their presence the royal halls of Holyrood.

## CHAPTER VII. MRS. BALIOL ASSISTS MR. CROFTANGRY IN HIS LITERARY

SPECULATIONS.

Such as I have described Mrs. Bethune Baliol, the reader will easily believe that, when I thought of the miscellaneous nature of my work, I rested upon the information she possessed, and her communicative disposition, as one of the principal supports of my enterprise. Indeed, she by no means disapproved of my proposed publication, though expressing herself very doubtful how far she could personally assist it—a doubt which might be, perhaps, set down to a little ladylike coquetry, which required to be sued for the boon she was not unwilling to grant. Or, perhaps, the good old lady, conscious that her unusual term of years must soon draw to a close, preferred bequeathing the materials in the shape of a legacy, to subjecting them to the judgment of a critical public during her lifetime.

Many a time I used, in our conversations of the Canongate, to resume my request of assistance, from a sense that my friend was the most valuable depository of Scottish traditions that was probably now to be found. This was a subject on which my mind was so much made up that, when I heard her carry her description of manners so far back beyond her own time, and describe how Fletcher of Salton spoke, how Graham of Claverhouse danced, what were the jewels worn by the famous Duchess of Lauderdale, and how she came by them, I could not help telling her I thought her some fairy, who cheated us by retaining the appearance of a mortal of our own day, when, in fact, she had witnessed the revolutions of centuries. She was much diverted when I required her to take some solemn oath that she had not danced at the balls given by Mary of Este, when her unhappy husband occupied Holyrood in a species of honourable banishment; [The Duke of York afterwards James II., frequently resided in Holyrood House when his religion rendered him an object of suspicion to the English Parliament.] or asked whether she could not recollect Charles the Second when he came to Scotland in 1650, and did not possess some slight recollections of the bold usurper who drove him beyond the Forth.

"BEAU COUSIN," she said, laughing, "none of these do I remember personally, but you must know there has been wonderfully little change on my natural temper from youth to age. From which it follows, cousin, that, being even now something too young in spirit for the years which Time has marked me in his calendar, I was, when a girl, a little too old for those of my own standing, and as much inclined at that period to keep the society of elder persons, as I am now disposed to admit the company of gay young fellows of fifty or sixty like yourself, rather than collect about me all the octogenarians. Now, although I do not actually come from Elfland, and therefore cannot boast any personal knowledge of the great personages you enquire about, yet I have seen and heard those who knew them well, and who have given me as distinct an account of them as I could give you myself of the Empress Queen, or Frederick of Prussia; and I will frankly add," said she, laughing and offering her BONBONNIERE, "that I HAVE heard so much of the years which immediately succeeded the Revolution, that I sometimes am apt to confuse the vivid descriptions fixed on my memory by the frequent and animated recitation of others, for things which I myself have actually witnessed. I caught myself but yesterday describing to Lord M—the riding of the last Scottish Parliament, with as much minuteness as if I had seen it, as my mother did, from the balcony in front of Lord Moray's Lodging in the Canongate."

"I am sure you must have given Lord M— a high treat."

"I treated him to a hearty laugh, I believe," she replied; "but it is you, you vile seducer of youth, who lead me into such follies. But I will be on my guard against my own weakness. I do not well know if the Wandering Jew is supposed to have a wife, but I should be sorry a decent middle-aged Scottish gentlewoman should be suspected of identity with such a supernatural person."

"For all that, I must torture you a little more, MA BELLE COUSINE, with my interrogatories; for how shall I ever turn author unless on the strength of the information which you have so often procured me on the ancient state of manners?"

"Stay, I cannot allow you to give your points of enquiry a name so very venerable, if I am expected to answer them. Ancient is a term for antediluvians. You may catechise me about the battle of Flodden, or ask particulars about Bruce and Wallace, under pretext of curiosity after ancient manners; and that last subject would wake my Baliol blood, you know."

"Well, but, Mrs. Baliol, suppose we settle our era: you do not call the accession of James the Sixth to the kingdom of Britain very ancient?"

"Umph! no, cousin; I think I could tell you more of that than folk nowadays remember. For instance, that as James was trooping towards England, bag and baggage, his journey was stopped near Cockenzie by meeting the funeral of the Earl of Winton, the old and faithful servant and follower of his ill-fated mother, poor Mary! It was an ill omen for the INFARE, and so was seen of it, cousin." [See Note 5.—Earl of Winton.]

I did not choose to prosecute this subject, well knowing Mrs. Bethune Baliol did not like to be much pressed on the subject of the Stewarts, whose misfortunes she pitied, the rather that her father had espoused their cause. And yet her attachment to the present dynasty being very sincere, and even ardent, more especially as her family had served his late Majesty both in peace and war, she experienced a little embarrassment in reconciling her opinions respecting the exiled family with those she entertained for the present. In fact, like many an old Jacobite, she was contented to be somewhat inconsistent on the subject, comforting herself that NOW everything stood as it ought to do, and that there was no use in looking back narrowly on the right or wrong of the matter half a century ago.

"The Highlands," I suggested, "should furnish you with ample subjects of recollection. You have witnessed the complete change of that primeval country, and have seen a race not far removed from the earliest period of society melted down into the great mass of civilization; and that could not happen without incidents striking in themselves, and curious as chapters in the history of the human race."

"It is very true," said Mrs. Baliol; "one would think it should have struck the observers greatly, and yet it scarcely did so. For me, I was no Highlander myself, and the Highland chiefs of old, of whom I certainly knew several, had little in their manners to distinguish them from the Lowland gentry, when they mixed in society in Edinburgh, and assumed the Lowland dress. Their peculiar character was for the clansmen at home; and you must not imagine that they swaggered about in plaids and broadswords at the Cross, or came to the Assembly Rooms in bonnets and kilts."

"I remember," said I, "that Swift, in his Journal, tells Stella he had dined in the house of a Scots nobleman, with two Highland chiefs, whom he had found as well-bred men as he had ever met with." [Extract of Journal to Stella.—"I dined to-day (12th March 1712) with Lord Treasurer and two gentlemen of the Highlands of Scotland, yet very polite men." SWIFT'S WORKS, VOL. III. p.7. EDIN. 1824.]

"Very likely," said my friend. "The extremes of society approach much more closely to each other than perhaps the Dean of Saint Patrick's expected. The savage is always to a certain degree polite. Besides, going always armed, and having a very punctilious idea of their own gentility and consequence, they usually behaved to each other and to the Lowlanders with a good deal of formal politeness, which sometimes even procured them the character of insincerity."

"Falsehood belongs to an early period of society, as well as the deferential forms which we style politeness," I replied. "A child does not see the least moral beauty in truth until he has been flogged half a dozen times. It is so easy, and apparently so natural, to deny what you cannot be easily convicted of, that a savage as well as a child lies to excuse himself almost as instinctively as he raises his hand to protect his head. The old saying, 'Confess and be hanged,' carries much argument in it. I observed a remark the other day in old Birrel. He mentions that M'Gregor of Glenstrae and some of his people had surrendered themselves to one of the Earls of Argyle, upon the express condition that they should be conveyed safe into England. The Maccallum Mhor of the day kept the word of promise, but it was only to the ear. He indeed sent his captives to Berwick, where they had an airing on the other side of the Tweed; but it was under the custody of a strong guard, by whom they were brought back to Edinburgh, and delivered to the executioner. This, Birrel calls keeping a Highlandman's promise." [See Note 6.—M'Gregor of Glenstrae.]

"Well," replied Mrs. Baliol, "I might add that many of the Highland chiefs whom I knew in former days had been brought up in France, which might improve their politeness, though perhaps it did not amend their sincerity. But considering that, belonging to the depressed and defeated faction in the state, they were compelled sometimes to use dissimulation, you must set their uniform fidelity to their friends; against their occasional falsehood to their enemies, and then you will not judge poor John Highlandman too severely. They were in a state of society where bright lights are strongly contrasted with deep shadows."

"It is to that point I would bring you, MA BELLE COUSINE; and therefore they are most proper subjects for composition."

"And you want to turn composer, my good friend, and set my old tales to some popular tune? But there have been too many composers, if that be the word, in the field before. The Highlands WERE indeed a rich mine; but they have, I think, been fairly wrought out, as a good tune is grinded into vulgarity when it descends to the hurdy-gurdy and the barrel-organ."

"If it be really tune," I replied, "it will recover its better qualities when it gets into the hands of better artists."

"Umph!" said Mrs. Baliol, tapping her box, "we are happy in our own good opinion this evening, Mr. Croftangry. And so you think you can restore the gloss to the tartan which it has lost by being dragged through so many fingers?"

"With your assistance to procure materials, my dear lady, much, I think, may be done."

"Well, I must do my best, I suppose, though all I know about the Gael is but of little consequence. Indeed, I gathered it chiefly from Donald MacLeish."

"And who might Donald MacLeish be?"

"Neither bard nor sennachie, I assure you, nor monk nor hermit, the approved authorities for old traditions. Donald was as good a postilion as ever drove a chaise and pair between Glencroe and Inverary. I assure you, when I give you my Highland anecdotes, you will hear much of Donald MacLeish. He was Alice Lambskin's beau and mine through a long Highland tour."

"But when am I to possess these anecdotes? you answer me as Harley did poor Prior—

'Let that be done which Mat doth say—
Yea, quoth the Earl, but not to-day.'"

"Well, MON BEAU COUSIN, if you begin to remind me of my cruelty, I must remind you it has struck nine on the Abbey clock, and it is time you were going home to Little Croftangry. For my promise to assist your antiquarian researches, be assured I will one day keep it to the utmost extent. It shall not be a Highlandman's promise, as your old citizen calls it."

I by this time suspected the purpose of my friend's procrastination; and it saddened my heart to reflect that I was not to get the information which I desired, excepting in the shape of a legacy. I found accordingly, in the packet transmitted to me after the excellent lady's death, several anecdotes respecting the Highlands, from which I have selected that which follows, chiefly on account of its possessing great power over the feelings of my critical housekeeper, Janet M'Evoy, who wept most bitterly when I read it to her.

It is, however, but a very simple tale, and may have no interest for persons beyond Janet's rank of life or understanding.

# THE HIGHLAND WIDOW

## CHAPTER I.

> It wound as near as near could be,
> But what it is she cannot tell;
> On the other side it seemed to be
> Of the huge broad-breasted old oak-tree.    COLERIDGE.

Mrs. Bethune Baliol's memorandum begins thus:—

It is five-and-thirty, or perhaps nearer forty years ago, since, to relieve the dejection of spirits occasioned by a great family loss sustained two or three months before, I undertook what was called the short Highland tour. This had become in some degree fashionable; but though the military roads were excellent, yet the accommodation was so indifferent that it was reckoned a little adventure to accomplish it. Besides, the Highlands, though now as peaceable as any part of King George's dominions, was a sound which still carried terror, while so many survived who had witnessed the insurrection of 1745; and a vague idea of fear was impressed on many as they looked from the towers of Stirling northward to the huge chain of mountains, which rises like a dusky rampart to conceal in its recesses a people whose dress, manners, and language differed still very much from those of their Lowland countrymen. For my part, I come of a race not greatly subject to apprehensions arising from imagination only. I had some Highland relatives; know several of their families of distinction; and though only having the company of my bower-maiden, Mrs. Alice Lambskin, I went on my journey fearless.

But then I had a guide and cicerone, almost equal to Greatheart in the Pilgrim's Progress, in no less a person than Donald MacLeish, the postilion whom I hired at Stirling, with a pair of able-bodied horses, as steady as Donald himself, to drag my carriage, my duenna, and myself, wheresoever it was my pleasure to go.

Donald MacLeish was one of a race of post-boys whom, I suppose, mail-coaches and steamboats have put out of fashion. They were to be found chiefly at Perth, Stirling, or Glasgow, where they and their horses were usually hired by travellers, or tourists, to accomplish such journeys of business or pleasure as they might have to perform in the land of the Gael. This class of persons approached to the character of what is called abroad a CONDUCTEUR; or might be compared to the sailing-master on board a British ship of war, who follows out after his own manner the course which the captain commands him to observe. You explained to your postilion the length of your tour, and the objects you were desirous it should embrace; and you found him perfectly competent to fix the places of rest or refreshment, with due attention that those should be chosen with reference to your convenience, and to any points of interest which you might desire to visit.

The qualifications of such a person were necessarily much superior to those of the "first ready," who gallops thrice-a-day over the same ten miles. Donald MacLeish, besides being quite alert at repairing all ordinary accidents to his horses and carriage, and in making shift to support them, where forage was scarce, with such substitutes as bannocks and cakes, was likewise a man of intellectual resources. He had acquired a general knowledge of the traditional stories of the country which he had traversed so often; and if encouraged (for Donald was a man of the most decorous reserve), he would willingly point out to you the site of the principal clan-battles, and recount the most remarkable legends by which the road, and the objects which occurred in travelling it, had been distinguished. There was some originality in the man's habits of thinking and expressing himself, his turn for legendary lore strangely contrasting with a portion of the knowing shrewdness belonging to his actual occupation, which made his conversation amuse the way well enough.

Add to this, Donald knew all his peculiar duties in the country which he traversed so frequently. He could tell, to a day, when they would "be killing" lamb at Tyndrum or Glenuilt; so that the stranger would have some chance of being fed like a Christian; and knew to a mile the last village where it was possible to procure a wheaten loaf for the guidance of those who were little familiar with the Land of Cakes. He was acquainted with the road every mile, and could tell to an inch which side of a Highland bridge was passable, which decidedly dangerous. [This is, or was at least, a necessary accomplishment. In one of the most beautiful districts of the Highlands was, not many years since, a bridge bearing this startling caution, "Keep to the right side, the left being dangerous."] In short, Donald MacLeish was not only our faithful attendant and steady servant, but our humble and obliging friend; and though I have known the half-classical cicerone of Italy, the talkative French valet-de-place, and even the muleteer of Spain, who piques himself on being a maize-eater, and whose honour is not to be questioned without danger, I do not think I have ever had so sensible and intelligent a guide.

Our motions were of course under Donald's direction; and it frequently happened, when the weather was serene, that we preferred halting to rest his horses even where there was no established stage, and taking our refreshment under a crag, from which leaped a waterfall, or beside the verge of a fountain, enamelled with verdant turf and wild-flowers. Donald had an eye for such spots, and though he had, I dare say, never read Gil Blas or Don Quixote, yet he chose such halting-places as Le Sage or Cervantes would have described. Very often, as he observed the pleasure I took in conversing with the country people, he would manage to fix our place of rest near a cottage, where there was some old Gael whose broadsword had blazed at Falkirk or Preston, and who seemed the frail yet faithful record of times which had passed away. Or he would contrive to quarter us, as far as a cup of tea went, upon the hospitality of some parish minister of worth and intelligence, or some country family of the better class, who mingled with the wild simplicity of their original manners, and their ready and hospitable welcome, a sort of courtesy belonging to a people, the lowest of whom are accustomed to consider themselves as being, according to the Spanish phrase, "as good gentlemen as the king, only not quite so rich."

To all such persons Donald MacLeish was well known, and his introduction passed as current as if we had brought letters from some high chief of the country.

Sometimes it happened that the Highland hospitality, which welcomed us with all the variety of mountain fare, preparations of milk and eggs, and girdle-cakes of various kinds, as well as more substantial dainties, according to the inhabitant's means of regaling the passenger, descended rather too exuberantly on Donald MacLeish in the shape of mountain dew. Poor Donald! he was on such occasions like Gideon's fleece—moist with the noble element, which, of course, fell not on us. But it was his only fault, and when pressed to drink DOCH-AN-DORROCH to my ladyship's good health, it would have been ill taken to have refused the pledge; nor was he willing to do such discourtesy. It was, I repeat, his only fault. Nor had we any great right to complain; for if it rendered him a little more talkative, it augmented his ordinary share of punctilious civility, and he only drove slower, and talked longer and more pompously, than when he had not come by a drop of usquebaugh. It was, we remarked, only on such occasions that Donald talked with an air of importance of the family of MacLeish; and we had no title to be scrupulous in censuring a foible, the consequences of which were confined within such innocent limits.

We became so much accustomed to Donald's mode of managing us, that we observed with some interest the art which he used to produce a little agreeable surprise, by concealing from us the spot where he proposed our halt to be made, when it was of an unusual and interesting character. This was so much his wont that, when he made apologies at setting off for being obliged to stop in some strange, solitary place till the horses should eat the corn which he brought on with them for that purpose, our imagination used to be on the stretch to guess what romantic retreat he had secretly fixed upon for our noontide baiting-place.

We had spent the greater part of the morning at the delightful village of Dalmally, and had gone upon the lake under the guidance of the excellent clergyman who was then incumbent at Glenorquhy, [This venerable and hospitable gentleman's name was MacIntyre.] and had heard a hundred legends of the stern chiefs of Loch Awe, Duncan with the thrum bonnet, and the other lords of the now mouldering towers of Kilchurn. [See Note 7.—Loch Awe.] Thus it was later than usual when we set out on our journey, after a hint or two from Donald concerning the length of the way to the next stage, as there was no good halting-place between Dalmally and Oban.

Having bid adieu to our venerable and kind cicerone, we proceeded on our tour, winding round the tremendous mountain called Cruachan Ben, which rushes down in all its majesty of rocks and wilderness on the lake, leaving only a pass, in which, notwithstanding its extreme strength, the warlike clan of MacDougal of Lorn were almost destroyed by the sagacious Robert Bruce. That King, the Wellington of his day, had accomplished, by a forced march, the unexpected manoeuvre of forcing a body of troops round the other side of the mountain, and thus placed them in the flank and in the rear of the men of Lorn, whom at the same time, he attacked in front. The great number of cairns yet visible as you descend the pass on the westward side shows the extent of the vengeance which Bruce exhausted on his inveterate and personal enemies. I am, you know, the sister of soldiers, and it has since struck me forcibly that the manoeuvre which Donald described, resembled those of Wellington or of Bonaparte. He was a great man Robert Bruce, even a Baliol must admit that; although it begins now to be allowed that his title to the crown was scarce so good as that of the unfortunate family with whom he contended. But let that pass. The slaughter had been the greater, as the deep and rapid river Awe is disgorged from the lake just in the rear of the fugitives, and encircles the base of the tremendous mountain; so that the retreat of the unfortunate fleers was intercepted on all sides by the inaccessible character of the country, which had seemed to promise them defence and protection. [See Note 8.—Battle betwixt the armies of the Bruce and MacDougal of Lorn.]

Musing, like the Irish lady in the song, "upon things which are long enough a-gone," [This is a line from a very pathetic ballad which I heard sung by one of the young ladies of Edgeworthstown in 1825. I do not know that it has been printed.] we felt no impatience at the slow and almost creeping pace with which our conductor proceeded along General Wade's military road, which never or rarely condescends to turn aside from the steepest ascent, but proceeds right up and down hill, with the indifference to height and hollow, steep or level, indicated by the old Roman engineers. Still, however, the substantial excellence of these great works—for such are the military highways in the Highlands—deserved the compliment of the poet, who, whether he came from our sister kingdom, and spoke in his own dialect, or whether he supposed those whom he addressed might have some national pretension to the second sight, produced the celebrated couplet,—

"Had you but seen these roads BEFORE they were made,
You would hold up your hands and bless General Wade."

Nothing, indeed, can be more wonderful than to see these wildernesses penetrated and pervious in every quarter by broad accesses of the best possible construction, and so superior to what the country could have demanded for many centuries for any pacific purpose of commercial intercourse. Thus the traces of war are sometimes happily accommodated to the purposes of peace. The victories of Bonaparte have been without results but his road over the Simplon will long be the communication betwixt peaceful countries, who will apply to the ends of commerce and friendly intercourse that gigantic work, which was formed for the ambitious purpose of warlike invasion.

While we were thus stealing along, we gradually turned round the shoulder of Ben Cruachan, and descending the course of the foaming and rapid Awe, left behind us the expanse of the majestic lake which gives birth to that impetuous river. The rocks and precipices which stooped down perpendicularly on our path on the right hand exhibited a few remains of the wood which once clothed them, but which had in later times been felled to supply, Donald MacLeish informed us, the iron foundries at the Bunawe. This made us fix our eyes with interest on one large oak, which grew on the left hand towards the river. It seemed a tree of extraordinary magnitude and picturesque beauty, and stood just where there appeared to be a few roods of open ground lying among huge stones, which had rolled down from the mountain. To add to the romance of the situation, the spot of clear ground extended round the foot of a proud-browed rock, from the summit of which leaped a mountain stream in a fall of sixty feet, in which it was dissolved into foam and dew. At the bottom of the fall the rivulet with difficulty collected, like a routed general, its dispersed forces, and, as if tamed by its descent, found a noiseless passage through the heath to join the Awe.

I was much struck with the tree and waterfall, and wished myself nearer them; not that I thought of sketch-book or portfolio—for in my younger days misses were not accustomed to black-lead pencils, unless they could use them to some good purpose—but merely to indulge myself with a closer view. Donald immediately opened the chaise door, but observed it was rough walking down the brae, and that I would see the tree better by keeping the road for a hundred yards farther, when it passed closer to the spot, for which he seemed, however, to have no predilection. "He knew," he said, "a far bigger tree than that nearer Bunawe, and it was a place where there was flat ground for the carriage to stand, which it could jimply do on these braes; but just as my leddyship liked."

My ladyship did choose rather to look at the fine tree before me than to pass it by in hopes of a finer; so we walked beside the carriage till we should come to a point, from which, Donald assured us, we might, without scrambling, go as near the tree as we chose, "though he wadna advise us to go nearer than the highroad."

There was something grave and mysterious in Donald's sun-browned countenance when he gave us this intimation, and his manner was so different from his usual frankness, that my female curiosity was set in motion. We walked on the whilst, and I found the tree, of which we had now lost sight by the intervention of some rising ground, was really more distant than I had at first supposed. "I could have sworn now," said I to my cicerone, "that yon tree and waterfall was the very place where you intended to make a stop to-day."

"The Lord forbid!" said Donald hastily.

"And for what, Donald? Why should you be willing to pass so pleasant a spot?"

"It's ower near Dalmally, my leddy, to corn the beasts; it would bring their dinner ower near their breakfast, poor things. An' besides, the place is not canny."

"Oh! then the mystery is out. There is a bogle or a brownie, a witch or a gyre-carlin, a bodach or a fairy, in the case?"

"The ne'er a bit, my leddy—ye are clean aff the road, as I may say. But if your leddyship will just hae patience, and wait till we are by the place and out of the glen, I'll tell ye all about it. There is no much luck in speaking of such things in the place they chanced in."

I was obliged to suspend my curiosity, observing, that if I persisted in twisting the discourse one way while Donald was twining it another, I should make his objection, like a hempen cord, just so much the tougher. At length the promised turn of the road brought us within fifty paces of the tree which I desired to admire, and I now saw to my surprise, that there was a human habitation among the cliffs which surrounded it. It was a hut of the least dimensions, and most miserable description that I ever saw even in the Highlands. The walls of sod, or DIVOT, as the Scotch call it, were not four feet high; the roof was of turf, repaired with reeds and sedges; the chimney was composed of clay, bound round by straw ropes; and the whole walls, roof, and chimney, were alike covered with the vegetation of house-leek, rye-grass, and moss common to decayed cottages formed of such materials. There was not the slightest vestige of a kale-yard, the usual accompaniment of the very worst huts; and of living things we saw nothing, save a kid which was browsing on the roof of the hut, and a goat, its mother, at some distance, feeding betwixt the oak and the river Awe.

"What man," I could not help exclaiming, "can have committed sin deep enough to deserve such a miserable dwelling!"

"Sin enough," said Donald MacLeish, with a half-suppressed groan; "and God he knoweth, misery enough too. And it is no man's dwelling neither, but a woman's."

"A woman's!" I repeated, "and in so lonely a place! What sort of a woman can she be?"

"Come this way, my leddy, and you may judge that for yourself," said Donald. And by advancing a few steps, and making a sharp turn to the left, we gained a sight of the side of the great broad-breasted oak, in the direction opposed to that in which we had hitherto seen it.

"If she keeps her old wont, she will be there at this hour of the day," said Donald; but immediately became silent, and pointed with his finger, as one afraid of being overheard. I looked, and beheld, not without some sense of awe, a female form seated by the stem of the oak, with her head drooping, her hands clasped, and a dark-coloured mantle drawn over her head, exactly as Judah is represented in the Syrian medals as seated under her palm-tree. I was infected with the fear and reverence which my guide seemed to entertain towards this solitary being, nor did I think of advancing towards her to obtain a nearer view until I had cast an enquiring look on Donald; to which he replied in a half whisper, "She has been a fearfu' bad woman, my leddy."

"Mad woman, said you," replied I, hearing him imperfectly; "then she is perhaps dangerous?"

"No—she is not mad," replied Donald; "for then it may be she would be happier than she is; though when she thinks on what she has done, and caused to be done, rather than yield up a hair-breadth of her ain wicked will, it is not likely she can be very well settled. But she neither is mad nor mischievous; and yet, my leddy, I think you had best not go nearer to her." And then, in a few hurried words, he made me acquainted with the story which I am now to tell more in detail. I heard the narrative with a mixture of horror and sympathy, which at once impelled me to approach the sufferer, and speak to her the words of comfort, or rather of pity, and at the same time made me afraid to do so.

This indeed was the feeling with which she was regarded by the Highlanders in the neighbourhood, who looked upon Elspat MacTavish, or the Woman of the Tree, as they called her, as the Greeks considered those who were pursued by the Furies, and endured the mental torment consequent on great criminal actions. They regarded such unhappy beings as Orestes and OEdipus, as being less the voluntary perpetrators of their crimes than as the passive instruments by which the terrible decrees of Destiny had been accomplished; and the fear with which they beheld them was not unmingled with veneration.

I also learned further from Donald MacLeish, that there was some apprehension of ill luck attending those who had the boldness to approach too near, or disturb the awful solitude of a being so unutterably miserable—that it was supposed that whosoever approached her must experience in some respect the contagion of her wretchedness.

It was therefore with some reluctance that Donald saw me prepare to obtain a nearer view of the sufferer, and that he himself followed to assist me in the descent down a very rough path. I believe his regard for me conquered some ominous feelings in his own breast, which connected his duty on this occasion with the presaging fear of lame horses, lost linch-pins, overturns, and other perilous chances of the postilion's life.

I am not sure if my own courage would have carried me so close to Elspat had he not followed. There was in her countenance the stern abstraction of hopeless and overpowering sorrow, mixed with the contending feelings of remorse, and of the pride which struggled to conceal it. She guessed, perhaps, that it was curiosity, arising out of her uncommon story, which induced me to intrude on her solitude; and she could not be pleased that a fate like hers had been the theme of a traveller's amusement. Yet the look with which she regarded me was one of scorn instead of embarrassment. The opinion of the world and all its children could not add or take an iota from her load of misery; and, save from the half smile that seemed to intimate the contempt of a being rapt by the very intensity of her affliction above the sphere of ordinary humanities, she seemed as indifferent to my gaze, as if she had been a dead corpse or a marble statue.

Elspat was above the middle stature. Her hair, now grizzled, was still profuse, and it had been of the most decided black. So were her eyes, in which, contradicting the stern and rigid features of her countenance, there shone the wild and troubled light that indicates an unsettled mind. Her hair was wrapt round a silver bodkin with some attention to neatness, and her dark mantle was disposed around her with a degree of taste, though the materials were of the most ordinary sort.

After gazing on this victim of guilt and calamity till I was ashamed to remain silent, though uncertain how I ought to address her, I began to express my surprise at her choosing such a desert and deplorable dwelling. She cut short these expressions of sympathy, by answering in a stern voice, without the least change of countenance or posture, "Daughter of the stranger, he has told you my story." I was silenced at once, and felt how little all earthly accommodation must seem to the mind which had such subjects as hers for rumination. Without again attempting to open the conversation, I took a piece of gold from my purse, (for Donald had intimated she lived on alms), expecting she would at least stretch her hand to receive it. But she neither accepted nor rejected the gift; she did not even seem to notice it, though twenty times as valuable, probably, as was usually offered. I was obliged to place it on her knee, saying involuntarily, as I did so,

"May God pardon you and relieve you!" I shall never forget the look which she cast up to Heaven, nor the tone in which she exclaimed, in the very words of my old friend John Home,—

"My beautiful—my brave!"

It was the language of nature, and arose from the heart of the deprived mother, as it did from that gifted imaginative poet while furnishing with appropriate expressions the ideal grief of Lady Randolph.

CHAPTER II.

> Oh, I'm come to the Low Country,
>   Och, och, ohonochie,
> Without a penny in my pouch
>   To buy a meal for me.
> I was the proudest of my clan,
>   Long, long may I repine;
> And Donald was the bravest man,
>   And Donald he was mine.        OLD SONG.

Elspat had enjoyed happy days, though her age had sunk into hopeless and inconsolable sorrow and distress. She was once the beautiful and happy wife of Hamish MacTavish, for whom his strength and feats of prowess had gained the title of MacTavish Mhor. His life was turbulent and dangerous, his habits being of the old Highland stamp which esteemed it shame to want anything that could be had for the taking. Those in the Lowland line who lay near him, and desired to enjoy their lives and property in quiet, were contented to pay him a small composition, in name of protection money, and comforted themselves with the old proverb that it was better to "fleech the deil than fight him." Others, who accounted such composition dishonourable, were often surprised by MacTavish Mhor and his associates and followers, who usually inflicted an adequate penalty, either in person or property, or both. The creagh is yet remembered in which he swept one hundred and fifty cows from Monteith in one drove; and how he placed the laird of Ballybught naked in a slough, for having threatened to send for a party of the Highland Watch to protect his property.

Whatever were occasionally the triumphs of this daring cateran, they were often exchanged for reverses; and his narrow escapes, rapid flights, and the ingenious stratagems with which he extricated himself from imminent danger, were no less remembered and admired than the exploits in which he had been successful. In weal or woe, through every species of fatigue, difficulty, and danger, Elspat was his faithful companion. She enjoyed with him the fits of occasional prosperity; and when adversity pressed them hard, her strength of mind, readiness of wit, and courageous endurance of danger and toil, are said often to have stimulated the exertions of her husband.

Their morality was of the old Highland cast—faithful friends and fierce enemies. The Lowland herds and harvests they accounted their own, whenever they had the means of driving off the one or of seizing upon the other; nor did the least scruple on the right of property interfere on such occasions. Hamish Mhor argued like the old Cretan warrior:

> "My sword, my spear, my shaggy shield,
>   They make me lord of all below;

> For he who dreads the lance to wield,
>   Before my shaggy shield must bow.
> His lands, his vineyards, must resign,
>   And all that cowards have is mine."

But those days of perilous, though frequently successful depredation, began to be abridged after the failure of the expedition of Prince Charles Edward. MacTavish Mhor had not sat still on that occasion, and he was outlawed, both as a traitor to the state and as a robber and cateran. Garrisons were now settled in many places where a red-coat had never before been seen, and the Saxon war-drum resounded among the most hidden recesses of the Highland mountains. The fate of MacTavish became every day more inevitable; and it was the more difficult for him to make his exertions for defence or escape, that Elspat, amid his evil days, had increased his family with an infant child, which was a considerable encumbrance upon the necessary rapidity of their motions.

At length the fatal day arrived. In a strong pass on the skirts of Ben Crunchan, the celebrated MacTavish Mhor was surprised by a detachment of the Sidier Roy. [The Red Soldier.] His wife assisted him heroically, charging his piece from time to time; and as they were in possession of a post that was nearly unassailable, he might have perhaps escaped if his ammunition had lasted. But at length his balls were expended, although it was not until he had fired off most of the silver buttons from his waistcoat; and the soldiers, no longer deterred by fear of the unerring marksman, who had slain three and wounded more of their number, approached his stronghold, and, unable to take him alive, slew him after a most desperate resistance.

All this Elspat witnessed and survived; for she had, in the child which relied on her for support, a motive for strength and exertion. In what manner she maintained herself it is not easy to say. Her only ostensible means of support were a flock of three or four goats, which she fed wherever she pleased on the mountain pastures, no one challenging the intrusion. In the general distress of the country, her ancient acquaintances had little to bestow; but what they could part with from their own necessities, they willingly devoted to the relief of others, From Lowlanders she sometimes demanded tribute, rather than requested alms. She had not forgotten she was the widow of MacTavish Mhor, or that the child who trotted by her knee might, such were her imaginations, emulate one day the fame of his father, and command the same influence which he had once exerted without control. She associated so little with others, went so seldom and so unwillingly from the wildest recesses of the mountains, where she usually dwelt with her goats, that she was quite unconscious of the great change which had taken place in the country around her—the substitution of civil order for military violence, and the strength gained by the law and its adherents over those who were called in Gaelic song, "the stormy sons of the sword." Her own diminished consequence and straitened circumstances she indeed felt, but for this the death of MacTavish Mhor was, in her apprehension, a sufficing reason; and she doubted not that she should rise to her former state of importance when Hamish Bean (or fair-haired James) should be able to wield the arms of his father. If, then, Elspat was repelled, rudely when she demanded anything necessary for her wants, or the accommodation of her little flock, by a churlish farmer, her threats of vengeance, obscurely expressed, yet terrible in their tenor, used frequently to extort, through fear of her maledictions, the relief which was denied to her necessities; and the trembling goodwife, who gave meal or money to the widow of MacTavish Mhor, wished in her heart that the stern old carlin had been burnt on the day her husband had his due.

Years thus ran on, and Hamish Bean grew up—not, indeed, to be of his father's size or strength, but to become an active, high-spirited, fair-haired youth, with a ruddy cheek, an eye like an eagle's, and all the agility, if not all the strength, of his formidable father, upon whose history and achievements his mother dwelt, in order to form her son's mind to a similar course of adventures. But the young see the present state of this changeful world more keenly than the old. Much attached to his mother, and disposed to do all in his power for her support, Hamish yet perceived, when he mixed with the world, that the trade of the cateran was now alike dangerous and discreditable, and that if he were to emulate his father's progress, it must be in some other line of warfare more consonant to the opinions of the present day.

As the faculties of mind and body began to expand, he became more sensible of the precarious nature of his situation, of the erroneous views of his mother, and her ignorance respecting the changes of the society with which she mingled so little. In visiting friends and neighbours, he became aware of the extremely reduced scale to which his parent was limited, and learned that she possessed little or nothing more than the absolute necessaries of life, and that these were sometimes on the point of failing. At times his success in fishing and the chase was able to add something to her subsistence; but he saw no regular means of contributing to her support, unless by stooping to servile labour, which, if he himself could have endured it, would, he knew, have been like a death's-wound to the pride of his mother.

Elspat, meanwhile, saw with surprise that Hamish Bean, although now tall and fit for the field, showed no disposition to enter on his father's scene of action. There was something of the mother at her heart, which prevented her from urging him in plain terms to take the field as a cateran, for the fear occurred of the perils into which the trade must conduct him; and when she would have spoken to him on the subject, it seemed to her heated imagination as if the ghost of her husband arose between them in his bloody tartans, and laying his finger on his lips, appeared to prohibit the topic. Yet she wondered at what seemed his want of spirit, sighed as she saw him from day to day lounging about in the long-skirted Lowland coat which the legislature had imposed upon the Gael instead of their own romantic garb, and thought how much nearer he would have resembled her husband had he been clad in the belted plaid and short hose, with his polished arms gleaming at his side.

Besides these subjects for anxiety, Elspat had others arising from the engrossing impetuosity of her temper. Her love of MacTavish Mhor had been qualified by respect and sometimes even by fear, for the cateran was not the species of man who submits to female government; but over his son she had exerted, at first during childhood, and afterwards in early youth, an imperious authority, which gave her maternal love a character of jealousy. She could not bear when Hamish, with advancing life, made repeated steps towards independence, absented himself from her cottage at such season and for such length of time as he chose, and seemed to consider, although maintaining towards her every possible degree of respect and kindness, that the control and responsibility of his actions rested on himself alone. This would have been of little consequence, could she have concealed her feelings within her own bosom; but the ardour and impatience of her passions made her frequently show her son that she conceived herself neglected and ill-used. When he was absent for any length of time from her cottage without giving intimation of his purpose, her resentment on his return used to be so unreasonable, that it naturally suggested to a young man fond of independence, and desirous to amend his situation in the world, to leave her, even for the very purpose of enabling him to provide for the parent whose egotistical demands on his filial attention tended to confine him to a desert, in which both were starving in hopeless and helpless indigence.

Upon one occasion, the son having been guilty of some independent excursion, by which the mother felt herself affronted and disobliged, she had been more than usually violent on his return, and awakened in Hamish a sense of displeasure, which clouded his brow and cheek. At length, as she persevered in her unreasonable resentment, his patience became exhausted, and taking his gun from the chimney corner, and muttering to himself the reply which his respect for his mother prevented him from speaking aloud, he was about to leave the hut which he had but barely entered.

"Hamish," said his mother, "are you again about to leave me?" But Hamish only replied by looking at and rubbing the lock of his gun.

"Ay, rub the lock of your gun," said his parent bitterly. "I am glad you have courage enough to fire it? though it be but at a roe-deer." Hamish started at this undeserved taunt, and cast a look of anger at her in reply. She saw that she had found the means of giving him pain.

"Yes," she said, "look fierce as you will at an old woman, and your mother; it would be long ere you bent your brow on the angry countenance of a bearded man."

"Be silent, mother, or speak of what you understand," said Hamish, much irritated, "and that is of the distaff and the spindle."

"And was it of spindle and distaff that I was thinking when I bore you away on my back through the fire of six of the Saxon soldiers, and you a wailing child? I tell you, Hamish, I know a hundredfold more of swords and guns than ever you will; and you will never learn so much of noble war by yourself, as you have seen when you were wrapped up in my plaid."

"You are determined, at least, to allow me no peace at home, mother; but this shall have an end," said Hamish, as, resuming his purpose of leaving the hut, he rose and went towards the door.

"Stay, I command you," said his mother—"stay! or may the gun you carry be the means of your ruin! may the road you are going be the track of your funeral!"

"What makes you use such words, mother?" said the young man, turning a little back; "they are not good, and good cannot come of them. Farewell just now! we are too angry to speak together—farewell! It will be long ere you see me again." And he departed, his mother, in the first burst of her impatience, showering after him her maledictions, and in the next invoking them on her own head, so that they might spare her son's. She passed that day and the next in all the vehemence of impotent and yet unrestrained passion, now entreating Heaven, and such powers as were familiar to her by rude tradition, to restore her dear son, "the calf of her heart;" now in impatient resentment, meditating with what bitter terms she should rebuke his filial disobedience upon his return, and now studying the most tender language to attach him to the cottage, which, when her boy was present, she would not, in the rapture of her affection, have exchanged for the apartments of Taymouth Castle.

Two days passed, during which, neglecting even the slender means of supporting nature which her situation afforded, nothing but the strength of a frame accustomed to hardships and privations of every kind could have kept her in existence, notwithstanding the anguish of her mind prevented her being sensible of her personal weakness. Her dwelling at this period was the same cottage near which I had found her, but then more habitable by the exertions of Hamish, by whom it had been in a great measure built and repaired.

It was on the third day after her son had disappeared, as she sat at the door rocking herself, after the fashion of her countrywomen when in distress, or in pain, that the then unwonted circumstance occurred of a passenger being seen on the highroad above the cottage. She cast but one glance at him. He was on horseback, so that it could not be Hamish; and Elspat cared not enough for any other being on earth to make her turn her eyes towards him a second time. The stranger, however, paused opposite to her cottage, and dismounting from his pony, led it down the steep and broken path which conducted to her door.

"God bless you, Elspat MacTavish!" She looked at the man as he addressed her in her native language, with the displeased air of one whose reverie is interrupted; but the traveller went on to say, "I bring you tidings of your son Hamish." At once, from being the most uninteresting object, in respect to Elspat, that could exist, the form of the stranger became awful in her eyes, as that of a messenger descended from heaven, expressly to pronounce upon her death or life. She started from her seat, and with hands convulsively clasped together, and held up to Heaven, eyes fixed on the stranger's countenance, and person stooping forward to him, she looked those inquiries which her faltering tongue could not articulate. "Your son sends you his dutiful remembrance, and this," said the messenger, putting into Elspat's hand a small purse containing four or five dollars.

"He is gone! he is gone!" exclaimed Elspat; "he has sold himself to be the servant of the Saxons, and I shall never more behold him! Tell me, Miles MacPhadraick—for now I know you—is it the price of the son's blood that you have put into the mother's hand?"

"Now, God forbid!" answered MacPhadraick, who was a tacksman, and had possession of a considerable tract of ground under his chief, a proprietor who lived about twenty miles off—"God forbid I should do wrong, or say wrong, to you, or to the son of MacTavish Mhor! I swear to you by the hand of my chief that your son is well, and will soon see you; and the rest he will tell you himself." So saying, MacPhadraick hastened back up the pathway, gained the road, mounted his pony, and rode upon his way.

CHAPTER III.

Elspat MacTavish remained gazing on the money as if the impress of the coin could have conveyed information how it was procured.

"I love not this MacPhadraick," she said to herself. "It was his race of whom the Bard hath spoken, saying, Fear them not when their words are loud as the winter's wind, but fear them when they fall on you like the sound of the thrush's song. And yet this riddle can be read but one way: My son hath taken the sword to win that, with strength like a man, which churls would keep him from with the words that frighten children." This idea, when once it occurred to her, seemed the more reasonable, that MacPhadraick, as she well knew, himself a cautious man, had so far encouraged her husband's practices as occasionally to buy cattle of MacTavish, although he must have well known how they were come by, taking care, however, that the transaction was so made as to be accompanied with great profit and absolute safety. Who so likely as MacPhadraick to indicate to a young cateran the glen in which he could commence his perilous trade with most prospect of success? Who so likely to convert his booty into money? The feelings which another might have experienced on believing that an only son had rushed forward on the same path in which his father had perished, were scarce known to the Highland mothers of that day. She thought of the death of MacTavish Mhor as that of a hero who had fallen in his proper trade of war, and who had not fallen unavenged. She feared less for her son's life than for his dishonour. She dreaded, on his account, the subjection to strangers, and the death-sleep of the soul which is brought on by what she regarded as slavery.

The moral principle which so naturally and so justly occurs to the mind of those who have been educated under a settled government of laws that protect the property of the weak against the incursions of the strong, was to poor Elspat a book sealed and a fountain closed. She had been taught to consider those whom they call Saxons as a race with whom the Gael were constantly at war; and she regarded every settlement of theirs within the reach of Highland incursion as affording a legitimate object of attack and plunder. Her feelings on this point had been strengthened and confirmed, not only by the desire of revenge for the death of her husband, but by the sense of general indignation entertained, not unjustly, through the Highlands of Scotland, on account of the barbarous and violent conduct of the victors after the battle of Culloden. Other Highland clans, too, she regarded as the fair objects of plunder, when that was possible, upon the score of ancient enmities and deadly feuds.

The prudence that might have weighed the slender means which the times afforded for resisting the efforts of a combined government, which had, in its less compact and established authority, been unable to put down the ravages of such lawless caterans as MacTavish Mhor, was unknown to a solitary woman whose ideas still dwelt upon her own early times. She imagined that her son had only to proclaim himself his father's successor in adventure and enterprise, and that a force of men, as gallant as those who had followed his father's banner, would crowd around to support it when again displayed. To her Hamish was the eagle who had only to soar aloft and resume his native place in the skies, without her being able to comprehend how many additional eyes would have watched his flight—how many additional bullets would have been directed at his bosom. To be brief, Elspat was one who viewed the present state of society with the same feelings with which she regarded the times that had passed away. She had been indigent, neglected, oppressed since the days that her husband had no longer been feared and powerful, and she thought that the term of her ascendence would return when her son had determined to play the part of his father. If she permitted her eye to glance farther into futurity, it was but to anticipate that she must be for many a day cold in the grave, with the coronach of her tribe cried duly over her, before her fair-haired Hamish could, according to her calculation, die with his hand on the basket-hilt of the red claymore. His father's hair was grey, ere, after a hundred dangers, he had fallen with his arms in his hands. That she should have seen and survived the sight was a natural consequence of the manners of that age. And better it was—such was her proud thought—that she had seen him so die, than to have witnessed his departure from life in a smoky hovel on a bed of rotten straw like an over-worn hound, or a bullock which died of disease. But the hour of her young, her brave Hamish, was yet far distant. He must succeed—he must conquer—like his father. And when he fell at length—for she anticipated for him no bloodless death—Elspat would ere then have lain long in the grave, and could neither see his death-struggle nor mourn over his grave-sod.

With such wild notions working in her brain, the spirit of Elspat rose to its usual pitch, or, rather, to one which seemed higher. In the emphatic language of Scripture, which in that idiom does not greatly differ from her own, she arose, she washed and changed her apparel, and ate bread, and was refreshed.

She longed eagerly for the return of her son, but she now longed not with the bitter anxiety of doubt and apprehension. She said to herself that much must be done ere he could in these times arise to be an eminent and dreaded leader. Yet when she saw him again, she almost expected him at the head of a daring band, with pipes playing and banners flying, the noble tartans fluttering free in the wind, in despite of the laws which had suppressed, under severe penalties, the use of the national garb and all the appurtenances of Highland chivalry. For all this, her eager imagination was content only to allow the interval of some days.

From the moment this opinion had taken deep and serious possession of her mind, her thoughts were bent upon receiving her son at the head of his adherents in the manner in which she used to adorn her hut for the return of his father.

The substantial means of subsistence she had not the power of providing, nor did she consider that of importance. The successful caterans would bring with them herds and flocks. But the interior of her hut was arranged for their reception, the usquebaugh was brewed or distilled in a larger quantity than it could have been supposed one lone woman could have made ready. Her hut was put into such order as might, in some degree, give it the appearance of a day of rejoicing. It was swept and decorated, with boughs of various kinds, like the house of a Jewess upon what is termed the Feast of the Tabernacles. The produce of the milk of her little flock was prepared in as great variety of forms as her skill admitted, to entertain her son and his associates whom she, expected to receive along with him.

But the principal decoration, which she sought with the greatest toil, was the cloudberry, a scarlet fruit, which is only found on very high hills; and these only in small quantities. Her husband, or perhaps one of his forefathers, had chosen this as the emblem of his family, because it seemed at once to imply, by its scarcity, the smallness of their clan, and, by the places in which it was found, the ambitious height of their pretensions.

For the time that these simple preparations of welcome endured, Elspat was in a state of troubled happiness. In fact, her only anxiety was that she might be able to complete all that she could do to welcome Hamish and the friends who she supposed must have attached themselves to his band, before they should arrive and find her unprovided for their reception.

But when such efforts as she could make had been accomplished, she once more had nothing left to engage her save the trifling care of her goats; and when these had been attended to, she had only to review her little preparations, renew such as were of a transitory nature, replace decayed branches and fading boughs, and then to sit down at her cottage-door and watch the road as it ascended on the one side from the banks of the Awe, and on the other wound round the heights of the mountain, with such a degree of accommodation to hill and level as the plan of the military engineer permitted. While so occupied, her imagination, anticipating the future from recollections of the past, formed out of the morning mist or the evening cloud the wild forms of an advancing band, which were then called "Sidier Dhu" (dark soldiers), dressed in their native tartan, and so named to distinguish them from the scarlet ranks of the British army. In this occupation she spent many hours of each morning and evening.

CHAPTER IV.

It was in vain that Elspat's eyes surveyed the distant path by the earliest light of the dawn and the latest glimmer of the twilight. No rising dust awakened the expectation of nodding plumes or flashing arms. The solitary traveller trudged listlessly along in his brown lowland greatcoat, his tartans dyed black or purple, to comply with or evade the law which prohibited their being worn in their variegated hues. The spirit of the Gael, sunk and broken by the severe though perhaps necessary laws, that proscribed the dress and arms which he considered as his birthright, was intimated by his drooping head and dejected appearance. Not in such depressed wanderers did Elspat recognise the light and free step of her son, now, as she concluded, regenerated from every sign of Saxon thraldom. Night by night, as darkness came, she removed from her unclosed door, to throw herself on her restless pallet, not to sleep, but to watch. The brave and the terrible, she said, walk by night. Their steps are heard in darkness, when all is silent save the whirlwind and the cataract. The timid deer comes only forth when the sun is upon the mountain's peak, but the bold wolf walks in the red light of the harvest-moon. She reasoned in vain; her son's expected summons did not call her from the lowly couch where she lay dreaming of his approach. Hamish came not.

"Hope deferred," saith the royal sage, "maketh the heart sick;" and strong as was Elspat's constitution, she began to experience that it was unequal to the toils to which her anxious and immoderate affection subjected her, when early one morning the appearance of a traveller on the lonely mountain-road, revived hopes which had begun to sink into listless despair. There was no sign of Saxon subjugation about the stranger. At a distance she could see the flutter of the belted-plaid that drooped in graceful folds behind him, and the plume that, placed in the bonnet, showed rank and gentle birth. He carried a gun over his shoulder, the claymore was swinging by his side with its usual appendages, the dirk, the pistol, and the SPORRAN MOLLACH. [The goat-skin pouch, worn by the Highlanders round their waist.] Ere yet her eye had scanned all these particulars, the light step of the traveller was hastened, his arm was waved in token of recognition—a moment more, and Elspat held in her arms her darling son, dressed in the garb of his ancestors, and looking, in her maternal eyes, the fairest among ten thousand!

The first outpouring of affection it would be impossible to describe. Blessings mingled with the most endearing epithets which her energetic language affords in striving to express the wild rapture of Elspat's joy. Her board was heaped hastily with all she had to offer, and the mother watched the young soldier, as he partook of the refreshment, with feelings how similar to, yet how different from, those with which she had seen him draw his first sustenance from her bosom!

When the tumult of joy was appeased, Elspat became anxious to know her son's adventures since they parted, and could not help greatly censuring his rashness for traversing the hills in the Highland dress in the broad sunshine, when the penalty was so heavy, and so many red soldiers were abroad in the country.

"Fear not for me, mother," said Hamish, in a tone designed to relieve her anxiety, and yet somewhat embarrassed; "I may wear the BREACAN [That which is variegated—that is, the tartan.] at the gate of Fort-Augustus, if I like it."

"Oh, be not too daring, my beloved Hamish, though it be the fault which best becomes thy father's son—yet be not too daring! Alas! they fight not now as in former days, with fair weapons and on equal terms, but take odds of numbers and of arms, so that the feeble and the strong are alike levelled by the shot of a boy. And do not think me unworthy to be called your father's widow and your mother because I speak thus; for God knoweth, that, man to man, I would peril thee against the best in Breadalbane, and broad Lorn besides."

"I assure you, my dearest mother," replied Hamish, "that I am in no danger. But have you seen MacPhadraick, mother? and what has he said to you on my account?"

"Silver he left me in plenty, Hamish; but the best of his comfort was that you were well, and would see me soon. But beware of MacPhadraick, my son; for when he called himself the friend of your father, he better loved the most worthless stirk in his herd than he did the life-blood of MacTavish Mhor. Use his services, therefore, and pay him for them, for it is thus we should deal with the unworthy; but take my counsel, and trust him not."

Hamish could not suppress a sigh, which seemed to Elspat to intimate that the caution came too late. "What have you done with him?" she continued, eager and alarmed. "I had money of him, and he gives not that without value; he is none of those who exchange barley for chaff. Oh, if you repent you of your bargain, and if it be one which you may break off without disgrace to your truth or your manhood, take back his silver, and trust not to his fair words."

"It may not be, mother," said Hamish; "I do not repent my engagement, unless that it must make me leave you soon."

"Leave me! how leave me? Silly boy, think you I know not what duty belongs to the wife or mother of a daring man? Thou art but a boy yet; and when thy father had been the dread of the country for twenty years, he did not despise my company and assistance, but often said my help was worth that of two strong gillies."

"It is not on that score, mother, but since I must leave the country—"

"Leave the country!" replied his mother, interrupting him. "And think you that I am like a bush, that is rooted to the soil where it grows, and must die if carried elsewhere? I have breathed other winds than these of Ben Cruachan. I have followed your father to the wilds of Ross and the impenetrable deserts of Y Mac Y Mhor. Tush, man! my limbs, old as they are, will bear me as far as your young feet can trace the way."

"Alas, mother," said the young man, with a faltering accent, "but to cross the sea—"

"The sea! who am I that I should fear the sea? Have I never been in a birling in my life—never known the Sound of Mull, the Isles of Treshornish, and the rough rocks of Harris?"

"Alas, mother, I go far—far from all of these. I am enlisted in one of the new regiments, and we go against the French in America."

"Enlisted!" uttered the astonished mother—"against MY will—without MY consent! You could not! you would not!" Then rising up, and assuming a posture of almost imperial command, "Hamish, you DARED not!"

"Despair, mother, dares everything," answered Hamish, in a tone of melancholy resolution. "What should I do here, where I can scarce get bread for myself and you, and when the times are growing daily worse? Would you but sit down and listen, I would convince you I have acted for the best."

With a bitter smile Elspat sat down, and the same severe ironical expression was on her features, as, with her lips firmly closed, she listened to his vindication.

Hamish went on, without being disconcerted by her expected displeasure. "When I left you, dearest mother, it was to go to MacPhadraick's house; for although I knew he is crafty and worldly, after the fashion of the Sassenach, yet he is wise, and I thought how he would teach me, as it would cost him nothing, in which way I could mend our estate in the world."

"Our estate in the world!" said Elspat, losing patience at the word; "and went you to a base fellow with a soul no better than that of a cowherd, to ask counsel about your conduct? Your father asked none, save of his courage and his sword."

"Dearest mother," answered Hamish, "how shall I convince you that you live in this land of our fathers as if our fathers were yet living? You walk as it were in a dream, surrounded by the phantoms of those who have been long with the dead. When my father lived and fought, the great respected the man of the strong right hand, and the rich feared him. He had protection from Macallum Mhor, and from Caberfae, and tribute from meaner men. [Caberfae—ANGLICE, the Stag's-head, the Celtic designation for the arms of the family of the high Chief of Seaforth.] That is ended, and his son would only earn a disgraceful and unpitied death by the practices which gave his father credit and power among those who wear the breacan. The land is conquered; its lights are quenched—Glengarry, Lochiel, Perth, Lord Lewis, all the high chiefs are dead or in exile. We may mourn for it, but we cannot help it. Bonnet, broadsword, and sporran—power, strength, and wealth, were all lost on Drummossie Muir."

"It is false!" said Elspat, fiercely; "you and such like dastardly spirits are quelled by your own faint hearts, not by the strength of the enemy; you are like the fearful waterfowl, to whom the least cloud in the sky seems the shadow of the eagle."

"Mother," said Hamish proudly, "lay not faint heart to my charge. I go where men are wanted who have strong arms and bold hearts too. I leave a desert, for a land where I may gather fame."

"And you leave your mother to perish in want, age, and solitude," said Elspat, essaying successively every means of moving a resolution which she began to see was more deeply rooted than she had at first thought.

"Not so, neither," he answered; "I leave you to comfort and certainty, which you have yet never known. Barcaldine's son is made a leader, and with him I have enrolled myself. MacPhadraick acts for him, and raises men, and finds his own in doing it."

"That is the truest word of the tale, were all the rest as false as hell," said the old woman, bitterly.

"But we are to find our good in it also," continued Hamish; "for Barcaldine is to give you a shieling in his wood of Letter-findreight, with grass for your goats, and a cow, when you please to have one, on the common; and my own pay, dearest mother, though I am far away, will do more than provide you with meal, and with all else you can want. Do not fear for me. I enter a private gentleman; but I will return, if hard fighting and regular duty can deserve it, an officer, and with half a dollar a day."

"Poor child!" replied Elspat, in a tone of pity mingled with contempt, "and you trust MacPhadraick?"

"I might mother," said Hamish, the dark red colour of his race crossing his forehead and cheeks, "for MacPhadraick knows the blood which flows in my veins, and is aware, that should he break trust with you, he might count the days which could bring Hamish back to Breadalbane, and number those of his life within three suns more. I would kill him at his own hearth, did he break his word with me—I would, by the great Being who made us both!"

The look and attitude of the young soldier for a moment overawed Elspat; she was unused to see him express a deep and bitter mood, which reminded her so strongly of his father. But she resumed her remonstrances in the same taunting manner in which she had commenced them.

"Poor boy!" she said; "and you think that at the distance of half the world your threats will be heard or thought of! But, go—go—place your neck under him of Hanover's yoke, against whom every true Gael fought to the death. Go, disown the royal Stewart, for whom your father, and his fathers, and your mother's fathers, have crimsoned many a field with their blood. Go, put your head under the belt of one of the race of Dermid, whose children murdered—Yes," she added, with a wild shriek, "murdered your mother's fathers in their peaceful dwellings in Glencoe! Yes," she again exclaimed, with a wilder and shriller scream, "I was then unborn, but my mother has told me—and I attended to the voice of MY mother—well I remember her words! They came in peace, and were received in friendship—and blood and fire arose, and screams and murder!" [See Note 9.—Massacre of Glencoe.]

"Mother," answered Hamish, mournfully, but with a decided tone, "all that I have thought over. There is not a drop of the blood of Glencoe on the noble hand of Barcaldine; with the unhappy house of Glenlyon the curse remains, and on them God hath avenged it."

"You speak like the Saxon priest already," replied his mother; "will you not better stay, and ask a kirk from Macallum Mhor, that you may preach forgiveness to the race of Dermid?"

"Yesterday was yesterday," answered Hamish, "and to-day is to-day. When the clans are crushed and confounded together, it is well and wise that their hatreds and their feuds should not survive their independence and their power. He that cannot execute vengeance like a man, should not harbour useless enmity like a craven. Mother, young Barcaldine is true and brave. I know that MacPhadraick counselled him that he should not let me take leave of you, lest you dissuaded me from my purpose; but he said, 'Hamish MacTavish is the son of a brave man, and he will not break his word.' Mother, Barcaldine leads an hundred of the bravest of the sons of the Gael in their native dress, and with their fathers' arms—heart to heart—shoulder to shoulder. I have sworn to go with him. He has trusted me, and I will trust him."

At this reply, so firmly and resolvedly pronounced, Elspat remained like one thunderstruck, and sunk in despair. The arguments which she had considered so irresistibly conclusive, had recoiled like a wave from a rock. After a long pause, she filled her son's quaigh, and presented it to him with an air of dejected deference and submission.

"Drink," she said, "to thy father's roof-tree, ere you leave it for ever; and tell me—since the chains of a new King, and of a new chief, whom your fathers knew not save as mortal enemies, are fastened upon the limbs of your father's son—tell me how many links you count upon them?"

Hamish took the cup, but looked at her as if uncertain of her meaning. She proceeded in a raised voice. "Tell me," she said, "for I have a right to know, for how many days the will of those you have made your masters permits me to look upon you? In other words, how many are the days of my life? for when you leave me, the earth has nought besides worth living for!"

"Mother," replied Hamish MacTavish, "for six days I may remain with you; and if you will set out with me on the fifth, I will conduct you in safety to your new dwelling. But if you remain here, then I will depart on the seventh by daybreak—then, as at the last moment, I MUST set out for Dunbarton, for if I appear not on the eighth day, I am subject to punishment as a deserter, and am dishonoured as a soldier and a gentleman."

"Your father's foot," she answered, "was free as the wind on the heath—it were as vain to say to him, where goest thou? as to ask that viewless driver of the clouds, wherefore blowest thou? Tell me under what penalty thou must—since go thou must, and go thou wilt—return to thy thraldom?"

"Call it not thraldom, mother; it is the service of an honourable soldier—the only service which is now open to the son of MacTavish Mhor."

"Yet say what is the penalty if thou shouldst not return?" replied Elspat.

"Military punishment as a deserter," answered Hamish, writhing, however, as his mother failed not to observe, under some internal feelings, which she resolved to probe to the uttermost.

"And that," she said, with assumed calmness, which her glancing eye disowned, "is the punishment of a disobedient hound, is it not?"

"Ask me no more, mother," said Hamish; "the punishment is nothing to one who will never deserve it."

"To me it is something," replied Elspat, "since I know better than thou, that where there is power to inflict, there is often the will to do so without cause. I would pray for thee, Hamish, and I must know against what evils I should beseech Him who leaves none unguarded, to protect thy youth and simplicity."

"Mother," said Hamish, "it signifies little to what a criminal may be exposed, if a man is determined not to be such. Our Highland chiefs used also to punish their vassals, and, as I have heard, severely. Was it not Lachlan MacIan, whom we remember of old, whose head was struck off by order of his chieftain for shooting at the stag before him?"

"Ay," said Elspat, "and right he had to lose it, since he dishonoured the father of the people even in the face of the assembled clan. But the chiefs were noble in their ire; they punished with the sharp blade, and not with the baton. Their punishments drew blood, but they did not infer dishonour. Canst thou say, the same for the laws under whose yoke thou hast placed thy freeborn neck?"

"I cannot, mother—I cannot," said Hamish mournfully. "I saw them punish a Sassenach for deserting as they called it, his banner. He was scourged—I own it—scourged like a hound who has offended an imperious master. I was sick at the sight—I confess it. But the punishment of dogs is only for those worse than dogs, who know not how to keep their faith."

"To this infamy, however, thou hast subjected thyself, Hamish," replied Elspat, "if thou shouldst give, or thy officers take, measure of offence against thee. I speak no more to thee on thy purpose. Were the sixth day from this morning's sun my dying day, and thou wert to stay to close mine eyes, thou wouldst run the risk of being lashed like a dog at a post—yes! unless thou hadst the gallant heart to leave me to die alone, and upon my desolate hearth, the last spark of thy father's fire, and of thy forsaken mother's life, to be extinguished together!"—Hamish traversed the hut with an impatient and angry pace.

"Mother," he said at length, "concern not yourself about such things. I cannot be subjected to such infamy, for never will I deserve it; and were I threatened with it, I should know how to die before I was so far dishonoured."

"There spoke the son of the husband of my heart!" replied Elspat, and she changed the discourse, and seemed to listen in melancholy acquiescence, when her son reminded her how short the time was which they were permitted to pass in each other's society, and entreated that it might be spent without useless and unpleasant recollections respecting the circumstances under which they must soon be separated.

Elspat was now satisfied that her son, with some of his father's other properties, preserved the haughty masculine spirit which rendered it impossible to divert him from a resolution which he had deliberately adopted. She assumed, therefore, an exterior of apparent submission to their inevitable separation; and if she now and then broke out into complaints and murmurs, it was either that she could not altogether suppress the natural impetuosity of her temper, or because she had the wit to consider that a total and unreserved acquiescence might have seemed to her son constrained and suspicious, and induced him to watch and defeat the means by which she still hoped to prevent his leaving her. Her ardent though selfish affection for her son, incapable of being qualified by a regard for the true interests of the unfortunate object of her attachment, resembled the instinctive fondness of the animal race for their offspring; and diving little farther into futurity than one of the inferior creatures, she only felt that to be separated from Hamish was to die.

In the brief interval permitted them, Elspat exhausted every art which affection could devise, to render agreeable to him the space which they were apparently to spend with each other. Her memory carried her far back into former days, and her stores of legendary history, which furnish at all times a principal amusement of the Highlander in his moments of repose, were augmented by an unusual acquaintance with the songs of ancient bards, and traditions of the most approved seannachies and tellers of tales. Her officious attentions to her son's accommodation, indeed, were so unremitted as almost to give him pain, and he endeavoured quietly to prevent her from taking so much personal toil in selecting the blooming heath for his bed, or preparing the meal for his refreshment. "Let me alone, Hamish," she would reply on such occasions; "you follow your own will in departing from your mother, let your mother have hers in doing what gives her pleasure while you remain."

So much she seemed to be reconciled to the arrangements which he had made in her behalf, that she could hear him speak to her of her removing to the lands of Green Colin, as the gentleman was called, on whose estate he had provided her an asylum. In truth, however, nothing could be farther from her thoughts. From what he had said during their first violent dispute, Elspat had gathered that, if Hamish returned not by the appointed time permitted by his furlough, he would incur the hazard of corporal punishment. Were he placed within the risk of being thus dishonoured, she was well aware that he would never submit to the disgrace by a return to the regiment where it might be inflicted. Whether she looked to any farther probable consequences of her unhappy scheme cannot be known; but the partner of MacTavish Mhor, in all his perils and wanderings, was familiar with an hundred instances of resistance or escape, by which one brave man, amidst a land of rocks, lakes, and mountains, dangerous passes, and dark forests, might baffle the pursuit of hundreds. For the future, therefore, she feared nothing; her sole engrossing object was to prevent her son from keeping his word with his commanding officer.

With this secret purpose, she evaded the proposal which Hamish repeatedly made, that they should set out together to take possession of her new abode; and she resisted it upon grounds apparently so natural to her character that her son was neither alarmed nor displeased. "Let me not," she said, "in the same short week, bid farewell to my only son, and to the glen in which I have so long dwelt. Let my eye, when dimmed with weeping for thee, still look around, for a while at least, upon Loch Awe and on Ben Cruachan."

Hamish yielded the more willingly to his mother's humour in this particular, that one or two persons who resided in a neighbouring glen, and had given their sons to Barcaldine's levy, were also to be provided for on the estate of the chieftain, and it was apparently settled that Elspat was to take her journey along with them when they should remove to their new residence. Thus, Hamish believed that he had at once indulged his mother's humour, and ensured her safety and accommodation. But she nourished in her mind very different thoughts and projects.

The period of Hamish's leave of absence was fast approaching, and more than once he proposed to depart, in such time as to ensure his gaining easily and early Dunbarton, the town where were the head-quarters of his regiment. But still his mother's entreaties, his own natural disposition to linger among scenes long dear to him, and, above all, his firm reliance in his speed and activity, induced him to protract his departure till the sixth day, being the very last which he could possibly afford to spend with his mother, if indeed he meant to comply with the conditions of his furlough.

## CHAPTER V.

> But for your son, believe it—oh, believe it—
> Most dangerously you have with him prevailed,
> If not most mortal to him.  CORIOLANUS.

On the evening which preceded his proposed departure, Hamish walked down to the river with his fishing-rod, to practise in the Awe, for the last time, a sport in which he excelled, and to find, at the same time, the means for making one social meal with his mother on something better than their ordinary cheer. He was as successful as usual, and soon killed a fine salmon. On his return homeward an incident befell him, which he afterwards related as ominous, though probably his heated imagination, joined to the universal turn of his countrymen for the marvellous, exaggerated into superstitious importance some very ordinary and accidental circumstance.

In the path which he pursued homeward, he was surprised to observe a person, who, like himself, was dressed and armed after the old Highland fashion. The first idea that struck him was, that the passenger belonged to his own corps, who, levied by government, and bearing arms under royal authority, were not amenable for breach of the statutes against the use of the Highland garb or weapons. But he was struck on perceiving, as he mended his pace to make up to his supposed comrade, meaning to request his company for the next day's journey, that the stranger wore a white cockade, the fatal badge which was proscribed in the Highlands. The stature of the man was tall, and there was something shadowy in the outline, which added to his size; and his mode of motion, which rather resembled gliding than walking, impressed Hamish with superstitious fears concerning the character of the being which thus passed before him in the twilight. He no longer strove to make up to the stranger, but contented himself with keeping him in view, under the superstition common to the Highlanders, that you ought neither to intrude yourself on such supernatural apparitions as you may witness, nor avoid their presence, but leave it to themselves to withhold or extend their communication, as their power may permit, or the purpose of their commission require.

Upon an elevated knoll by the side of the road, just where the pathway turned down to Elspat's hut, the stranger made a pause, and seemed to await Hamish's coming up. Hamish, on his part, seeing it was necessary he should pass the object of his suspicion, mustered up his courage, and approached the spot where the stranger had placed himself; who first pointed to Elspat's hut, and made, with arm and head, a gesture prohibiting Hamish to approach it, then stretched his hand to the road which led to the southward, with a motion which seemed to enjoin his instant departure in that direction. In a moment afterwards the plaided form was gone—Hamish did not exactly say vanished, because there were rocks and stunted trees enough to have concealed him; but it was his own opinion that he had seen the spirit of MacTavish Mhor, warning him to commence his instant journey to Dunbarton, without waiting till morning, or again visiting his mother's hut.

In fact, so many accidents might arise to delay his journey, especially where there were many ferries, that it became his settled purpose, though he could not depart without bidding his mother adieu, that he neither could nor would abide longer than for that object; and that the first glimpse of next day's sun should see him many miles advanced towards Dunbarton. He descended the path, therefore, and entering the cottage, he communicated, in a hasty and troubled voice, which indicated mental agitation, his determination to take his instant departure. Somewhat to his surprise, Elspat appeared not to combat his purpose, but she urged him to take some refreshment ere he left her for ever. He did so hastily, and in silence, thinking on the approaching separation, and scarce yet believing it would take place without a final struggle with his mother's fondness. To his surprise, she filled the quaigh with liquor for his parting cup.

"Go," she said, "my son, since such is thy settled purpose; but first stand once more on thy mother's hearth, the flame on which will be extinguished long ere thy foot shall again be placed there."

"To your health, mother!" said Hamish; "and may we meet again in happiness, in spite of your ominous words."

"It were better not to part," said his mother, watching him as he quaffed the liquor, of which he would have held it ominous to have left a drop.

"And now," she said, muttering the words to herself, "go—if thou canst go."

"Mother," said Hamish, as he replaced on the table the empty quaigh, "thy drink is pleasant to the taste, but it takes away the strength which it ought to give."

"Such is its first effect, my son," replied Elspat. "But lie down upon that soft heather couch, shut your eyes but for a moment, and, in the sleep of an hour, you shall have more refreshment than in the ordinary repose of three whole nights, could they be blended into one."

"Mother," said Hamish, upon whose brain the potion was now taking rapid effect, "give me my bonnet—I must kiss you and begone—yet it seems as if my feet were nailed to the floor."

"Indeed," said his mother, "you will be instantly well, if you will sit down for half an hour—but half an hour. It is eight hours to dawn, and dawn were time enough for your father's son to begin such a journey."

"I must obey you, mother—I feel I must," said Hamish inarticulately; "but call me when the moon rises."

He sat down on the bed, reclined back, and almost instantly was fast asleep. With the throbbing glee of one who has brought to an end a difficult and troublesome enterprise, Elspat proceeded tenderly to arrange the plaid of the unconscious slumberer, to whom her extravagant affection was doomed to be so fatal, expressing, while busied in her office, her delight, in tones of mingled tenderness and triumph. "Yes," she said, "calf of my heart, the moon shall arise and set to thee, and so shall the sun; but not to light thee from the land of thy fathers, or tempt thee to serve the foreign prince or the feudal enemy! To no son of Dermid shall I be delivered, to be fed like a bondswoman; but he who is my pleasure and my pride shall be my guard and my protector. They say the Highlands are changed; but I see Ben Cruachan rear his crest as high as ever into the evening sky; no one hath yet herded his kine on the depths of Loch Awe; and yonder oak does not yet bend like a willow. The children of the mountains will be such as their fathers, until the mountains themselves shall be levelled with the strath. In these wild forests, which used to support thousands of the brave, there is still surely subsistence and refuge left for one aged woman, and one gallant youth of the ancient race and the ancient manners."

While the misjudging mother thus exulted in the success of her stratagem, we may mention to the reader that it was founded on the acquaintance with drugs and simples which Elspat, accomplished in all things belonging to the wild life which she had led, possessed in an uncommon degree, and which she exercised for various purposes. With the herbs, which she knew how to select as well as how to distil, she could relieve more diseases than a regular medical person could easily believe. She applied some to dye the bright colours of the tartan; from others she compounded draughts of various powers, and unhappily possessed the secret of one which was strongly soporific. Upon the effects of this last concoction, as the reader doubtless has anticipated, she reckoned with security on delaying Hamish beyond the period for which his return was appointed; and she trusted to his horror for the apprehended punishment to which he was thus rendered liable, to prevent him from returning at all.

Sound and deep, beyond natural rest, was the sleep of Hamish MacTavish on that eventful evening, but not such the repose of his mother. Scarce did she close her eyes from time to time, but she awakened again with a start, in the terror that her son had arisen and departed; and it was only on approaching his couch, and hearing his deep-drawn and regular breathing, that she reassured herself of the security of the repose in which he was plunged.

Still, dawning, she feared, might awaken him, notwithstanding the unusual strength of the potion with which she had drugged his cup. If there remained a hope of mortal man accomplishing the journey, she was aware that Hamish would attempt it, though he were to die from fatigue upon the road. Animated by this new fear, she studied to exclude the light, by stopping all the crannies and crevices through which, rather than through any regular entrance, the morning beams might find access to her miserable dwelling; and this in order to detain amid its wants and wretchedness the being on whom, if the world itself had been at her disposal, she would have joyfully conferred it.

Her pains were bestowed unnecessarily. The sun rose high above the heavens, and not the fleetest stag in Breadalbane, were the hounds at his heels, could have sped, to save his life, so fast as would have been necessary to keep Hamish's appointment. Her purpose was fully attained—her son's return within the period assigned was impossible. She deemed it equally impossible, that he would ever dream of returning, standing, as he must now do, in the danger of an infamous punishment. By degrees, and at different times, she had gained from him a full acquaintance with the predicament in which he would be placed by failing to appear on the day appointed, and the very small hope he could entertain of being treated with lenity.

It is well known, that the great and wise Earl of Chatham prided himself on the scheme, by which he drew together for the defence of the colonies those hardy Highlanders, who, until his time, had been the objects of doubt, fear, and suspicion, on the part of each successive administration. But some obstacles occurred, from the peculiar habits and temper of this people, to the execution of his patriotic project. By nature and habit, every Highlander was accustomed to the use of arms, but at the same time totally unaccustomed to, and impatient of, the restraints imposed by discipline upon regular troops. They were a species of militia, who had no conception of a camp as their only home. If a battle was lost, they dispersed to save themselves, and look out for the safety of their families; if won, they went back to their glens to hoard up their booty, and attend to their cattle and their farms. This privilege of going and coming at pleasure, they would not be deprived of even by their chiefs, whose authority was in most other respects so despotic. It followed as a matter of course, that the new-levied Highland recruits could scarce be made to comprehend the nature of a military engagement, which compelled a man to serve in the army longer than he pleased; and perhaps, in many instances, sufficient care was not taken at enlisting to explain to them the permanency of the engagement which they came under, lest such a disclosure should induce them to change their mind. Desertions were therefore become numerous from the newly-raised regiment, and the veteran general who commanded at Dunbarton saw no better way of checking them than by causing an unusually severe example to be made of a deserter from an English corps. The young Highland regiment was obliged to attend upon the punishment, which struck a people, peculiarly jealous of personal honour, with equal horror and disgust, and not unnaturally indisposed some of them to the service. The old general, however, who had been regularly bred in the German wars, stuck to his own opinion, and gave out in orders that the first Highlander who might either desert, or fail to appear at the expiry of his furlough, should be brought to the halberds, and punished like the culprit whom they had seen in that condition. No man doubted that General — would keep his word rigorously whenever severity was required, and Elspat, therefore, knew that her son, when he perceived that due compliance with his orders was impossible, must at the same time consider the degrading punishment denounced against his defection as inevitable, should he place himself within the general's power. [See Note 10.—Fidelity of the Highlanders.]

When noon was well passed, new apprehensions came on the mind of the lonely woman. Her son still slept under the influence of the draught; but what if, being stronger than she had ever known it administered, his health or his reason should be affected by its potency? For the first time, likewise, notwithstanding her high ideas on the subject of parental authority, she began to dread the resentment of her son, whom her heart told her she had wronged. Of late, she had observed that his temper was less docile, and his determinations, especially upon this late occasion of his enlistment, independently formed, and then boldly carried through. She remembered the stern wilfulness of his father when he accounted himself ill-used, and began to dread that Hamish, upon finding the deceit she had put upon him, might resent it even to the extent of cutting her off, and pursuing his own course through the world alone. Such were the alarming and yet the reasonable apprehensions which began to crowd upon the unfortunate woman, after the apparent success of her ill-advised stratagem.

It was near evening when Hamish first awoke, and then he was far from being in the full possession either of his mental or bodily powers. From his vague expressions and disordered pulse, Elspat at first experienced much apprehension; but she used such expedients as her medical knowledge suggested, and in the course of the night she had the satisfaction to see him sink once more into a deep sleep, which probably carried off the greater part of the effects of the drug, for about sunrising she heard him arise, and call to her for his bonnet. This she had purposely removed, from a fear that he might awaken and depart in the night-time, without her knowledge.

"My bonnet—my bonnet," cried Hamish; "it is time to take farewell. Mother, your drink was too strong—the sun is up—but with the next morning I will still see the double summit of the ancient Dun. My bonnet—my bonnet, mother; I must be instant in my departure." These expressions made it plain that poor Hamish was unconscious that two nights and a day had passed since he had drained the fatal quaigh, and Elspat had now to venture on what she felt as the almost perilous, as well as painful, task of explaining her machinations.

"Forgive me, my son," she said, approaching Hamish, and taking him by the hand with an air of deferential awe, which perhaps she had not always used to his father, even when in his moody fits.

"Forgive you, mother!—for what?" said Hamish, laughing; "for giving me a dram that was too strong, and which my head still feels this morning, or for hiding my bonnet to keep me an instant longer? Nay, do YOU forgive ME. Give me the bonnet, and let that be done which now must be done. Give me my bonnet, or I go without it; surely I am not to be delayed by so trifling a want as that—I, who have gone for years with only a strap of deer's hide to tie back my hair. Trifle not, but give it me, or I must go bareheaded, since to stay is impossible."

"My son," said Elspat, keeping fast hold of his hand, "what is done cannot be recalled. Could you borrow the wings of yonder eagle, you would arrive at the Dun too late for what you purpose—too soon for what awaits you there. You believe you see the sun rising for the first time since you have seen him set; but yesterday beheld him climb Ben Cruachan, though your eyes were closed to his light."

Hamish cast upon his mother a wild glance of extreme terror, then instantly recovering himself, said, "I am no child to be cheated out of my purpose by such tricks as these. Farewell, mother! each moment is worth a lifetime."

"Stay," she said, "my dear, my deceived son, run not on infamy and ruin. Yonder I see the priest upon the high-road on his white horse. Ask him the day of the month and week; let him decide between us."

With the speed of an eagle, Hamish darted up the acclivity, and stood by the minister of Glenorquhy, who was pacing out thus early to administer consolation to a distressed family near Bunawe.

The good man was somewhat startled to behold an armed Highlander, then so unusual a sight, and apparently much agitated, stop his horse by the bridle, and ask him with a faltering voice the day of the week and month. "Had you been where you should have been yesterday, young man," replied the clergyman, "you would have known that it was God's Sabbath; and that this is Monday, the second day of the week, and twenty-first of the month."

"And this is true?" said Hamish.

"As true," answered the surprised minister, "as that I yesterday preached the word of God to this parish. What ails you, young man?—are you sick?—are you in your right mind?"

Hamish made no answer, only repeated to himself the first expression of the clergyman, "Had you been where you should have been yesterday;" and so saying, he let go the bridle, turned from the road, and descended the path towards the hut, with the look and pace of one who was going to execution. The minister looked after him with surprise; but although he knew the inhabitant of the hovel, the character of Elspat had not invited him to open any communication with her, because she was generally reputed a Papist, or rather one indifferent to all religion, except some superstitious observances which had been handed down from her parents. On Hamish the Reverend Mr. Tyrie had bestowed instructions when he was occasionally thrown in his way; and if the seed fell among the brambles and thorns of a wild and uncultivated disposition, it had not yet been entirely checked or destroyed. There was something so ghastly in the present expression of the youth's features that the good man was tempted to go down to the hovel, and inquire whether any distress had befallen the inhabitants, in which his presence might be consoling and his ministry useful. Unhappily he did not persevere in this resolution, which might have saved a great misfortune, as he would have probably become a mediator for the unfortunate young man; but a recollection of the wild moods of such Highlanders as had been educated after the old fashion of the country, prevented his interesting himself in the widow and son of the far-dreaded robber, MacTavish Mhor, and he thus missed an opportunity, which he afterwards sorely repented, of doing much good.

When Hamish MacTavish entered his mother's hut, it was only to throw himself on the bed he had left, and exclaiming, "Undone, undone!" to give vent, in cries of grief and anger, to his deep sense of the deceit which had been practised on him, and of the cruel predicament to which he was reduced.

Elspat was prepared for the first explosion of her son's passion, and said to herself, "It is but the mountain torrent, swelled by the thunder shower. Let us sit and rest us by the bank; for all its present tumult, the time will soon come when we may pass it dryshod." She suffered his complaints and his reproaches, which were, even in the midst of his agony, respectful and affectionate, to die away without returning any answer; and when, at length, having exhausted all the exclamations of sorrow which his language, copious in expressing the feelings of the heart, affords to the sufferer, he sunk into a gloomy silence, she suffered the interval to continue near an hour ere she approached her son's couch.

"And now," she said at length, with a voice in which the authority of the mother was qualified by her tenderness, "have you exhausted your idle sorrows, and are you able to place what you have gained against what you have lost? Is the false son of Dermid your brother, or the father of your tribe, that you weep because you cannot bind yourself to his belt, and become one of those who must do his bidding? Could you find in yonder distant country the lakes and the mountains that you leave behind you here? Can you hunt the deer of Breadalbane in the forests of America, or will the ocean afford you the silver-scaled salmon of the Awe? Consider, then, what is your loss, and, like a wise man, set it against what you have won."

"I have lost all, mother," replied Hamish, "since I have broken my word, and lost my honour. I might tell my tale, but who, oh, who would believe me?" The unfortunate young man again clasped his hands together, and, pressing them to his forehead, hid his face upon the bed.

Elspat was now really alarmed, and perhaps wished the fatal deceit had been left unattempted. She had no hope or refuge saving in the eloquence of persuasion, of which she possessed no small share, though her total ignorance of the world as it actually existed rendered its energy unavailing. She urged her son, by every tender epithet which a parent could bestow, to take care for his own safety.

"Leave me," she said, "to baffle your pursuers. I will save your life—I will save your honour. I will tell them that my fair-haired Hamish fell from the Corrie Dhu (black precipice) into the gulf, of which human eye never beheld the bottom. I will tell them this, and I will fling your plaid on the thorns which grow on the brink of the precipice, that they may believe my words. They will believe, and they will return to the Dun of the double-crest; for though the Saxon drum can call the living to die, it cannot recall the dead to their slavish standard. Then will we travel together far northward to the salt lakes of Kintail, and place glens and mountains betwixt us and the sons of Dermid. We will visit the shores of the dark lake; and my kinsmen—for was not my mother of the children of Kenneth, and will they not remember us with the old love?—my kinsmen will receive us with the affection of the olden time, which lives in those distant glens, where the Gael still dwell in their nobleness, unmingled with the churl Saxons, or with the base brood that are their tools and their slaves."

The energy of the language, somewhat allied to hyperbole, even in its most ordinary expressions, now seemed almost too weak to afford Elspat the means of bringing out the splendid picture which she presented to her son of the land in which she proposed to him to take refuge. Yet the colours were few with which she could paint her Highland paradise. "The hills," she said, "were higher and more magnificent than those of

Breadalbane—Ben Cruachan was but a dwarf to Skooroora. The lakes were broader and larger, and abounded not only with fish, but with the enchanted and amphibious animal which gives oil to the lamp. [The seals are considered by the Highlanders as enchanted princes.] The deer were larger and more numerous; the white-tusked boar, the chase of which the brave loved best, was yet to be roused in those western solitudes; the men were nobler, wiser, and stronger than the degenerate brood who lived under the Saxon banner. The daughters of the land were beautiful, with blue eyes and fair hair, and bosoms of snow; and out of these she would choose a wife for Hamish, of blameless descent, spotless fame, fixed and true affection, who should be in their summer bothy as a beam of the sun, and in their winter abode as the warmth of the needful fire."

Such were the topics with which Elspat strove to soothe the despair of her son, and to determine him, if possible, to leave the fatal spot, on which he seemed resolved to linger. The style of her rhetoric was poetical, but in other respects resembled that which, like other fond mothers, she had lavished on Hamish, while a child or a boy, in order to gain his consent to do something he had no mind to; and she spoke louder, quicker, and more earnestly, in proportion as she began to despair of her words carrying conviction.

On the mind of Hamish her eloquence made no impression. He knew far better than she did the actual situation of the country, and was sensible that, though it might be possible to hide himself as a fugitive among more distant mountains, there was now no corner in the Highlands in which his father's profession could be practised, even if he had not adopted, from the improved ideas of the time when he lived, the opinion that the trade of the cateran was no longer the road to honour and distinction. Her words were therefore poured into regardless ears, and she exhausted herself in vain in the attempt to paint the regions of her mother's kinsmen in such terms as might tempt Hamish to accompany her thither. She spoke for hours, but she spoke in vain. She could extort no answer, save groans and sighs and ejaculations, expressing the extremity of despair.

At length, starting on her feet, and changing the monotonous tone in which she had chanted, as it were, the praises of the province of refuge, into the short, stern language of eager passion—"I am a fool," she said, "to spend my words upon an idle, poor-spirited, unintelligent boy, who crouches like a hound to the lash. Wait here, and receive your taskmasters, and abide your chastisement at their hands; but do not think your mother's eyes will behold it. I could not see it and live. My eyes have looked often upon death, but never upon dishonour. Farewell, Hamish! We never meet again."

She dashed from the hut like a lapwing, and perhaps for the moment actually entertained the purpose which she expressed, of parting with her son for ever. A fearful sight she would have been that evening to any who might have met her wandering through the wilderness like a restless spirit, and speaking to herself in language which will endure no translation. She rambled for hours, seeking rather than shunning the most dangerous paths. The precarious track through the morass, the dizzy path along the edge of the precipice or by the banks of the gulfing river, were the roads which, far from avoiding, she sought with eagerness, and traversed with reckless haste. But the courage arising from despair was the means of saving the life which (though deliberate suicide was rarely practised in the Highlands) she was perhaps desirous of terminating. Her step on the verge of the precipice was firm as that of the wild goat. Her eye, in that state of excitation, was so keen as to discern, even amid darkness, the perils which noon would not have enabled a stranger to avoid.

Elspat's course was not directly forward, else she had soon been far from the bothy in which she had left her son. It was circuitous, for that hut was the centre to which her heartstrings were chained, and though she wandered around it, she felt it impossible to leave the vicinity. With the first beams of morning she returned to the hut. Awhile she paused at the wattled door, as if ashamed that lingering fondness should have brought her back to the spot which she had left with the purpose of never returning; but there was yet more of fear and anxiety in her hesitation—of anxiety, lest her fair-haired son had suffered from the effects of her potion—of fear, lest his enemies had come upon him in the night. She opened the door of the hut gently, and entered with noiseless step. Exhausted with his sorrow and anxiety, and not entirely relieved perhaps from the influence of the powerful opiate, Hamish Bean again slept the stern, sound sleep by which the Indians are said to be overcome during the interval of their torments. His mother was scarcely sure that she actually discerned his form on the bed, scarce certain that her ear caught the sound of his breathing. With a throbbing heart, Elspat went to the fireplace in the centre of the hut, where slumbered, covered with a piece of turf, the glimmering embers of the fire, never extinguished on a Scottish hearth until the indwellers leave the mansion for ever.

"Feeble greishogh," [Greishogh, a glowing ember.] she said, as she lighted, by the help of a match, a splinter of bog pine which was to serve the place of a candle—"weak greishogh, soon shalt thou be put out for ever, and may Heaven grant that the life of Elspat MacTavish have no longer duration than thine!"

While she spoke she raised the blazing light towards the bed, on which still lay the prostrate limbs of her son, in a posture that left it doubtful whether he slept or swooned. As she advanced towards him, the light flashed upon his eyes—he started up in an instant, made a stride forward with his naked dirk in his hand, like a man armed to meet a mortal enemy, and exclaimed, "Stand off!—on thy life, stand off!"

"It is the word and the action of my husband," answered Elspat; "and I know by his speech and his step the son of MacTavish Mhor."

"Mother," said Hamish, relapsing from his tone of desperate firmness into one of melancholy expostulation—"oh, dearest mother, wherefore have you returned hither?"

"Ask why the hind comes back to the fawn," said Elspat, "why the cat of the mountain returns to her lodge and her young. Know you, Hamish, that the heart of the mother only lives in the bosom of the child."

"Then will it soon cease to throb," said Hamish, "unless it can beat within a bosom that lies beneath the turf. Mother, do not blame me. If I weep, it is not for myself but for you; for my sufferings will soon be over, but yours—oh, who but Heaven shall set a boundary to them?"

Elspat shuddered and stepped backward, but almost instantly resumed her firm and upright position and her dauntless bearing.

"I thought thou wert a man but even now," she said, "and thou art again a child. Hearken to me yet, and let us leave this place together. Have I done thee wrong or injury? if so, yet do not avenge it so cruelly. See, Elspat MacTavish, who never kneeled before even to a priest, falls prostrate before her own son, and craves his forgiveness." And at once she threw herself on her knees before the young man, seized on his hand, and kissing it an hundred times, repeated as often, in heart-breaking accents, the most earnest entreaties for forgiveness. "Pardon," she exclaimed, "pardon, for the sake of your father's ashes—pardon, for the sake of the pain with which I bore thee, the care with which I nurtured thee!—Hear it, Heaven, and behold it, Earth—the mother asks pardon of her child, and she is refused!"

It was in vain that Hamish endeavoured to stem this tide of passion, by assuring his mother, with the most solemn asseverations, that he forgave entirely the fatal deceit which she had practised upon him.

"Empty words," she said, "idle protestations, which are but used to hide the obduracy of your resentment. Would you have me believe you, then leave the hut this instant, and retire from a country which every hour renders more dangerous. Do this, and I may think you have forgiven me; refuse it, and again I call on moon and stars, heaven and earth, to witness the unrelenting resentment with which you prosecute your mother for a fault, which, if it be one, arose out of love to you."

"Mother," said Hamish, "on this subject you move me not. I will fly before no man. If Barcaldine should send every Gael that is under his banner, here, and in this place, will I abide them; and when you bid me fly, you may as well command yonder mountain to be loosened from its foundations. Had I been sure of the road by which they are coming hither, I had spared them the pains of seeking me; but I might go by the mountain, while they perchance came by the lake. Here I will abide my fate; nor is there in Scotland a voice of power enough to bid me stir from hence, and be obeyed."

"Here, then, I also stay," said Elspat, rising up and speaking with assumed composure. "I have seen my husband's death—my eyelids shall not grieve to look on the fall of my son. But MacTavish Mhor died as became the brave, with his good sword in his right hand; my son will perish like the bullock that is driven to the shambles by the Saxon owner who had bought him for a price."

"Mother," said the unhappy young man, "you have taken my life. To that you have a right, for you gave it; but touch not my honour! It came to me from a brave train of ancestors, and should be sullied neither by man's deed nor woman's speech. What I shall do, perhaps I myself yet know not; but tempt me no farther by reproachful words—you have already made wounds more than you can ever heal."

"It is well, my son," said Elspat, in reply. "Expect neither farther complaint nor remonstrance from me; but let us be silent, and wait the chance which Heaven shall send us."

The sun arose on the next morning, and found the bothy silent as the grave. The mother and son had arisen, and were engaged each in their separate task—Hamish in preparing and cleaning his arms with the greatest accuracy, but with an air of deep dejection. Elspat, more restless in her agony of spirit, employed herself in making ready the food which the distress of yesterday had induced them both to dispense with for an unusual number of hours. She placed it on the board before her son so soon as it was prepared, with the words of a Gaelic poet, "Without daily food, the husbandman's ploughshare stands still in the furrow; without daily food, the sword of the warrior is too heavy for his hand. Our bodies are our slaves, yet they must be fed if we would have their service. So spake in ancient days the Blind Bard to the warriors of Fion."

The young man made no reply, but he fed on what was placed before him, as if to gather strength for the scene which he was to undergo. When his mother saw that he had eaten what sufficed him, she again filled the fatal quaigh, and proffered it as the conclusion of the repast. But he started aside with a convulsive gesture, expressive at once of fear and abhorrence.

"Nay, my son," she said, "this time surely, thou hast no cause of fear."

"Urge me not, mother," answered Hamish—"or put the leprous toad into a flagon, and I will drink; but from that accursed cup, and of that mind-destroying potion, never will I taste more!"

"At your pleasure, my son," said Elspat, haughtily, and began, with much apparent assiduity, the various domestic tasks which had been interrupted during the preceding day. Whatever was at her heart, all anxiety seemed banished from her looks and demeanour. It was but from an over-activity of bustling exertion that it might have been perceived, by a close observer, that her actions were spurred by some internal cause of painful excitement; and such a spectator, too, might also have observed how often she broke off the snatches of songs or tunes which she hummed, apparently without knowing what she was doing, in order to cast a hasty glance from the door of the hut. Whatever might be in the mind of Hamish, his demeanour was directly the reverse of that adopted by his mother. Having finished the task of cleaning and preparing his arms, which he arranged within the hut, he sat himself down before the door of the bothy, and watched the opposite hill, like the fixed sentinel who expects the approach of an enemy. Noon found him in the same unchanged posture, and it was an hour after that period, when his mother, standing beside him, laid her hand on his shoulder, and said, in a tone indifferent, as if she had been talking of some friendly visit, "When dost thou expect them?"

"They cannot be here till the shadows fall long to the eastward," replied Hamish; "that is, even supposing the nearest party, commanded by Sergeant Allan Breack Cameron, has been commanded hither by express from Dunbarton, as it is most likely they will."

"Then enter beneath your mother's roof once more; partake the last time of the food which she has prepared; after this, let them come, and thou shalt see if thy mother is an useless encumbrance in the day of strife. Thy hand, practised as it is, cannot fire these arms so fast as I can load them; nay, if it is necessary, I do not myself fear the flash or the report, and my aim has been held fatal."

"In the name of Heaven, mother, meddle not with this matter!" said Hamish. "Allan Breack is a wise man and a kind one, and comes of a good stem. It may be, he can promise for our officers that they will touch me with no infamous punishment; and if they offer me confinement in the dungeon, or death by the musket, to that I may not object."

"Alas, and wilt thou trust to their word, my foolish child? Remember the race of Dermid were ever fair and false; and no sooner shall they have gyves on thy hands, than they will strip thy shoulders for the scourge."

"Save your advice, mother," said Hamish, sternly; "for me, my mind is made up."

But though he spoke thus, to escape the almost persecuting urgency of his mother, Hamish would have found it, at that moment, impossible to say upon what course of conduct he had thus fixed. On one point alone he was determined—namely, to abide his destiny, be what it might, and not to add to the breach of his word, of which he had been involuntarily rendered guilty, by attempting to escape from punishment. This act of self-devotion he conceived to be due to his own honour and that of his countrymen. Which of his comrades would in future be trusted, if he should be considered as having broken his word, and betrayed the confidence of his officers? and whom but Hamish Bean MacTavish would the Gael accuse for having verified and confirmed the suspicions which the Saxon General was well known to entertain against the good faith of the Highlanders? He was, therefore, bent firmly to abide his fate. But whether his intention was to yield himself peaceably into the bands of the party who should come to apprehend him, or whether he purposed, by a show of resistance, to provoke them to kill him on the spot, was a question which he could not himself have answered. His desire to see Barcaldine, and explain the cause of his absence at the appointed time, urged him to the one course; his fear of the degrading punishment, and of his mother's bitter upbraidings, strongly instigated the latter and the more dangerous purpose. He left it to chance to decide when the crisis should arrive; nor did he tarry long in expectation of the catastrophe.

Evening approached; the gigantic shadows of the mountains streamed in darkness towards the east, while their western peaks were still glowing with crimson and gold. The road which winds round Ben Cruachan was fully visible from the door of the bothy, when a party of five Highland soldiers, whose arms glanced in the sun, wheeled suddenly into sight from the most distant extremity, where the highway is hidden behind the mountain. One of the party walked a little before the other four, who marched regularly and in files, according to the rules of military discipline. There was no dispute, from the firelocks which they carried, and the plaids and bonnets which they wore, that they were a party of Hamish's regiment, under a non-commissioned officer; and there could be as little doubt of the purpose of their appearance on the banks of Loch Awe.

"They come briskly forward"—said the widow of MacTavish Mhor;—"I wonder how fast or how slow some of them will return again! But they are five, and it is too much odds for a fair field. Step back within the hut, my son, and shoot from the loophole beside the door. Two you may bring down ere they quit the highroad for the footpath—there will remain but three; and your father, with my aid, has often stood against that number."

Hamish Bean took the gun which his mother offered, but did not stir from the door of the hut. He was soon visible to the party on the highroad, as was evident from their increasing their pace to a run—the files, however, still keeping together like coupled greyhounds, and advancing with great rapidity. In far less time than would have been accomplished by men less accustomed to the mountains, they had left the highroad, traversed the narrow path, and approached within pistol-shot of the bothy, at the door of which stood Hamish, fixed like a statue of stone, with his firelock in his hand, while his mother, placed behind him, and almost driven to frenzy by the violence of her passions, reproached him in the strongest terms which despair could invent, for his want of resolution and faintness of heart. Her words increased the bitter gall which was arising in the young man's own spirit, as he observed the unfriendly speed with which his late comrades were eagerly making towards him, like hounds towards the stag when he is at bay. The untamed and angry passions which he inherited from father and mother, were awakened by the supposed hostility of those who pursued him; and the restraint under which these passions had been hitherto held by his sober judgment began gradually to give way. The sergeant now called to him, "Hamish Bean MacTavish, lay down your arms and surrender."

"Do YOU stand, Allan Breack Cameron, and command your men to stand, or it will be the worse for us all."

"Halt, men," said the sergeant, but continuing himself to advance. "Hamish, think what you do, and give up your gun; you may spill blood, but you cannot escape punishment."

"The scourge—the scourge—my son, beware the scourge!" whispered his mother.

"Take heed, Allan Breack," said Hamish. "I would not hurt you willingly, but I will not be taken unless you can assure me against the Saxon lash."

"Fool!" answered Cameron, "you know I cannot. Yet I will do all I can. I will say I met you on your return, and the punishment will be light; but give up your musket—Come on, men."

Instantly he rushed forward, extending his arm as if to push aside the young man's levelled firelock. Elspat exclaimed, "Now, spare not your father's blood to defend your father's hearth!" Hamish fired his piece, and Cameron dropped dead. All these things happened, it might be said, in the same moment of time. The soldiers rushed forward and seized Hamish, who, seeming petrified with what he had done, offered not the least resistance. Not so his mother, who, seeing the men about to put handcuffs on her son, threw herself on the soldiers with such fury, that it required two of them to hold her, while the rest secured the prisoner.

"Are you not an accursed creature," said one of the men to Hamish, "to have slain your best friend, who was contriving, during the whole march, how he could find some way of getting you off without punishment for your desertion?"

"Do you hear THAT, mother?" said Hamish, turning himself as much towards her as his bonds would permit; but the mother heard nothing, and saw nothing. She had fainted on the floor of her hut. Without waiting for her recovery, the party almost immediately began their homeward march towards Dunbarton, leading along with them their prisoner. They thought it necessary, however, to stay for a little space at the village of Dalmally, from which they despatched a party of the inhabitants to bring away the body of their unfortunate leader, while they themselves repaired to a magistrate, to state what had happened, and require his instructions as to the farther course to be pursued. The crime being of a military character, they were instructed to march the prisoner to Dunbarton without delay.

The swoon of the mother of Hamish lasted for a length of time—the longer perhaps that her constitution, strong as it was, must have been much exhausted by her previous agitation of three days' endurance. She was roused from her stupor at length by female voices, which cried the coronach, or lament for the dead, with clapping of hands and loud exclamations; while the melancholy note of a lament, appropriate to the clan Cameron, played on the bagpipe, was heard from time to time.

Elspat started up like one awakened from the dead, and without any accurate recollection of the scene which had passed before her eyes. There were females in the hut who were swathing the corpse in its bloody plaid before carrying it from the fatal spot. "Women," she said, starting up and interrupting their chant at once and their labour—"Tell me, women, why sing you the dirge of MacDhonuil Dhu in the house of MacTavish Mhor?"

"She-wolf, be silent with thine ill-omened yell," answered one of the females, a relation of the deceased, "and let us do our duty to our beloved kinsman. There shall never be coronach cried, or dirge played, for thee or thy bloody wolf-burd. [Wolf-brood—that is, wolf-cub.] The ravens shall eat him from the gibbet, and the foxes and wild-cats shall tear thy corpse upon the hill. Cursed be he that would sain [Bless.] your bones, or add a stone to your cairn!"

"Daughter of a foolish mother," answered the widow of MacTavish Mhor, "know that the gibbet with which you threaten us is no portion of our inheritance. For thirty years the Black Tree of the Law, whose apples are dead men's bodies, hungered after the beloved husband of my heart; but he died like a brave man, with the sword in his hand, and defrauded it of its hopes and its fruit."

"So shall it not be with thy child, bloody sorceress," replied the female mourner, whose passions were as violent as those of Elspat herself. "The ravens shall tear his fair hair to line their nests, before the sun sinks beneath the Treshornish islands."

These words recalled to Elspat's mind the whole history of the last three dreadful days. At first she stood fixed, as if the extremity of distress had converted her into stone; but in a minute, the pride and violence of her temper, outbraved as she thought herself on her own threshold, enabled her to reply, "Yes, insulting hag, my fair-haired boy may die, but it will not be with a white hand. It has been dyed in the blood of his enemy, in the best blood of a Cameron—remember that; and when you lay your dead in his grave, let it be his best epitaph that he was killed by Hamish Bean for essaying to lay hands on the son of MacTavish Mhor on his own threshold. Farewell—the shame of defeat, loss, and slaughter remain with the clan that has endured it!"

The relative of the slaughtered Cameron raised her voice in reply; but Elspat, disdaining to continue the objurgation, or perhaps feeling her grief likely to overmaster her power of expressing her resentment, had left the hut, and was walking forth in the bright moonshine.

The females who were arranging the corpse of the slaughtered man hurried from their melancholy labour to look after her tall figure as it glided away among the cliffs. "I am glad she is gone," said one of the younger persons who assisted. "I would as soon dress a corpse when the great fiend himself—God sain us!—stood visibly before us, as when Elspat of the Tree is amongst us. Ay, ay, even overmuch intercourse hath she had with the enemy in her day."

"Silly woman," answered the female who had maintained the dialogue with the departed Elspat, "thinkest thou that there is a worse fiend on earth, or beneath it, than the pride and fury of an offended woman, like yonder bloody-minded hag? Know that blood has been as familiar to her as the dew to the mountain daisy. Many and many a brave man has she caused to breathe their last for little wrong they had done to her or theirs. But her hough-sinews are cut, now that her wolf-burd must, like a murderer as he is, make a murderer's end."

Whilst the women thus discoursed together, as they watched the corpse of Allan Breack Cameron, the unhappy cause of his death pursued her lonely way across the mountain. While she remained within sight of the bothy, she put a strong constraint on herself, that by no alteration of pace or gesture she might afford to her enemies the triumph of calculating the excess of her mental agitation, nay, despair. She stalked, therefore, with a slow rather than a swift step, and, holding herself upright, seemed at once to endure with firmness that woe which was passed, and bid defiance to that which was about to come. But when she was beyond the sight of those who remained in the hut, she could no longer suppress the extremity of her agitation. Drawing her mantle wildly round her, she stopped at the first knoll, and climbing to its summit, extended her arms up to the bright moon, as if accusing heaven and earth for her misfortunes, and uttered scream on scream, like those of an eagle whose nest has been plundered of her brood. Awhile she vented her grief in these inarticulate cries, then rushed on her way with a hasty and unequal step, in the vain hope of overtaking the party which was conveying her son a prisoner to Dunbarton. But her strength, superhuman as it seemed, failed her in the trial; nor was it possible for her, with her utmost efforts, to accomplish her purpose.

Yet she pressed onward, with all the speed which her exhausted frame could exert. When food became indispensable, she entered the first cottage. "Give me to eat," she said. "I am the widow of MacTavish Mhor—I am the mother of Hamish MacTavish Bean,—give me to eat, that I may once more see my fair-haired son." Her demand was never refused, though granted in many cases with a kind of struggle between compassion and aversion in some of those to whom she applied, which was in others qualified by fear. The share she had had in occasioning the death of Allan Breack Cameron, which must probably involve that of her own son, was not accurately known; but, from a knowledge of her violent passions and former habits of life, no one doubted that in one way or other she had been the cause of the catastrophe, and Hamish Bean was considered, in the slaughter which he had committed, rather as the instrument than as the accomplice of his mother.

This general opinion of his countrymen was of little service to the unfortunate Hamish. As his captain, Green Colin, understood the manners and habits of his country, he had no difficulty in collecting from Hamish the particulars accompanying his supposed desertion, and the subsequent death of the non-commissioned officer. He felt the utmost compassion for a youth, who had thus fallen a victim to the extravagant and fatal fondness of a parent. But he had no excuse to plead which could rescue his unhappy recruit from the doom which military discipline and the award of a court-martial denounced against him for the crime he had committed.

No time had been lost in their proceedings, and as little was interposed betwixt sentence and execution. General — had determined to make a severe example of the first deserter who should fall into his power, and here was one who had defended himself by main force, and slain in the affray the officer sent to take him into custody. A fitter subject for punishment could not have occurred, and Hamish was sentenced to immediate execution. All which the interference of his captain in his favour could procure was that he should die a soldier's death; for there had been a purpose of executing him upon the gibbet.

The worthy clergyman of Glenorquhy chanced to be at Dunbarton, in attendance upon some church courts, at the time of this catastrophe. He visited his unfortunate parishioner in his dungeon, found him ignorant indeed, but not obstinate, and the answers which he received from him, when conversing on religious topics, were such as induced him doubly to regret that a mind naturally pure and noble should have remained unhappily so wild and uncultivated.

When he ascertained the real character and disposition of the young man, the worthy pastor made deep and painful reflections on his own shyness and timidity, which, arising out of the evil fame that attached to the lineage of Hamish, had restrained him from charitably endeavouring to bring this strayed sheep within the great fold. While the good minister blamed his cowardice in times past, which had deterred him from risking his person, to save, perhaps, an immortal soul, he resolved no longer to be governed by such timid counsels, but to endeavour, by application to his officers, to obtain a reprieve, at least, if not a pardon, for the criminal, in whom he felt so unusually interested, at once from his docility of temper and his generosity of disposition.

Accordingly the divine sought out Captain Campbell at the barracks within the garrison. There was a gloomy melancholy on the brow of Green Colin, which was not lessened, but increased, when the clergyman stated his name, quality, and errand. "You cannot tell me better of the young man than I am disposed to believe," answered the Highland officer; "you cannot ask me to do more in his behalf than I am of myself inclined, and have already endeavoured to do. But it is all in vain. General — is half a Lowlander, half an Englishman. He has no idea of the high and enthusiastic character which in these mountains often brings exalted virtues in contact with great crimes, which, however, are less offences of the heart than errors of the understanding. I have gone so far as to tell him, that in this young man he was putting to death the best and the bravest of my company, where all, or almost all, are good and brave. I explained to him by what strange delusion the culprit's apparent desertion was occasioned, and how little his heart was accessory to the crime which his hand unhappily committed. His answer was, 'These are Highland visions, Captain Campbell, as unsatisfactory and vain as those of the second sight. An act of gross desertion may, in any case, be palliated under the plea of intoxication; the murder of an officer may be as easily coloured over with that of temporary insanity. The example must be made, and if it has fallen on a man otherwise a good recruit, it will have the greater effect.' Such being the general's unalterable purpose," continued Captain Campbell, with a sigh, "be it your care, reverend sir, that your penitent prepare by break of day tomorrow for that great change which we shall all one day be subjected to."

"And for which," said the clergyman, "may God prepare us all, as I in my duty will not be wanting to this poor youth!"

Next morning, as the very earliest beams of sunrise saluted the grey towers which crown the summit of that singular and tremendous rock, the soldiers of the new Highland regiment appeared on the parade, within the Castle of Dunbarton, and having fallen into order, began to move downward by steep staircases, and narrow passages towards the external barrier-gate, which is at the very bottom of the rock. The wild wailings of the pibroch were heard at times, interchanged with the drums and fifes, which beat the Dead March.

The unhappy criminal's fate did not, at first, excite that general sympathy in the regiment which would probably have arisen had he been executed for desertion alone. The slaughter of the unfortunate Allan Breack had given a different colour to Hamish's offence; for the deceased was much beloved, and besides belonged to a numerous and powerful clan, of whom there were many in the ranks. The unfortunate criminal, on the contrary, was little known to, and scarcely connected with, any of his regimental companions. His father had been, indeed, distinguished for his strength and manhood; but he was of a broken clan, as those names were called who had no chief to lead them to battle.

It would have been almost impossible in another case to have turned out of the ranks of the regiment the party necessary for execution of the sentence; but the six individuals selected for that purpose, were friends of the deceased, descended, like him, from the race of MacDhonuil Dhu; and while they prepared for the dismal task which their duty imposed, it was not without a stern feeling of gratified revenge. The leading company of the regiment began now to defile from the barrier-gate, and was followed by the others, each successively moving and halting according to the orders of the adjutant, so as to form three sides of an oblong square, with the ranks faced inwards. The fourth, or blank side of the square, was closed up by the huge and lofty precipice on which the Castle rises. About the centre of the procession, bare-headed, disarmed, and with his hands bound, came the unfortunate victim of military law. He was deadly pale, but his step was firm and his eye as bright as ever. The clergyman walked by his side; the coffin, which was to receive his mortal remains, was borne before him. The looks of his comrades were still, composed, and solemn. They felt for the youth, whose handsome form and manly yet submissive deportment had, as soon as he was distinctly visible to them, softened the hearts of many, even of some who had been actuated by vindictive feelings.

The coffin destined for the yet living body of Hamish Bean was placed at the bottom of the hollow square, about two yards distant from the foot of the precipice, which rises in that place as steep as a stone wall to the height of three or four hundred feet. Thither the prisoner was also led, the clergyman still continuing by his side, pouring forth exhortations of courage and consolation, to which the youth appeared to listen with respectful devotion. With slow, and, it seemed, almost unwilling steps, the firing party entered the square, and were drawn up facing the prisoner, about ten yards distant. The clergyman was now about to retire. "Think, my son," he said, "on what I have told you, and let your hope be rested on the anchor which I have given. You will then exchange a short and miserable existence here for a life in which you will experience neither sorrow nor pain. Is there aught else which you can entrust to me to execute for you?"

The youth looked at his sleeve buttons. They were of gold, booty perhaps which his father had taken from some English officer during the civil wars. The clergyman disengaged them from his sleeves.

"My mother!" he said with some effort—"give them to my poor mother! See her, good father, and teach her what she should think of all this. Tell her Hamish Bean is more glad to die than ever he was to rest after the longest day's hunting. Farewell, sir—farewell!"

The good man could scarce retire from the fatal spot. An officer afforded him the support of his arm. At his last look towards Hamish, he beheld him alive and kneeling on the coffin; the few that were around him had all withdrawn. The fatal word was given, the rock rung sharp to the sound of the discharge, and Hamish, falling forward with a groan, died, it may be supposed, without almost a sense of the passing agony.

Ten or twelve of his own company then came forward, and laid with solemn reverence the remains of their comrade in the coffin, while the Dead March was again struck up, and the several companies, marching in single files, passed the coffin one by one, in order that all might receive from the awful spectacle the warning which it was peculiarly intended to afford. The regiment was then marched off the ground, and reascended the ancient cliff, their music, as usual on such occasions, striking lively strains, as if sorrow, or even deep thought, should as short a while as possible be the tenant of the soldier's bosom.

At the same time the small party, which we before mentioned, bore the bier of the ill-fated Hamish to his humble grave, in a corner of the churchyard of Dunbarton, usually assigned to criminals. Here, among the dust of the guilty, lies a youth, whose name, had he survived the ruin of the fatal events by which he was hurried into crime, might have adorned the annals of the brave.

The minister of Glenorquhy left Dunbarton immediately after he had witnessed the last scene of this melancholy catastrophe. His reason acquiesced in the justice of the sentence, which required blood for blood, and he acknowledged that the vindictive character of his countrymen required to be powerfully restrained by the strong curb of social law. But still he mourned over the individual victim. Who may arraign the bolt of Heaven when it bursts among the sons of the forest? yet who can refrain from mourning when it selects for the object of its blighting aim the fair stem of a young oak, that promised to be the pride of the dell in which it flourished? Musing on these melancholy events, noon found him engaged in the mountain passes, by which he was to return to his still distant home.

Confident in his knowledge of the country, the clergyman had left the main road, to seek one of those shorter paths, which are only used by pedestrians, or by men, like the minister, mounted on the small, but sure-footed, hardy, and sagacious horses of the country. The place which he now traversed was in itself gloomy and desolate, and tradition had added to it the terror of superstition, by affirming it was haunted by an evil spirit, termed CLOGHT-DEARG—that is, Redmantle—who at all times, but especially at noon and at midnight, traversed the glen, in enmity both to man and the inferior creation, did such evil as her power was permitted to extend to, and afflicted with ghastly terrors those whom she had not license otherwise to hurt.

The minister of Glenorquhy had set his face in opposition to many of these superstitions, which he justly thought were derived from the dark ages of Popery, perhaps even from those of paganism, and unfit to be entertained or believed by the Christians of an enlightened age. Some of his more attached parishioners considered him as too rash in opposing the ancient faith of their fathers; and though they honoured the moral intrepidity of their pastor, they could not avoid entertaining and expressing fears that he would one day fall a victim to his temerity, and be torn to pieces in the glen of the Cloght-dearg, or some of those other haunted wilds, which he appeared rather to have a pride and pleasure in traversing alone, on the days and hours when the wicked spirits were supposed to have especial power over man and beast.

These legends came across the mind of the clergyman, and, solitary as he was, a melancholy smile shaded his cheek, as he thought of the inconsistency of human nature, and reflected how many brave men, whom the yell of the pibroch would have sent headlong against fixed bayonets, as the wild bull rushes on his enemy, might have yet feared to encounter those visionary terrors, which he himself, a man of peace, and in ordinary perils no way remarkable for the firmness of his nerves, was now risking without hesitation.

As he looked around the scene of desolation, he could not but acknowledge, in his own mind, that it was not ill chosen for the haunt of those spirits, which are said to delight in solitude and desolation. The glen was so steep and narrow that there was but just room for the meridian sun to dart a few scattered rays upon the gloomy and precarious stream which stole through its recesses, for the most part in silence, but occasionally murmuring sullenly against the rocks and large stones which seemed determined to bar its further progress. In winter, or in the rainy season, this small stream was a foaming torrent of the most formidable magnitude, and it was at such periods that it had torn open and laid bare the broad-faced and huge fragments of rock which, at the season of which we speak, hid its course from the eye, and seemed disposed totally to interrupt its course. "Undoubtedly," thought the clergyman, "this mountain rivulet, suddenly swelled by a waterspout or thunderstorm, has often been the cause of those accidents which, happening in the glen called by her name, have been ascribed to the agency of the Cloght-dearg."

Just as this idea crossed his mind, he heard a female voice exclaim, in a wild and thrilling accent, "Michael Tyrie! Michael Tyrie!" He looked round in astonishment, and not without some fear. It seemed for an instant, as if the evil being, whose existence he had disowned, was about to appear for the punishment of his incredulity. This alarm did not hold him more than an instant, nor did it prevent his replying in a firm voice, "Who calls? and where are you?"

"One who journeys in wretchedness, between life and death," answered the voice; and the speaker, a tall female, appeared from among the fragments of rocks which had concealed her from view.

As she approached more closely, her mantle of bright tartan, in which the red colour much predominated, her stature, the long stride with which she advanced, and the writhen features and wild eyes which were visible from under her curch, would have made her no inadequate representative of the spirit which gave name to the valley. But Mr. Tyrie instantly knew her as the Woman of the Tree, the widow of MacTavish Mhor, the now childless mother of Hamish Bean. I am not sure whether the minister would not have endured the visitation of the Cloght-dearg herself, rather than the shock of Elspat's presence, considering her crime and her misery. He drew up his horse instinctively, and stood endeavouring to collect his ideas, while a few paces brought her up to his horse's head.

"Michael Tyrie," said she, "the foolish women of the Clachan [The village; literally, the stones.] hold thee as a god—be one to me, and say that my son lives. Say this, and I too will be of thy worship; I will bend my knees on the seventh day in thy house of worship, and thy God shall be my God."

"Unhappy woman," replied the clergyman, "man forms not pactions with his Maker as with a creature of clay like himself. Thinkest thou to chaffer with Him, who formed the earth, and spread out the heavens, or that thou canst offer aught of homage or devotion that can be worth acceptance in his eyes? He hath asked obedience, not sacrifice; patience under the trials with which He afflicts us, instead of vain bribes, such as man offers to his changeful brother of clay, that he may be moved from his purpose."

"Be silent, priest!" answered the desperate woman; "speak not to me the words of thy white book. Elspat's kindred were of those who crossed themselves and knelt when the sacring bell was rung, and she knows that atonement can be made on the altar for deeds done in the field. Elspat had once flocks and herds, goats upon the cliffs, and cattle in the strath. She wore gold around her neck and on her hair—thick twists, as those worn by the heroes of old. All these would she have resigned to the priest—all these; and if he wished for the ornaments of a gentle lady, or the sporran of a high chief, though they had been great as Macallum Mhor himself, MacTavish Mhor would have procured them, if Elspat had promised them. Elspat is now poor, and has nothing to give. But the Black Abbot of Inchaffray would have bidden her scourge her shoulders, and macerate her feet by pilgrimage; and he would have granted his pardon to her when he saw that her blood had flowed, and that her flesh had been torn. These were the priests who had indeed power even with the most powerful; they threatened the great men of the earth with the word of their mouth, the sentence of their book, the blaze of their torch, the sound of their sacring bell. The mighty bent to their will, and unloosed at the word of the priests those whom they had bound in their wrath, and set at liberty, unharmed, him whom they had sentenced to death, and for whose blood they had thirsted. These were a powerful race, and might well ask the poor to kneel, since their power could humble the proud. But you!—against whom are ye strong, but against women who have been guilty of folly, and men who never wore sword? The priests of old were like the winter torrent which fills this hollow valley, and rolls these massive rocks against each other as easily as the boy plays with the ball which he casts before him. But you!—you do but resemble the summer-stricken stream, which is turned aside by the rushes, and stemmed by a bush of sedges. Woe worth you, for there is no help in you!"

The clergyman was at no loss to conceive that Elspat had lost the Roman Catholic faith without gaining any other, and that she still retained a vague and confused idea of the composition with the priesthood, by confession, alms, and penance, and of their extensive power, which, according to her notion, was adequate, if duly propitiated, even to effecting her son's safety. Compassionating her situation, and allowing for her errors and ignorance, he answered her with mildness.

"Alas, unhappy woman! Would to God I could convince thee as easily where thou oughtest to seek, and art sure to find, consolation, as I can assure you with a single word, that were Rome and all her priesthood once more in the plenitude of their power, they could not, for largesse or penance, afford to thy misery an atom of aid or comfort—Elspat MacTavish, I grieve to tell you the news."

"I know them without thy speech," said the unhappy woman. "My son is doomed to die."

"Elspat," resumed the clergyman, "he WAS doomed, and the sentence has been executed."

The hapless mother threw her eyes up to heaven, and uttered a shriek so unlike the voice of a human being, that the eagle which soared in middle air answered it as she would have done the call of her mate.

"It is impossible!" she exclaimed—"it is impossible! Men do not condemn and kill on the same day! Thou art deceiving me. The people call thee holy—hast thou the heart to tell a mother she has murdered her only child?"

"God knows," said the priest, the tears falling fast from his eyes, "that were it in my power, I would gladly tell better tidings. But these which I bear are as certain as they are fatal. My own ears heard the death-shot, my own eyes beheld thy son's death—thy son's funeral. My tongue bears witness to what my ears heard and my eyes saw."

The wretched female clasped her bands close together, and held them up towards heaven like a sibyl announcing war and desolation, while, in impotent yet frightful rage, she poured forth a tide of the deepest imprecations. "Base Saxon churl!" she exclaimed—"vile hypocritical juggler! May the eyes that looked tamely on the death of my fair-haired boy be melted in their sockets with ceaseless tears, shed for those that are nearest and most dear to thee! May the ears that heard his death-knell be dead hereafter to all other sounds save the screech of the raven, and the hissing of the adder! May the tongue that tells me of his death and of my own crime, be withered in thy mouth—or better, when thou wouldst pray with thy people, may the Evil One guide it, and give voice to blasphemies instead of blessings, until men shall fly in terror from thy presence, and the thunder of heaven be launched against thy head, and stop for ever thy cursing and accursed voice! Begone, with this malison! Elspat will never, never again bestow so many words upon living man."

She kept her word. From that day the world was to her a wilderness, in which she remained without thought, care, or interest, absorbed in her own grief, indifferent to every thing else.

With her mode of life, or rather of existence, the reader is already as far acquainted as I have the power of making him. Of her death, I can tell him nothing. It is supposed to have happened several years after she had attracted the attention of my excellent friend Mrs. Bethune Baliol. Her benevolence, which was never satisfied with dropping a sentimental tear, when there was room for the operation of effective charity, induced her to make various attempts to alleviate the condition of this most wretched woman. But all her exertions could only render Elspat's means of subsistence less precarious—a circumstance which, though generally interesting even to the most wretched outcasts, seemed to her a matter of total indifference. Every attempt to place any person in her hut to take charge of her miscarried, through the extreme resentment with which she regarded all intrusion on her solitude, or by the timidity of those who had been pitched upon to be inmates with the terrible Woman of the Tree. At length, when Elspat became totally unable (in appearance at least) to turn herself on the wretched settle which served her for a couch, the humanity of Mr. Tyrie's successor sent two women to attend upon the last moments of the solitary, which could not, it was judged, be far distant, and to avert the possibility that she might perish for want of assistance or food, before she sunk under the effects of extreme age or mortal malady.

It was on a November evening, that the two women appointed for this melancholy purpose arrived at the miserable cottage which we have already described. Its wretched inmate lay stretched upon the bed, and seemed almost already a lifeless corpse, save for the wandering of the fierce dark eyes, which rolled in their sockets in a manner terrible to look upon, and seemed to watch with surprise and indignation the motions of the strangers, as persons whose presence was alike unexpected and unwelcome. They were frightened at her looks; but, assured in each other's company, they kindled a fire, lighted a candle, prepared food, and made other arrangements for the discharge of the duty assigned them.

The assistants agreed they should watch the bedside of the sick person by turns; but, about midnight, overcome by fatigue, (for they had walked far that morning), both of them fell fast asleep. When they awoke, which was not till after the interval of some hours, the hut was empty, and the patient gone. They rose in terror, and went to the door of the cottage, which was latched as it had been at night. They looked out into the darkness, and called upon their charge by her name. The night-raven screamed from the old oak-tree, the fox howled on the hill, the hoarse waterfall replied with its echoes; but there was no human answer. The terrified women did not dare to make further search till morning should appear; for the sudden disappearance of a creature so frail as Elspat, together with the wild tenor of her history, intimidated them from stirring from the hut. They remained, therefore, in dreadful terror, sometimes thinking they heard her voice without, and at other times, that sounds of a different description were mingled with the mournful sigh of the night-breeze, or the dashing of the cascade. Sometimes, too, the latch rattled, as if some frail and impotent hand were in vain attempting to lift it, and ever and anon they expected the entrance of their terrible patient, animated by supernatural strength, and in the company, perhaps, of some being more dreadful than herself. Morning came at length. They sought brake, rock, and thicket in vain. Two hours after daylight, the minister himself appeared, and, on the report of the watchers, caused the country to be alarmed, and a general and exact search to be made through the whole neighbourhood of the cottage and the oak-tree. But it was all in vain. Elspat MacTavish was never found, whether dead or alive; nor could there ever be traced the slightest circumstance to indicate her fate.

The neighbourhood was divided concerning the cause of her disappearance. The credulous thought that the evil spirit, under whose influence she seemed to have acted, had carried her away in the body; and there are many who are still unwilling, at untimely hours, to pass the oak-tree, beneath which, as they allege, she may still be seen seated according to her wont. Others less superstitious supposed, that had it been possible to search the gulf of the Corri Dhu, the profound deeps of the lake, or the whelming eddies of the river, the remains of Elspat MacTavish might have been discovered—as nothing was more natural, considering her state of body and mind, than that she should have fallen in by accident, or precipitated herself intentionally, into one or other of those places of sure destruction. The clergyman entertained an opinion of his own. He thought that, impatient of the watch which was placed over her, this unhappy woman's instinct had taught her, as it directs various domestic animals, to withdraw herself from the sight of her own race, that the death-struggle might take place in some secret den, where, in all probability, her mortal relics would never meet the eyes of mortals. This species of instinctive feeling seemed to him of a tenor with the whole course of her unhappy life, and most likely to influence her when it drew to a conclusion.

End of THE HIGHLAND WIDOW.

MR. CROFTANGRY INTRODUCES ANOTHER TALE.

Together both on the high lawns appeared.
Under the opening eyelids of the morn
They drove afield.           ELEGY ON LYCIDAS.

I have sometimes wondered why all the favourite occupations and pastimes of mankind go to the disturbance of that happy state of tranquillity, that OTIUM, as Horace terms it, which he says is the object of all men's prayers, whether preferred from sea or land; and that the undisturbed repose, of which we are so tenacious, when duty or necessity compels us to abandon it, is precisely what we long to exchange for a state of excitation, as soon as we may prolong it at our own pleasure. Briefly, you have only to say to a man, "Remain at rest," and you instantly inspire the love of labour. The sportsman toils like his gamekeeper, the master of the pack takes as severe exercise as his whipper-in, the statesman or politician drudges more than the professional lawyer; and, to come to my own case, the volunteer author subjects himself to the risk of painful criticism, and the assured certainty of mental and manual labour, just as completely as his needy brother, whose necessities compel him to assume the pen.

These reflections have been suggested by an annunciation on the part of Janet, "that the little Gillie-whitefoot was come from the printing-office."

"Gillie-blackfoot you should call him, Janet," was my response, "for he is neither more nor less than an imp of the devil, come to torment me for COPY, for so the printers call a supply of manuscript for the press."

"Now, Cot forgie your honour," said Janet; "for it is no like your ainsell to give such names to a faitherless bairn."

"I have got nothing else to give him, Janet; he must wait a little."

"Then I have got some breakfast to give the bit gillie," said Janet; "and he can wait by the fireside in the kitchen, till your honour's ready; and cood enough for the like of him, if he was to wait your honour's pleasure all day."

"But, Janet," said I to my little active superintendent, on her return to the parlour, after having made her hospitable arrangements, "I begin to find this writing our Chronicles is rather more tiresome than I expected, for here comes this little fellow to ask for manuscript—that is, for something to print—and I have got none to give him."

"Your honour can be at nae loss. I have seen you write fast and fast enough; and for subjects, you have the whole Highlands to write about, and I am sure you know a hundred tales better than that about Hamish MacTavish, for it was but about a young cateran and an auld carlin, when all's done; and if they had burned the rudas quean for a witch, I am thinking, may be they would not have tyned their coals—and her to gar her ne'er-do-weel son shoot a gentleman Cameron! I am third cousin to the Camerons mysel'—my blood warms to them. And if you want to write about deserters, I am sure there were deserters enough on the top of Arthur's Seat, when the MacRaas broke out, and on that woeful day beside Leith Pier—ohonari!"—

Here Janet began to weep, and to wipe her eyes with her apron. For my part, the idea I wanted was supplied, but I hesitated to make use of it. Topics, like times, are apt to become common by frequent use. It is only an ass like Justice Shallow, who would pitch upon the over-scutched tunes, which the carmen whistled, and try to pass them off as his FANCIES and his GOOD-NIGHTS. Now, the Highlands, though formerly a rich mine for original matter, are, as my friend Mrs. Bethune Baliol warned me, in some degree worn out by the incessant labour of modern romancers and novelists, who, finding in those remote regions primitive habits and manners, have vainly imagined that the public can never tire of them; and so kilted Highlanders are to be found as frequently, and nearly of as genuine descent, on the shelves of a circulating library, as at a Caledonian ball. Much might have been made at an earlier time out of the history of a Highland regiment, and the singular revolution of ideas which must have taken place in the minds of those who composed it, when exchanging their native hills for the battle-fields of the Continent, and their simple, and sometimes indolent domestic habits for the regular exertions demanded by modern discipline. But the market is forestalled. There is Mrs. Grant of Laggan, has drawn the manners, customs, and superstitions of the mountains in their natural unsophisticated state; [Letters from the Mountains, 3 vols.—Essays on the Superstitions of the Highlanders—The Highlanders, and other Poems, etc.] and my friend, General Stewart of Garth, [The gallant and amiable author of the History of the Highland

Regiments, in whose glorious services his own share had been great, went out Governor of St Lucia in 1828, and died in that island on the 18th of December 1829,—no man more regretted, or perhaps by a wider circle of friends and acquaintance.] in giving the real history of the Highland regiments, has rendered any attempt to fill up the sketch with fancy-colouring extremely rash and precarious. Yet I, too, have still a lingering fancy to add a stone to the cairn; and without calling in imagination to aid the impressions of juvenile recollection, I may just attempt to embody one or two scenes illustrative of the Highland character, and which belong peculiarly to the Chronicles of the Canongate, to the grey-headed eld of whom they are as familiar as to Chrystal Croftangry. Yet I will not go back to the days of clanship and claymores. Have at you, gentle reader, with a tale of Two Drovers. An oyster may be crossed in love, says the gentle Tilburina—and a drover may be touched on a point of honour, says the Chronicler of the Canongate.

THE TWO DROVERS.

CHAPTER I.

It was the day after Doune Fair when my story commences. It had been a brisk market. Several dealers had attended from the northern and midland counties in England, and English money had flown so merrily about as to gladden the hearts of the Highland farmers. Many large droves were about to set off for England, under the protection of their owners, or of the topsmen whom they employed in the tedious, laborious, and responsible office of driving the cattle for many hundred miles, from the market where they had been purchased, to the fields or farmyards where they were to be fattened for the shambles.

The Highlanders in particular are masters of this difficult trade of driving, which seems to suit them as well as the trade of war. It affords exercise for all their habits of patient endurance and active exertion. They are required to know perfectly the drove-roads, which lie over the wildest tracts of the country, and to avoid as much as possible the highways, which distress the feet of the bullocks, and the turnpikes, which annoy the spirit of the drover; whereas on the broad green or grey track which leads across the pathless moor, the herd not only move at ease and without taxation, but, if they mind their business, may pick up a mouthful of food by the way. At night the drovers usually sleep along with their cattle, let the weather be what it will; and many of these hardy men do not once rest under a roof during a journey on foot from Lochaber to Lincolnshire. They are paid very highly, for the trust reposed is of the last importance, as it depends on their prudence, vigilance, and honesty whether the cattle reach the final market in good order, and afford a profit to the grazier. But as they maintain themselves at their own expense, they are especially economical in that particular. At the period we speak of, a Highland drover was victualled for his long and toilsome journey with a few handfulls of oatmeal and two or three onions, renewed from time to time, and a ram's horn filled with whisky, which he used regularly, but sparingly, every night and morning. His dirk, or

SKENE-DHU, (that is, black-knife), so worn as to be concealed beneath the arm, or by the folds of the plaid, was his only weapon, excepting the cudgel with which he directed the movements of the cattle. A Highlander was never so happy as on these occasions. There was a variety in the whole journey, which exercised the Celt's natural curiosity and love of motion. There were the constant change of place and scene, the petty adventures incidental to the traffic, and the intercourse with the various farmers, graziers, and traders, intermingled with occasional merry-makings, not the less acceptable to Donald that they were void of expense. And there was the consciousness of superior skill; for the Highlander, a child amongst flocks, is a prince amongst herds, and his natural habits induce him to disdain the shepherd's slothful life, so that he feels himself nowhere more at home than when following a gallant drove of his country cattle in the character of their guardian.

Of the number who left Doune in the morning, and with the purpose we have described, not a GLUNAMIE of them all cocked his bonnet more briskly, or gartered his tartan hose under knee over a pair of more promising SPIOGS, (legs), than did Robin Oig M'Combich, called familiarly Robin Oig, that is young, or the Lesser, Robin. Though small of stature, as the epithet Oig implies, and not very strongly limbed, he was as light and alert as one of the deer of his mountains. He had an elasticity of step which, in the course of a long march, made many a stout fellow envy him; and the manner in which he busked his plaid and adjusted his bonnet argued a consciousness that so smart a John Highlandman as himself would not pass unnoticed among the Lowland lasses. The ruddy cheek, red lips, and white teeth set off a countenance which had gained by exposure to the weather a healthful and hardy rather than a rugged hue. If Robin Oig did not laugh, or even smile frequently—as, indeed, is not the practice among his countrymen—his bright eyes usually gleamed from under his bonnet with an expression of cheerfulness ready to be turned into mirth.

The departure of Robin Oig was an incident in the little town, in and near which he had many friends, male and female. He was a topping person in his way, transacted considerable business on his own behalf, and was entrusted by the best farmers in the Highlands, in preference to any other drover in that district. He might have increased his business to any extent had he condescended to manage it by deputy; but except a lad or two, sister's sons of his own, Robin rejected the idea of assistance, conscious, perhaps, how much his reputation depended upon his attending in person to the practical discharge of his duty in every instance. He remained, therefore, contented with the highest premium given to persons of his description, and comforted himself with the hopes that a few journeys to England might enable him to conduct business on his own account, in a manner becoming his birth. For Robin Oig's father, Lachlan M'Combich (or SON OF MY FRIEND, his actual clan surname being M'Gregor), had been so called by the celebrated Rob Roy, because of the particular friendship which had subsisted between the grandsire of Robin and that renowned cateran. Some people even said that Robin Oig derived his Christian name from one as renowned in the wilds of Loch Lomond as ever was his namesake Robin Hood in the precincts of merry Sherwood. "Of such ancestry," as James Boswell says, "who would not be proud?" Robin Oig was proud accordingly; but his frequent visits to England and to the Lowlands had given him tact enough to know that pretensions which still gave him a little right to distinction in his own lonely glen, might be both obnoxious and ridiculous if preferred elsewhere. The pride of birth, therefore, was like the miser's treasure—the secret subject of his contemplation, but never exhibited to strangers as a subject of boasting.

Many were the words of gratulation and good-luck which were bestowed on Robin Oig. The judges commended his drove, especially Robin's own property, which were the best of them. Some thrust out their snuff-mulls for the parting pinch, others tendered the DOCH-AN-DORRACH, or parting cup. All cried, "Good-luck travel out with you and come home with you. Give you luck in the Saxon market—brave notes in the LEABHAR-DHU," (black pocket-book), "and plenty of English gold in the SPORRAN" (pouch of goat-skin).

The bonny lasses made their adieus more modestly, and more than one, it was said, would have given her best brooch to be certain that it was upon her that his eye last rested as he turned towards the road.

Robin Oig had just given the preliminary "HOO-HOO!" to urge forward the loiterers of the drove, when there was a cry behind him:—

"Stay, Robin—bide a blink. Here is Janet of Tomahourich—auld Janet, your father's sister."

"Plague on her, for an auld Highland witch and spaewife," said a farmer from the Carse of Stirling; "she'll cast some of her cantrips on the cattle."

"She canna do that," said another sapient of the same profession. "Robin Oig is no the lad to leave any of them without tying Saint Mungo's knot on their tails, and that will put to her speed the best witch that ever flew over Dimayet upon a broomstick."

It may not be indifferent to the reader to know that the Highland cattle are peculiarly liable to be TAKEN, or infected, by spells and witchcraft, which judicious people guard against by knitting knots of peculiar complexity on the tuft of hair which terminates the animal's tail.

But the old woman who was the object of the farmer's suspicion seemed only busied about the drover, without paying any attention to the drove. Robin, on the contrary, appeared rather impatient of her presence.

"What auld-world fancy," he said, "has brought you so early from the ingle-side this morning, Muhme? I am sure I bid you good-even, and had your God-speed, last night."

"And left me more siller than the useless old woman will use till you come back again, bird of my bosom," said the sibyl. "But it is little I would care for the food that nourishes me, or the fire that warms me, or for God's blessed sun itself, if aught but weel should happen to the grandson of my father. So let me walk the DEASIL round you, that you may go safe out into the far foreign land, and come safe home."

Robin Oig stopped, half embarrassed, half laughing, and signing to those around that he only complied with the old woman to soothe her humour. In the meantime, she traced around him, with wavering steps, the propitiation, which some have thought has been derived from the Druidical mythology. It consists, as is well known, in the person who makes the DEASIL walking three times round the person who is the object of the ceremony, taking care to move according to the course of the sun. At once, however, she stopped short, and exclaimed, in a voice of alarm and horror, "Grandson of my father, there is blood on your hand."

"Hush, for God's sake, aunt!" said Robin Oig. "You will bring more trouble on yourself with this TAISHATARAGH" (second sight) "than you will be able to get out of for many a day."

The old woman only repeated, with a ghastly look, "There is blood on your hand, and it is English blood. The blood of the Gael is richer and redder. Let us see—let us—"

Ere Robin Oig could prevent her, which, indeed, could only have been by positive violence, so hasty and peremptory were her proceedings, she had drawn from his side the dirk which lodged in the folds of his plaid, and held it up, exclaiming, although the weapon gleamed clear and bright in the sun, "Blood, blood—Saxon blood again. Robin Oig M'Combich, go not this day to England!"

"Prutt, trutt," answered Robin Oig, "that will never do neither—it would be next thing to running the country. For shame, Muhme—give me the dirk. You cannot tell by the colour the difference betwixt the blood of a black bullock and a white one, and you speak of knowing Saxon from Gaelic blood. All men have their blood from Adam, Muhme. Give me my skene-dhu, and let me go on my road. I should have been half way to Stirling brig by this time. Give me my dirk, and let me go."

"Never will I give it to you," said the old woman—"Never will I quit my hold on your plaid—unless you promise me not to wear that unhappy weapon."

The women around him urged him also, saying few of his aunt's words fell to the ground; and as the Lowland farmers continued to look moodily on the scene, Robin Oig determined to close it at any sacrifice.

"Well, then," said the young drover, giving the scabbard of the weapon to Hugh Morrison, "you Lowlanders care nothing for these freats. Keep my dirk for me. I cannot give it you, because it was my father's; but your drove follows ours, and I am content it should be in your keeping, not in mine.—Will this do, Muhme?"

"It must," said the old woman—"that is, if the Lowlander is mad enough to carry the knife."

The strong Westlandman laughed aloud.

"Goodwife," said he, "I am Hugh Morrison from Glenae, come of the Manly Morrisons of auld lang syne, that never took short weapon against a man in their lives. And neither needed they. They had their broadswords, and I have this bit supple"—showing a formidable cudgel; "for dirking ower the board, I leave that to John Highlandman.—Ye needna snort, none of you Highlanders, and you in especial, Robin. I'll keep the bit knife, if you are feared for the auld spaewife's tale, and give it back to you whenever you want it."

Robin was not particularly pleased with some part of Hugh Morrison's speech; but he had learned in his travels more patience than belonged to his Highland constitution originally, and he accepted the service of the descendant of the Manly Morrisons without finding fault with the rather depreciating manner in which it was offered.

"If he had not had his morning in his head, and been but a Dumfriesshire hog into the boot, he would have spoken more like a gentleman. But you cannot have more of a sow than a grumph. It's shame my father's knife should ever slash a haggis for the like of him."

Thus saying, (but saying it in Gaelic), Robin drove on his cattle, and waved farewell to all behind him. He was in the greater haste, because he expected to join at Falkirk a comrade and brother in profession, with whom he proposed to travel in company.

Robin Oig's chosen friend was a young Englishman, Harry Wakefield by name, well known at every northern market, and in his way as much famed and honoured as our Highland driver of bullocks. He was nearly six feet high, gallantly formed to keep the rounds at Smithfield, or maintain the ring at a wrestling match; and although he might have been overmatched, perhaps, among the regular professors of the Fancy, yet, as a yokel or rustic, or a chance customer, he was able to give a bellyful to any amateur of the pugilistic art. Doncaster races saw him in his glory, betting his guinea, and generally successfully; nor was there a main fought in Yorkshire, the feeders being persons of celebrity, at which he was not to be seen if business permitted. But though a SPRACK lad, and fond of pleasure and its haunts, Harry Wakefield was steady, and not the cautious Robin Oig M'Combich himself was more attentive to the main chance. His holidays were holidays indeed; but his days of work were dedicated to steady and persevering labour. In countenance and temper, Wakefield was the model of Old England's merry yeomen, whose clothyard shafts, in so many hundred battles, asserted her superiority over the nations, and whose good sabres, in our own time, are her cheapest and most assured defence. His mirth was readily excited; for, strong in limb and constitution, and fortunate in circumstances, he was disposed to be pleased with every thing about him, and such difficulties as he might occasionally encounter were, to a man of his energy, rather matter of amusement than serious annoyance. With all the merits of a sanguine temper, our young English drover was not without his defects. He was irascible, sometimes to the verge of being quarrelsome; and perhaps not the less inclined to bring his disputes to a pugilistic decision, because he found few antagonists able to stand up to him in the boxing ring.

It is difficult to say how Harry Wakefield and Robin Oig first became intimates, but it is certain a close acquaintance had taken place betwixt them, although they had apparently few common subjects of conversation or of interest, so soon as their talk ceased to be of bullocks. Robin Oig, indeed, spoke the English language rather imperfectly upon any other topics but stots and kyloes, and Harry Wakefield could never bring his broad Yorkshire tongue to utter a single word of Gaelic. It was in vain Robin spent a whole morning, during a walk over Minch Moor, in attempting to teach his companion to utter, with true precision, the shibboleth LLHU, which is the Gaelic for a calf. From Traquair to Murder Cairn, the hill rung with the discordant attempts of the Saxon upon the unmanageable monosyllable, and the heartfelt laugh which followed every failure. They had, however, better modes of awakening the echoes; for Wakefield could sing many a ditty to the praise of Moll, Susan, and Cicely, and Robin Oig had a particular gift at whistling interminable pibrochs through all their involutions, and what was more agreeable to his companion's southern ear, knew many of the northern airs, both lively and pathetic, to which Wakefield learned to pipe a bass. Thus, though Robin could hardly have comprehended his companion's stories about horse-racing, and cock-fighting, or fox-hunting, and although his own legends of clan-fights and CREAGHS, varied with talk of Highland goblins and fairy folk, would have been caviare to his companion, they contrived, nevertheless to find a degree of pleasure in each other's company, which had for three years back induced them to join company and travel together, when the direction of their journey permitted. Each, indeed, found his advantage in this companionship; for where could the Englishman have found a guide through the Western Highlands like Robin Oig M'Combich? and when they were on what Harry called the RIGHT side of the Border, his patronage, which was extensive, and his purse, which was heavy, were at all times at the service of his Highland friend, and on many occasions his liberality did him genuine yeoman's service.

CHAPTER II.

Were ever two such loving friends!—
  How could they disagree?
Oh, thus it was, he loved him dear,
  And thought how to requite him,
And having no friend left but he,

He did resolve to fight him.     DUKE UPON DUKE.

The pair of friends had traversed with their usual cordiality the grassy wilds of Liddesdale, and crossed the opposite part of Cumberland, emphatically called The Waste. In these solitary regions the cattle under the charge of our drovers derived their subsistence chiefly by picking their food as they went along the drove-road, or sometimes by the tempting opportunity of a START AND OWERLOUP, or invasion of the neighbouring pasture, where an occasion presented itself. But now the scene changed before them. They were descending towards a fertile and enclosed country, where no such liberties could be taken with impunity, or without a previous arrangement and bargain with the possessors of the ground. This was more especially the case, as a great northern fair was upon the eve of taking place, where both the Scotch and English drover expected to dispose of a part of their cattle, which it was desirable to produce in the market rested and in good order. Fields were therefore difficult to be obtained, and only upon high terms. This necessity occasioned a temporary separation betwixt the two friends, who went to bargain, each as he could, for the separate accommodation of his herd. Unhappily it chanced that both of them, unknown to each other, thought of bargaining for the ground they wanted on the property of a country gentleman of some fortune, whose estate lay in the neighbourhood. The English drover applied to the bailiff on the property, who was known to him. It chanced that the Cumbrian Squire, who had entertained some suspicions of his manager's honesty, was taking occasional measures to ascertain how far they were well founded, and had desired that any enquiries about his enclosures, with a view to occupy them for a temporary purpose, should be referred to himself. As however, Mr. Ireby had gone the day before upon a journey of some miles distance to the northward, the bailiff chose to consider the check upon his full powers as for the time removed, and concluded that he should best consult his master's interest, and perhaps his own, in making an agreement with Harry Wakefield. Meanwhile, ignorant of what his comrade was doing, Robin Oig, on his side, chanced to be overtaken by a good-looking smart little man upon a pony, most knowingly hogged and cropped, as was then the fashion, the rider wearing tight leather breeches, and long-necked bright spurs. This cavalier asked one or two pertinent questions about markets and the price of stock. So Robin, seeing him a well-judging civil gentleman, took the freedom to ask him whether he could let him know if there was any grass-land to be let in that neighbourhood, for the temporary accommodation of his drove. He could not have put the question to more willing ears. The gentleman of the buckskins was the proprietor, with whose bailiff Harry Wakefield had dealt, or was in the act of dealing.

"Thou art in good luck, my canny Scot," said Mr. Ireby, "to have spoken to me, for I see thy cattle have done their day's work, and I have at my disposal the only field within three miles that is to be let in these parts."

"The drove can pe gang two, three, four miles very pratty weel indeed"—said the cautious Highlander; "put what would his honour pe axing for the peasts pe the head, if she was to tak the park for twa or three days?"

"We won't differ, Sawney, if you let me have six stots for winterers, in the way of reason."

"And which peasts wad your honour pe for having?"

"Why—let me see—the two black—the dun one—yon doddy—him with the twisted horn—the brockit—How much by the head?"

"Ah," said Robin, "your honour is a shudge—a real shudge. I couldna have set off the pest six peasts petter mysel'—me that ken them as if they were my pairns, puir things."

"Well, how much per head, Sawney?" continued Mr. Ireby.

"It was high markets at Doune and Falkirk," answered Robin.

And thus the conversation proceeded, until they had agreed on the PRIX JUSTE for the bullocks, the Squire throwing in the temporary accommodation of the enclosure for the cattle into the boot, and Robin making, as he thought, a very good bargain, provided the grass was but tolerable. The Squire walked his pony alongside of the drove, partly to show him the way, and see him put into possession of the field, and partly to learn the latest news of the northern markets.

They arrived at the field, and the pasture seemed excellent. But what was their surprise when they saw the bailiff quietly inducting the cattle of Harry Wakefield into the grassy Goshen which had just been assigned to those of Robin Oig M'Combich by the proprietor himself! Squire Ireby set spurs to his horse, dashed up to his servant, and learning what had passed between the parties, briefly informed the English drover that his bailiff had let the ground without his authority, and that he might seek grass for his cattle wherever he would, since he was to get none there. At the same time he rebuked his servant severely for having transgressed his commands, and ordered him instantly to assist in ejecting the hungry and weary cattle of Harry Wakefield, which were just beginning to enjoy a meal of unusual plenty, and to introduce those of his comrade, whom the English drover now began to consider as a rival.

The feelings which arose in Wakefield's mind would have induced him to resist Mr. Ireby's decision; but every Englishman has a tolerably accurate sense of law and justice, and John Fleecebumpkin, the bailiff, having acknowledged that he had exceeded his commission, Wakefield saw nothing else for it than to collect his hungry and disappointed charge, and drive them on to seek quarters elsewhere. Robin Oig saw what had happened with regret, and hastened to offer to his English friend to share with him the disputed possession. But Wakefield's pride was severely hurt, and he answered disdainfully, "Take it all, man—take it all; never make two bites of a cherry. Thou canst talk over the gentry, and blear a plain man's eye. Out upon you, man. I would not kiss any man's dirty latchets for leave to bake in his oven."

Robin Oig, sorry but not surprised at his comrade's displeasure, hastened to entreat his friend to wait but an hour till he had gone to the Squire's house to receive payment for the cattle he had sold, and he would come back and help him to drive the cattle into some convenient place of rest, and explain to him the whole mistake they had both of them fallen into. But the Englishman continued indignant: "Thou hast been selling, hast thou? Ay, ay; thou is a cunning lad for kenning the hours of bargaining. Go to the devil with thyself, for I will ne'er see thy fause loon's visage again—thou should be ashamed to look me in the face."

"I am ashamed to look no man in the face," said Robin Oig, something moved; "and, moreover, I will look you in the face this blessed day, if you will bide at the Clachan down yonder."

"Mayhap you had as well keep away," said his comrade; and turning his back on his former friend, he collected his unwilling associates, assisted by the bailiff, who took some real and some affected interest in seeing Wakefield accommodated.

After spending some time in negotiating with more than one of the neighbouring farmers, who could not, or would not, afford the accommodation desired, Henry Wakefield at last, and in his necessity, accomplished his point by means of the landlord of the alehouse at which Robin Oig and he had agreed to pass the night, when they first separated from each other. Mine host was content to let him turn his cattle on a piece of barren moor, at a price little less than the bailiff had asked for the disputed enclosure; and the wretchedness of the pasture, as well as the price paid for it, were set down as exaggerations of the breach of faith and friendship of his Scottish crony. This turn of Wakefield's passions was encouraged by the bailiff, (who had his own reasons for being offended against poor Robin, as having been the unwitting cause of his falling into disgrace with his master), as well as by the innkeeper, and two or three chance guests, who stimulated the drover in his resentment against his quondam associate—some from the ancient grudge against the Scots, which, when it exists anywhere, is to be found lurking in the Border counties, and some from the general love of mischief, which characterises mankind in all ranks of life, to the honour of Adam's children be it spoken. Good John Barleycorn also, who always heightens and exaggerates the prevailing passions, be they angry or kindly, was not wanting in his offices on this occasion, and confusion to false friends and hard masters was pledged in more than one tankard.

In the meanwhile Mr. Ireby found some amusement in detaining the northern drover at his ancient hall. He caused a cold round of beef to be placed before the Scot in the butler's pantry, together with a foaming tankard of home-brewed, and took pleasure in seeing the hearty appetite with which these unwonted edibles were discussed by Robin Oig M'Combich. The Squire himself lighting his pipe, compounded between his patrician dignity and his love of agricultural gossip, by walking up and down while he conversed with his guest.

"I passed another drove," said the Squire, "with one of your countrymen behind them. They were something less beasts than your drove—doddies most of them. A big man was with them. None of your kilts, though, but a decent pair of breeches. D'ye know who he may be?"

"Hout aye; that might, could, and would be Hughie Morrison. I didna think he could hae peen sae weel up. He has made a day on us; but his Argyleshires will have wearied shanks. How far was he pehind?"

"I think about six or seven miles," answered the Squire, "for I passed them at the Christenbury Crag, and I overtook you at the Hollan Bush. If his beasts be leg-weary, he will be maybe selling bargains."

"Na, na, Hughie Morrison is no the man for pargains—ye maun come to some Highland body like Robin Oig hersel' for the like of these. Put I maun pe wishing you goot night, and twenty of them, let alane ane, and I maun down to the Clachan to see if the lad Harry Waakfelt is out of his humdudgeons yet."

The party at the alehouse were still in full talk, and the treachery of Robin Oig still the theme of conversation, when the supposed culprit entered the apartment. His arrival, as usually happens in such a case, put an instant stop to the discussion of which he had furnished the subject, and he was received by the company assembled with that chilling silence which, more than a thousand exclamations, tells an intruder that he is unwelcome. Surprised and offended, but not appalled by the reception which he experienced, Robin entered with an undaunted and even a haughty air, attempted no greeting, as he saw he was received with none, and placed himself by the side of the fire, a little apart from a table at which Harry Wakefield, the bailiff, and two or three other persons, were seated. The ample Cumbrian kitchen would have afforded plenty of room, even for a larger separation.

Robin thus seated, proceeded to light his pipe, and call for a pint of twopenny.

"We have no twopence ale," answered Ralph Heskett the landlord; "but as thou find'st thy own tobacco, it's like thou mayst find thy own liquor too—it's the wont of thy country, I wot."

"Shame, goodman," said the landlady, a blithe, bustling housewife, hastening herself to supply the guest with liquor. "Thou knowest well enow what the strange man wants, and it's thy trade to be civil, man. Thou shouldst know, that if the Scot likes a small pot, he pays a sure penny."

Without taking any notice of this nuptial dialogue, the Highlander took the flagon in his hand, and addressing the company generally, drank the interesting toast of "Good markets" to the party assembled.

"The better that the wind blew fewer dealers from the north," said one of the farmers, "and fewer Highland runts to eat up the English meadows."

"Saul of my pody, put you are wrang there, my friend," answered Robin, with composure; "it is your fat Englishmen that eat up our Scots cattle, puir things."

"I wish there was a summat to eat up their drovers," said another; "a plain Englishman canna make bread within a kenning of them."

"Or an honest servant keep his master's favour but they will come sliding in between him and the sunshine," said the bailiff.

"If these pe jokes," said Robin Oig, with the same composure, "there is ower mony jokes upon one man."

"It is no joke, but downright earnest," said the bailiff. "Harkye, Mr. Robin Ogg, or whatever is your name, it's right we should tell you that we are all of one opinion, and that is, that you, Mr. Robin Ogg, have behaved to our friend Mr. Harry Wakefield here, like a raff and a blackguard."

"Nae doubt, nae doubt," answered Robin, with great composure; "and you are a set of very pretty judges, for whose prains or pehaviour I wad not gie a pinch of sneeshing. If Mr. Harry Waakfelt kens where he is wranged, he kens where he may be righted."

"He speaks truth," said Wakefield, who had listened to what passed, divided between the offence which he had taken at Robin's late behaviour, and the revival of his habitual feelings of regard.

He now rose, and went towards Robin, who got up from his seat as he approached, and held out his hand.

"That's right, Harry—go it—serve him out," resounded on all sides—"tip him the nailer—show him the mill."

"Hold your peace all of you, and be—," said Wakefield; and then addressing his comrade, he took him by the extended hand, with something alike of respect and defiance. "Robin," he said, "thou hast used me ill enough this day; but if you mean, like a frank fellow, to shake hands, and take a tussle for love on the sod, why I'll forgie thee, man, and we shall be better friends than ever."

"And would it not pe petter to pe cood friends without more of the matter?" said Robin; "we will be much petter friendships with our panes hale than proken."

Harry Wakefield dropped the hand of his friend, or rather threw it from him.

"I did not think I had been keeping company for three years with a coward."

"Coward pelongs to none of my name," said Robin, whose eyes began to kindle, but keeping the command of his temper. "It was no coward's legs or hands, Harry Waakfelt, that drew you out of the fords of Frew, when you was drifting ower the plack rock, and every eel in the river expected his share of you."

"And that is true enough, too," said the Englishman, struck by the appeal.

"Adzooks!" exclaimed the bailiff—"sure Harry Wakefield, the nattiest lad at Whitson Tryste, Wooler Fair, Carlisle Sands, or Stagshaw Bank, is not going to show white feather? Ah, this comes of living so long with kilts and bonnets—men forget the use of their daddles."

"I may teach you, Master Fleecebumpkin, that I have not lost the use of mine," said Wakefield and then went on. "This will never do, Robin. We must have a turn-up, or we shall be the talk of the country-side. I'll be d—d if I hurt thee—I'll put on the gloves gin thou like. Come, stand forward like a man."

"To be peaten like a dog," said Robin; "is there any reason in that? If you think I have done you wrong, I'll go before your shudge, though I neither know his law nor his language."

A general cry of "No, no—no law, no lawyer! a bellyful and be friends," was echoed by the bystanders.

"But," continued Robin, "if I am to fight, I have no skill to fight like a jackanapes, with hands and nails."

"How would you fight then?" said his antagonist; "though I am thinking it would be hard to bring you to the scratch anyhow."

"I would fight with proadswords, and sink point on the first plood drawn—like a gentlemans."

A loud shout of laughter followed the proposal, which indeed had rather escaped from poor Robin's swelling heart, than been the dictate of his sober judgment.

"Gentleman, quotha!" was echoed on all sides, with a shout of unextinguishable laughter; "a very pretty gentleman, God wot.—Canst get two swords for the gentleman to fight with, Ralph Heskett?"

"No, but I can send to the armoury at Carlisle, and lend them two forks, to be making shift with in the meantime."

"Tush, man," said another, "the bonny Scots come into the world with the blue bonnet on their heads, and dirk and pistol at their belt."

"Best send post," said Mr. Fleecebumpkin, "to the Squire of Corby Castle, to come and stand second to the GENTLEMAN."

In the midst of this torrent of general ridicule, the Highlander instinctively griped beneath the folds of his plaid,

"But it's better not," he said in his own language. "A hundred curses on the swine-eaters, who know neither decency nor civility!"

"Make room, the pack of you," he said, advancing to the door.

But his former friend interposed his sturdy bulk, and opposed his leaving the house; and when Robin Oig attempted to make his way by force, he hit him down on the floor, with as much ease as a boy bowls down a nine-pin.

"A ring, a ring!" was now shouted, until the dark rafters, and the hams that hung on them, trembled again, and the very platters on the BINK clattered against each other. "Well done, Harry"—"Give it him home, Harry"—"Take care of him now—he sees his own blood!"

Such were the exclamations, while the Highlander, starting from the ground, all his coldness and caution lost in frantic rage, sprung at his antagonist with the fury, the activity, and the vindictive purpose of an incensed tiger-cat. But when could rage encounter science and temper? Robin Oig again went down in the unequal contest; and as the blow was necessarily a severe one, he lay motionless on the floor of the kitchen. The landlady ran to offer some aid, but Mr. Fleecebumpkin would not permit her to approach.

"Let him alone," he said, "he will come to within time, and come up to the scratch again. He has not got half his broth yet."

"He has got all I mean to give him, though," said his antagonist, whose heart began to relent towards his old associate; "and I would rather by half give the rest to yourself, Mr. Fleecebumpkin, for you pretend to know a thing or two, and Robin had not art enough even to peel before setting to, but fought with his plaid dangling about him.—Stand up, Robin, my man! All friends now; and let me hear the man that will speak a word against you, or your country, for your sake."

Robin Oig was still under the dominion of his passion, and eager to renew the onset; but being withheld on the one side by the peacemaking Dame Heskett, and on the other, aware that Wakefield no longer meant to renew the combat, his fury sunk into gloomy sullenness.

"Come, come, never grudge so much at it, man," said the brave-spirited Englishman, with the placability of his country; "shake hands, and we will be better friends than ever."

"Friends!" exclaimed Robin Oig with strong emphasis—"friends! Never. Look to yourself, Harry Waakfelt."

"Then the curse of Cromwell on your proud Scots stomach, as the man says in the play, and you may do your worst, and be d——d; for one man can say nothing more to another after a tussle, than that he is sorry for it."

On these terms the friends parted. Robin Oig drew out, in silence, a piece of money, threw it on the table, and then left the alehouse. But turning at the door, he shook his hand at Wakefield, pointing with his forefinger upwards, in a manner which might imply either a threat or a caution. He then disappeared in the moonlight.

Some words passed after his departure, between the bailiff, who piqued himself on being a little of a bully, and Harry Wakefield, who, with generous inconsistency, was now not indisposed to begin a new combat in defence of Robin Oig's reputation, "although he could not use his daddles like an Englishman, as it did not come natural to him." But Dame Heskett prevented this second quarrel from coming to a head by her peremptory interference. "There should be no more fighting in her house," she said; "there had been too much already.—And you, Mr. Wakefield, may live to learn," she added, "what it is to make a deadly enemy out of a good friend."

"Pshaw, dame! Robin Oig is an honest fellow, and will never keep malice."

"Do not trust to that; you do not know the dour temper of the Scots, though you have dealt with them so often. I have a right to know them, my mother being a Scot."

"And so is well seen on her daughter," said Ralph Heskett.

This nuptial sarcasm gave the discourse another turn. Fresh customers entered the tap-room or kitchen, and others left it. The conversation turned on the expected markets, and the report of prices from different parts both of Scotland and England. Treaties were commenced, and Harry Wakefield was lucky enough to find a chap for a part of his drove, and at a very considerable profit—an event of consequence more than sufficient to blot out all remembrances of the unpleasant scuffle in the earlier part of the day. But there remained one party from whose mind that recollection could not have been wiped away by the possession of every head of cattle betwixt Esk and Eden.

This was Robin Oig M'Combich. "That I should have had no weapon," he said, "and for the first time in my life! Blighted be the tongue that bids the Highlander part with the dirk. The dirk—ha! the English blood! My Muhme's word! When did her word fall to the ground?"

The recollection of the fatal prophecy confirmed the deadly intention which instantly sprang up in his mind.

"Ha! Morrison cannot be many miles behind; and if it were an hundred, what then?"

His impetuous spirit had now a fixed purpose and motive of action, and he turned the light foot of his country towards the wilds, through which he knew, by Mr. Ireby's report, that Morrison was advancing. His mind was wholly engrossed by the sense of injury—injury sustained from a friend; and by the desire of vengeance on one whom he now accounted his most bitter enemy. The treasured ideas of self-importance and self-opinion—of ideal birth and quality, had become more precious to him, (like the hoard to the miser) because he could only enjoy them in secret. But that hoard was pillaged—the idols which he had secretly worshipped had been desecrated and profaned. Insulted, abused, and beaten, he was no longer worthy, in his own opinion, of the name he bore, or the lineage which he belonged to. Nothing was left to him—nothing but revenge; and as the reflection added a galling spur to every step, he determined it should be as sudden and signal as the offence.

When Robin Oig left the door of the alehouse, seven or eight English miles at least lay betwixt Morrison and him. The advance of the former was slow, limited by the sluggish pace of his cattle; the latter left behind him stubble-field and hedgerow, crag and dark heath, all glittering with frost-rime in the broad November moonlight, at the rate of six miles an hour. And now the distant lowing of Morrison's cattle is heard; and now they are seen creeping like moles in size and slowness of motion on the broad face of the moor; and now he meets them—passes them, and stops their conductor.

"May good betide us," said the Westlander. "Is this you, Robin M'Combich, or your wraith?"

"It is Robin Oig M'Combich," answered the Highlander, "and it is not. But never mind that, put pe giving me the skene-dhu."

"What! you are for back to the Highlands! The devil! Have you selt all off before the fair? This beats all for quick markets!"

"I have not sold—I am not going north—maype I will never go north again. Give me pack my dirk, Hugh Morrison, or there will pe words petween us."

"Indeed, Robin, I'll be better advised before I gie it back to you; it is a wanchancy weapon in a Highlandman's hand, and I am thinking you will be about some harns-breaking."

"Prutt, trutt! let me have my weapon," said Robin Oig impatiently.

"Hooly and fairly," said his well-meaning friend. "I'll tell you what will do better than these dirking doings. Ye ken Highlander, and Lowlander, and Border-men are a' ae man's bairns when you are over the Scots dyke. See, the Eskdale callants, and fighting Charlie of Liddesdale, and the Lockerby lads, and the four Dandies of Lustruther, and a wheen mair grey plaids, are coming up behind; and if you are wranged, there is the hand of a Manly Morrison, we'll see you righted, if Carlisle and Stanwix baith took up the feud."

"To tell you the truth," said Robin Oig, desirous of eluding the suspicions of his friend, "I have enlisted with a party of the Black Watch, and must march off to-morrow morning."

"Enlisted! Were you mad or drunk? You must buy yourself off. I can lend you twenty notes, and twenty to that, if the drove sell."

"I thank you—thank ye, Hughie; but I go with good-will the gate that I am going. So the dirk, the dirk!"

"There it is for you then, since less wunna serve. But think on what I was saying. Waes me, it will be sair news in the braes of Balquidder that Robin Oig M'Combich should have run an ill gate, and ta'en on."

"Ill news in Balquidder, indeed!" echoed poor Robin. "But Cot speed you, Hughie, and send you good marcats. Ye winna meet with Robin Oig again, either at tryste or fair."

So saying, he shook hastily the hand of his acquaintance, and set out in the direction from which he had advanced, with the spirit of his former pace.

"There is something wrang with the lad," muttered the Morrison to himself; "but we will maybe see better into it the morn's morning."

But long ere the morning dawned, the catastrophe of our tale had taken place. It was two hours after the affray had happened, and it was totally forgotten by almost every one, when Robin Oig returned to Heskett's inn. The place was filled at once by various sorts of men, and with noises corresponding to their character. There were the grave low sounds of men engaged in busy traffic, with the laugh, the song, and the riotous jest of those who had nothing to do but to enjoy themselves. Among the last was Harry Wakefield, who, amidst a grinning group of smock-frocks, hobnailed shoes, and jolly English physiognomies, was trolling forth the old ditty,—

"What though my name be Roger,
  Who drives the plough and cart—"

when he was interrupted by a well-known voice saying in a high and stern voice, marked by the sharp Highland accent, "Harry Waakfelt—if you be a man stand up!"

"What is the matter?—what is it?" the guests demanded of each other.

"It is only a d—d Scotsman," said Fleecebumpkin, who was by this time very drunk, "whom Harry Wakefield helped to his broth to-day, who is now come to have HIS CAULD KAIL het again."

"Harry Waakfelt," repeated the same ominous summons, "stand up, if you be a man!"

There is something in the tone of deep and concentrated passion, which attracts attention and imposes awe, even by the very sound. The guests shrunk back on every side, and gazed at the Highlander as he stood in the middle of them, his brows bent, and his features rigid with resolution.

"I will stand up with all my heart, Robin, my boy, but it shall be to shake hands with you, and drink down all unkindness. It is not the fault of your heart, man, that you don't know how to clench your hands."

By this time he stood opposite to his antagonist, his open and unsuspecting look strangely contrasted with the stern purpose, which gleamed wild, dark, and vindictive in the eyes of the Highlander.

"'Tis not thy fault, man, that, not having the luck to be an Englishman, thou canst not fight more than a school-girl."

"I can fight," answered Robin Oig sternly, but calmly, "and you shall know it. You, Harry Waakfelt, showed me to-day how the Saxon churls fight; I show you now how the Highland Dunnie-wassel fights."

He seconded the word with the action, and plunged the dagger, which he suddenly displayed, into the broad breast of the English yeoman, with such fatal certainty and force that the hilt made a hollow sound against the breast-bone, and the double-edged point split the very heart of his victim. Harry Wakefield fell and expired with a single groan. His assassin next seized the bailiff by the collar, and offered the bloody poniard to his throat, whilst dread and surprise rendered the man incapable of defence.

"It were very just to lay you peside him," he said, "but the blood of a pase pickthank shall never mix on my father's dirk, with that of a brave man."

As he spoke, he cast the man from him with so much force that he fell on the floor, while Robin, with his other hand, threw the fatal weapon into the blazing turf-fire.

"There," he said, "take me who likes—and let fire cleanse blood if it can."

The pause of astonishment still continuing, Robin Oig asked for a peace-officer, and a constable having stepped out, he surrendered himself to his custody.

"A bloody night's work you have made of it," said the constable.

"Your own fault," said the Highlander. "Had you kept his hands off me twa hours since, he would have been now as well and merry as he was twa minutes since."

"It must be sorely answered," said the peace-officer.

"Never you mind that—death pays all debts; it will pay that too."

The horror of the bystanders began now to give way to indignation, and the sight of a favourite companion murdered in the midst of them, the provocation being, in their opinion, so utterly inadequate to the excess of vengeance, might have induced them to kill the perpetrator of the deed even upon the very spot. The constable, however, did his duty on this occasion, and with the assistance of some of the more reasonable persons present, procured horses to guard the prisoner to Carlisle, to abide his doom at the next assizes. While the escort was preparing, the prisoner neither expressed the least interest, nor attempted the slightest reply. Only, before he was carried from the fatal apartment, he desired to look at the dead body, which, raised from the floor, had been deposited upon the large table (at the head of which Harry Wakefield had presided but a few minutes before, full of life, vigour, and animation), until the surgeons should examine the mortal wound. The face of the corpse was decently covered with a napkin. To the surprise and horror of the bystanders, which displayed itself in a general AH! drawn through clenched teeth and half-shut lips, Robin Oig removed the cloth, and gazed with a mournful but steady eye on the lifeless visage, which had been so lately animated that the smile of good-humoured confidence in his own strength, of conciliation at once and contempt towards his enemy, still curled his lip. While those present expected that the wound, which had so lately flooded the apartment with gore, would send forth fresh streams at the touch of the homicide, Robin Oig replaced the covering with the brief exclamation, "He was a pretty man!"

My story is nearly ended. The unfortunate Highlander stood his trial at Carlisle. I was myself present, and as a young Scottish lawyer, or barrister at least, and reputed a man of some quality, the politeness of the Sheriff of Cumberland offered me a place on the bench. The facts of the case were proved in the manner I have related them; and whatever might be at first the prejudice of the audience against a crime so un-English as that of assassination from revenge, yet when the rooted national prejudices of the prisoner had been explained, which made him consider himself as stained with indelible dishonour, when subjected to personal violence—when his previous patience, moderation, and endurance were considered—the generosity of the English audience was inclined to regard his crime as the wayward aberration of a false idea of honour rather than as flowing from a heart naturally savage, or perverted by habitual vice. I shall never forget the charge of the venerable judge to the jury, although not at that time liable to be much affected either by that which was eloquent or pathetic.

"We have had," he said, "in the previous part of our duty" (alluding to some former trials), "to discuss crimes which infer disgust and abhorrence, while they call down the well-merited vengeance of the law. It is now our still more melancholy task to apply its salutary though severe enactments to a case of a very singular character, in which the crime (for a crime it is, and a deep one) arose less out of the malevolence of the heart, than the error of the understanding—less from any idea of committing wrong, than from an unhappily perverted notion of that which is right. Here we have two men, highly esteemed, it has been stated, in their rank of life, and attached, it seems, to each other as friends, one of whose lives has been already sacrificed to a punctilio, and the other is about to prove the vengeance of the offended laws; and yet both may claim our commiseration at least, as men acting in ignorance of each other's national prejudices, and unhappily misguided rather than voluntarily erring from the path of right conduct.

"In the original cause of the misunderstanding, we must in justice give the right to the prisoner at the bar. He had acquired possession of the enclosure, which was the object of competition, by a legal contract with the proprietor, Mr. Ireby; and yet, when accosted with reproaches undeserved in themselves, and galling, doubtless, to a temper at least sufficiently susceptible of passion, he offered notwithstanding, to yield up half his acquisition, for the sake of peace and good neighbourhood, and his amicable proposal was rejected with scorn. Then follows the scene at Mr. Heskett the publican's, and you will observe how the stranger was treated by the deceased, and, I am sorry to observe, by those around, who seem to have urged him in a manner which was aggravating in the highest degree. While he asked for peace and for composition, and offered submission to a magistrate, or to a mutual arbiter, the prisoner was insulted by a whole company, who seem on this occasion to have forgotten the national maxim of 'fair play;' and while attempting to escape from the place in peace, he was intercepted, struck down, and beaten to the effusion of his blood.

"Gentlemen of the jury, it was with some impatience that I heard my learned brother who opened the case for the crown give an unfavourable turn to the prisoner's conduct on this occasion. He said the prisoner was afraid to encounter his antagonist in fair fight, or to submit to the laws of the ring; and that therefore, like a cowardly Italian, he had recourse to his fatal stiletto, to murder the man whom he dared not meet in manly encounter. I observed the prisoner shrink from this part of the accusation with the abhorrence natural to a brave man; and as I would wish to make my words impressive when I point his real crime, I must secure his opinion of my impartiality by rebutting everything that seems to me a false accusation. There can be no doubt that the prisoner is a man of resolution—too much resolution. I wish to Heaven that he had less—or, rather that he had had a better education to regulate it.

"Gentlemen, as to the laws my brother talks of, they may be known in the bull-ring, or the bear-garden, or the cock-pit, but they are not known here. Or, if they should be so far admitted as furnishing a species of proof that no malice was intended in this sort of combat, from which fatal accidents do sometimes arise, it can only be so admitted when both parties are IN PARI CASU, equally acquainted with, and equally willing to refer themselves to, that species of arbitrament. But will it be contended that a man of superior rank and education is to be subjected, or is obliged to subject himself, to this coarse and brutal strife, perhaps in opposition to a younger, stronger, or more skilful opponent? Certainly even the pugilistic code, if founded upon the fair play of Merry Old England, as my brother alleges it to be, can contain nothing so preposterous. And, gentlemen of the jury, if the laws would support an English gentleman, wearing, we will suppose, his sword, in defending himself by force against a violent personal aggression of the nature offered to this prisoner, they will not less protect a foreigner and a stranger, involved in the same unpleasing circumstances. If, therefore, gentlemen of the jury, when thus pressed by a VIS MAJOR, the object of obloquy to a whole company, and of direct violence from one at least, and, as he might reasonably apprehend, from more, the panel had produced the weapon which his countrymen, as we are informed, generally carry about their persons, and the same unhappy circumstance had ensued which you have heard detailed in evidence, I could not in my conscience have asked from you a verdict of murder. The prisoner's personal defence might indeed, even in that case, have gone more or less beyond the MODERAMEN INCULPATAE TUTELAE, spoken of by lawyers; but the punishment incurred would have been that of manslaughter, not of murder. I beg leave to add that I should have thought this milder species of charge was demanded in the case supposed, notwithstanding the statute of James I. cap. 8, which takes the case of slaughter by stabbing with a short weapon, even without MALICE PREPENSE, out of the benefit of clergy. For this statute of stabbing, as it is termed, arose out of a temporary cause; and as the real guilt is the same, whether the slaughter be committed by the dagger, or by sword or pistol, the benignity of the modern law places them all on the same, or nearly the same, footing.

"But, gentlemen of the jury, the pinch of the case lies in the interval of two hours interposed betwixt the reception of the injury and the fatal retaliation. In the heat of affray and CHAUDE MELEE, law, compassionating the infirmities of humanity, makes allowance for the passions which rule such a stormy moment—for the sense of present pain, for the apprehension of further injury, for the difficulty of ascertaining with due accuracy the precise degree of violence which is necessary to protect the person of the individual, without annoying or injuring the assailant more than is absolutely necessary. But the time necessary to walk twelve miles, however speedily performed, was an interval sufficient for the prisoner to have recollected himself; and the violence with which he carried his purpose into effect, with so many circumstances of deliberate determination, could neither be induced by the passion of anger, nor that of fear. It was the purpose and the act of predetermined revenge, for which law neither can, will, nor ought to have sympathy or allowance.

"It is true, we may repeat to ourselves, in alleviation of this poor man's unhappy action, that his case is a very peculiar one. The country which he inhabits was, in the days of many now alive, inaccessible to the laws, not only of England, which have not even yet penetrated thither, but to those to which our neighbours of Scotland are subjected, and which must be supposed to be, and no doubt actually are, founded upon the general principles of justice and equity which pervade every civilized country. Amongst their mountains, as among the North American Indians, the various tribes were wont to make war upon each other, so that each man was obliged to go armed for his own protection. These men, from the ideas which they entertained of their own descent and of their own consequence, regarded themselves as so many cavaliers or men-at-arms, rather than as the peasantry of a peaceful country. Those laws of the ring, as my brother terms them, were unknown to the race of warlike mountaineers; that decision of quarrels by no other weapons than those which nature has given every man must to them have seemed as vulgar and as preposterous as to the NOBLESSE of France. Revenge, on the other hand, must have been as familiar to their habits of society as to those of the Cherokees or Mohawks. It is indeed, as described by Bacon, at bottom a kind of wild untutored justice; for the fear of retaliation must withhold the hands of the oppressor where there is no regular law to check daring violence. But though all this may be granted, and though we may allow that, such having been the case of the Highlands in the days of the prisoner's fathers, many of the opinions and sentiments must still continue to influence the present generation, it cannot, and ought not, even in this most painful case, to alter the administration of the law, either in your hands, gentlemen of the jury, or in mine. The first object of civilisation is to place the general protection of the law, equally administered, in the room of that wild justice which every man cut and carved for himself, according to the length of his sword and the strength of his arm. The law says to the subjects, with a voice only inferior to that of the Deity, 'Vengeance is mine.' The instant that there is time for passion to cool, and reason to interpose, an injured party must become aware that the law assumes the exclusive cognisance of the right and wrong betwixt the parties, and opposes her inviolable buckler to every attempt of the private party to right himself. I repeat that this unhappy man ought personally to be the object rather of our pity than our abhorrence, for he failed in his ignorance, and from mistaken notions of honour. But his crime is not the less that of murder, gentlemen, and, in your high and important office, it is your duty so to find. Englishmen have their angry passions as well as Scots; and should this man's action remain unpunished, you may unsheath, under various pretences, a thousand daggers betwixt the Land's-End and the Orkneys."

The venerable Judge thus ended what, to judge by his apparent emotion, and by the tears which filled his eyes, was really a painful task. The jury, according to his instructions, brought in a verdict of Guilty; and Robin Oig M'Combich, ALIAS McGregor, was sentenced to death, and left for execution, which took place accordingly. He met his fate with great firmness, and acknowledged the justice of his sentence. But he repelled indignantly the observations of those who accused him of attacking an unarmed man. "I give a life for the life I took," he said, "and what can I do more?" [See Note 11.—Robert Donn's Poems.]

NOTES.

NOTES TO CHRONICLES OF THE CANONGATE.

Note 1.—HOLYROOD.

The reader may be gratified with Hector Boece's narrative of the original foundation of the famous abbey of Holyrood, or the Holy Cross, as given in Bellenden's translation:—

"Eftir death of Alexander the first, his brothir David come out of Ingland, and wes crownit at Scone, the yeir of God MCXXIV yeiris, and did gret justice, eftir his coronation, in all partis of his realme. He had na weris during the time of King Hary; and wes so pietuous, that he sat daylie in judgement, to caus his pure commonis to have justice; and causit the actionis of his noblis to be decidit be his othir jugis. He gart ilk juge redres the skaithis that come to the party be his wrang sentence; throw quhilk, he decorit his realm with mony nobil actis, and ejeckit the vennomus custome of riotus cheir, quhilk wes inducit afore be Inglismen, quhen thay com with Quene Margaret; for the samin wes noisum to al gud maneris, makand his pepil tender and effeminat.

"In the fourt yeir of his regne, this nobill prince come to visie the madin Castell of Edinburgh. At this time, all the boundis of Scotland were ful of woddis, lesouris, and medois; for the countre wes more gevin to store of bestiall, than ony productioun of cornis; and about this castell was ane gret forest, full of haris, hindis, toddis, and siclike maner of beistis. Now was the Rude Day cumin, called the Exaltation of the Croce; and, becaus the samin wes ane hie solempne day, the king past to his contemplation. Eftir the messis wer done with maist solempnitie and reverence, comperit afore him mony young and insolent baronis of Scotland, richt desirus to haif sum plesur and solace, be chace of hundis in the said forest. At this time wes with the king ane man of singulare and devoit life, namit Alkwine, channon eftir the ordour of Sanct Augustine, quhilk well lang time confessoure, afore, to King David in Ingland, the time that he wes Erle of Huntingtoun and Northumbirland. This religious man dissuadit the king, be mony reasonis, to pas to this huntis; and allegit the day wes so solempne, be reverence of the haly croce, that he suld gif him erar, for that day, to contemplation, than ony othir exersition. Nochteles, his dissuasion is litill avalit; for the king wes finallie so provokit, be inoportune solicitatioun of his baronis, that he past, nochtwithstanding the solempnite of this day, to his hountis. At last, quhen he wes cumin throw the vail that lyis to the gret eist fra the said castell, quhare now lyis the Canongait, the staik past throw the wod with sic noyis and din of rachis and bugillis, that all the bestis were rasit fra thair dennis. Now wes the king cumin to the fute of the crag, and all his nobilis severit, heir and thair, fra him, at thair game and solace; quhen suddenlie apperit to his sicht the fairist hart that evir wes sene afore with levand creature. The noyis and din of this hart rinnand, as apperit, with awful and braid tindis, maid the kingis hors so effrayit, that na renzeis micht hald him, bot ran, perforce, ouir mire and mossis, away with the king. Nochteles, the hart followit so fast, that he dang baith the king and his hors to the ground. Than the king kest abak his handis betwix the tindis of this hart, to haif savit him fra the strak thairof; and the haly croce slaid, incontinent, in his handis. The hart fled away with gret violence, and evanist in the same place quhare now springis the Rude Well. The pepil richt affrayitly, returnit to him out of all partis of the wod, to comfort him efter his trubill; and fell on kneis, devotly adoring the haly croce; for it was not cumin but sum hevinly providence, as weill apperis; for thair is na man can schaw of quhat mater it is of, metal or tre. Sone eftir, the king returnit to his castell; and in the nicht following, he was admonist, be ane vision in his sleip, to big ane abbay of channonis regular in the same place quhare he gat the croce. Als sone as he was awalkinnit, he schew his visione to Alkwine, his confessoure; and he na thing suspended his gud mind, bot erar inflammit him with maist fervent devotion thairto. The king, incontinent, send his traist servandis in France and Flanderis, and brocht richt crafty masonis to big this abbay; syne dedicat it in the honour of this haly croce. The croce remanit continewally in the said abbay, to the time of King David Bruce; quhilk was unhappily tane with it at Durame, quhare it is haldin yit in gret veneration."—BOECE, BOOK 12, CH. 16.

It is by no means clear what Scottish prince first built a palace, properly so called, in the precincts of this renowned seat of sanctity. The abbey, endowed by successive sovereigns and many powerful nobles with munificent gifts of lands and tithes, came, in process of time, to be one of the most important of the ecclesiastical corporations of Scotland; and as early as the days of Robert Bruce, parliaments were held occasionally within its buildings. We have evidence that James IV. had a royal lodging adjoining to the cloister; but it is generally agreed that the first considerable edifice for the accommodation of the royal family erected here was that of James V., anno 1525, great part of which still remains, and forms the north-western side of the existing palace. The more modern buildings which complete the quadrangle were erected by King Charles II. The name of the old conventual church was used as the parish church of the Canongate from the period of the Reformation, until James II. claimed it for his chapel royal, and had it fitted up accordingly in a style of splendour which grievously outraged the feelings of his Presbyterian subjects. The roof of this fragment of a once magnificent church fell in in the year 1768, and it has remained ever since in a state of desolation. For fuller particulars, see the PROVINCIAL ANTIQUITIES OF SCOTLAND, or the HISTORY OF HOLYROOD, BY MR. CHARLES MACKIE.

The greater part of this ancient palace is now again occupied by his Majesty Charles the Tenth of France, and the rest of that illustrious family, which, in former ages so closely connected by marriage and alliance with the house of Stewart, seems to have been destined to run a similar career of misfortune. REQUIESCANT IN PACE!

Note 2.—STEELE, A COVENANTER, SHOT BY CAPTAIN CREICHTON.

The following extract from Swift's Life of Creichton gives the particulars of the bloody scene alluded to in the text:—

"Having drank hard one night, I (Creichton) dreamed that I had found Captain David Steele, a notorious rebel, in one of the five farmers' houses on a mountain in the shire of Clydesdale, and parish of Lismahago, within eight miles of Hamilton, a place that I was well acquainted with. This man was head of the rebels since the affair of Airs-Moss, having succeeded to Hackston, who had been there taken, and afterward hanged, as the reader has already heard; for, as to Robert Hamilton, who was then Commander-in-chief at Bothwell Bridge, he appeared no more among them, but fled, as it was believed, to Holland.

"Steele, and his father before him, held a farm in the estate of Hamilton, within two or three miles of that town. When he betook himself to arms, the farm lay waste, and the Duke could find no other person who would venture to take it; whereupon his Grace sent several messages to Steele, to know the reason why he kept the farm waste. The Duke received no other answer than that he would keep it waste, in spite of him and the king too; whereupon his Grace, at whose table I had always the honour to be a welcome guest, desired I would use my endeavours to destroy that rogue, and I would oblige him for ever."

"I return to my story. When I awaked out of my dream, as I had done before in the affair of Wilson (and I desire the same apology I made in the introduction to these Memoirs may serve for both), I presently rose, and ordered thirty-six dragoons to be at the place appointed by break of day. When we arrived thither, I sent a party to each of the five farmers' houses. This villain Steele had murdered above forty of the king's subjects in cold blood, and, as I was informed, had often laid snares to entrap me; but it happened that, although he usually kept a gang to attend him, yet at this time he had none, when he stood in the greatest need. One of the party found him in one of the farmers' houses, just as I happened to dream. The dragoons first searched all the rooms below without success, till two of them hearing somebody stirring over their heads, went up a pair of turnpike stairs. Steele had put on his clothes while the search was making below; the chamber where he lay was called the Chamber of Deese, [Or chamber of state; so called from the DAIS, or canopy and elevation of floor, which distinguished the part of old halls which was occupied by those of high rank. Hence the phrase was obliquely used to signify state in general.] which is the name given to a room where the laird lies when he comes to a tenant's house. Steele suddenly opening the door, fired a blunderbuss down at the two dragoons, as they were coming up the stairs; but the bullets grazing against the side of the turnpike, only wounded, and did not kill them. Then Steele violently threw himself down the stairs among them, and made towards the door to save his life, but lost it upon the spot; for the dragoons who guarded the house dispatched him with their broadswords. I was not with the party when he was killed, being at that time employed in searching one of the other houses, but I soon found what had happened, by hearing the noise of the shot made with the blunderbuss; from whence I returned straight to Lanark, and immediately sent one of the dragoons express to General Drummond at Edinburgh."—SWIFT'S WORKS, VOL.XII. (MEMOIRS OF CAPTAIN JOHN CREICHTON), pages 57-59, Edit. Edinb. 1824.

Woodrow gives a different account of this exploit:—"In December this year, (1686), David Steil, in the parish of Lismahagow, was surprised in the fields by Lieutenant

Creichton, and after his surrender of himself on quarters, he was in a very little time most barbarously shot, and lies buried in the churchyard there."

Note 3.—IRON RASP.

The ingenious Mr. R. CHAMBERS'S Traditions of Edinburgh give the following account of the forgotten rasp or risp:—

"This house had a PIN or RISP at the door, instead of the more modern convenience—a knocker. The pin, rendered interesting by the figure which it makes in Scottish song, was formed of a small rod of iron, twisted or notched, which was placed perpendicularly, starting out a little from the door, and bore a small ring of the same metal, which an applicant for admittance drew rapidly up and down the NICKS, so as to produce a grating sound. Sometimes the rod was simply stretched across the VIZZYING hole, a convenient aperture through which the porter could take cognisance of the person applying; in which case it acted also as a stanchion. These were almost all disused about sixty years ago, when knockers were generally substituted as more genteel. But knockers at that time did not long remain in repute, though they have never been altogether superseded, even by bells, in the Old Town. The comparative merit of knockers and pins was for a long time a subject of doubt, and many knockers got their heads twisted off in the course of the dispute."—CHAMBERS'S TRADITIONS OF EDINBURGH.

Note 4.—COUNTESS OF EGLINTON.

Susannah Kennedy, daughter of Sir Archibald Kennedy of Cullean, Bart., by Elizabeth Lesly, daughter of David Lord Newark, third wife of Alexander 9th Earl of Eglinton, and mother of the 10th and 11th Earls. She survived her husband, who died 1729, no less than fifty-seven years, and died March 1780, in her ninety-first year. Allan Ramsay's Gentle Shepherd, published 1726, is dedicated to her, in verse, by Hamilton of Bangour.

The following account of this distinguished lady is taken from Boswell's Life of Johnson by Mr. Croker:—

"Lady Margaret Dalrymple, only daughter of John, Earl of Stair, married in 1700, to Hugh, third Earl of Loudoun. She died in 1777, aged ONE HUNDRED. Of this venerable lady, and of the Countess of Eglintoune, whom Johnson visited next day, he thus speaks in his JOURNEY:—'Length of life is distributed impartially to very different modes of life, in very different climates; and the mountains have no greater examples of age than the Lowlands, where I was introduced to two ladies of high quality, one of whom (Lady Loudoun) in her ninety-fourth year, presided at her table with the full exercise of all her powers, and the other (Lady Eglintoun) had attained her eighty-fourth year, without any diminution of her vivacity, and little reason to accuse time of depredations on her beauty.'"

"Lady Eglintoune, though she was now in her eighty-fifth year, and had lived in the retirement of the country for almost half a century, was still a very agreeable woman. She was of the noble house of Kennedy, and had all the elevation which the consciousness of such birth inspires. Her figure was majestic, her manners high-bred, her reading extensive, and her conversation elegant. She had been the admiration of the gay circles of life, and the patroness of poets. Dr. Johnson was delighted with his reception here. Her principles in church and state were congenial with his. She knew all his merit, and had heard much of him from her son, Earl Alexander, who loved to cultivate the acquaintance of men of talents in every department."

"In the course of our conversation this day, it came out that Lady Eglintoune was married the year before Dr. Johnson was born; upon which she graciously said to him, that she might have been his mother, and that she now adopted him, and when we were going away, she embraced him, saying, 'My dear son, farewell!' My friend was much pleased with this day's entertainment, and owned that I had done well to force him out."

"At Sir Alexander Dick's, from that absence of mind to which every man is at times subject, I told, in a blundering manner, Lady Eglintoune's complimentary adoption of Dr. Johnson as her son; for I unfortunately stated that her ladyship adopted him as her son, in consequence of her having been married the year AFTER he was born. Dr. Johnson instantly corrected me. 'Sir, don't you perceive that you are defaming the Countess? For, supposing me to be her son, and that she was not married till the year after my birth, I must have been her NATURAL son.' A young lady of quality who was present very handsomely said, 'Might not the son have justified the fault?' My friend was much flattered by this compliment, which he never forgot. When in more than ordinary spirits, and talking of his journey in Scotland, he has called to me, 'Boswell, what was it that the young lady of quality said of me at Sir Alexander Dick's?' Nobody will doubt that I was happy in repeating it."

Note 5.—EARL OF WINTON.

The incident here alluded to is thus narrated in Nichols' Progresses of James I., Vol.III. p.306:—

"The family" (of Winton) "owed its first elevation to the union of Sir Christopher Seton with a sister of King Robert Bruce. With King James VI. they acquired great favour, who, having created his brother Earl of Dunfermline in 1599, made Robert, seventh Lord Seton, Earl of Winton in 1600. Before the King's accession to the English throne, his Majesty and the Queen were frequently at Seton, where the Earl kept a very hospitable table, at which all foreigners of quality were entertained on their visits to Scotland. His Lordship died in 1603, and was buried on the 5th of April, on the very day the King left Edinburgh for England. His Majesty, we are told, was pleased to rest himself at the south-west round of the orchard of Seton, on the highway, till the funeral was over, that he might not withdraw the noble company; and he said that he had lost a good, faithful, and loyal subject."—NICHOLS' PROGRESSES OF K. JAMES I., VOL.III. p.306.

Note 6.—MACGREGOR OF GLENSTRAE.

"The 2 of Octr: (1603) Allaster MacGregor of Glenstrae tane be the laird Arkynles, bot escapit againe; bot after taken be the Earle of Argyll the 4 of Januarii, and brought to Edr: the 9 of Januar: 1604, wt: 18 mae of hes friendes MacGregors. He wes convoyit to Berwick be the gaird, conform to the Earle's promes; for he promesit to put him out of Scottis grund: Sua, he keipit an Hielandman's promes, in respect he sent the gaird to convoy him out of Scottis grund; bot yai wer not directit to pairt wt: him, bot to fetche him bak againe. The 18 of Januar, he came at evin againe to Edinburghe; and upone the 20 day, he was hangit at the crosse, and ij of his freindes and name, upon ane gallows: himself being chieff, he was hangit his awin hight above the rest of hes freindis."—BIRRELL'S DIARY, (IN DALZELL'S FRAGMENTS OF SCOTTISH HISTORY),pp.60,61.

NOTES TO THE HIGHLAND WIDOW.

Note 7.—LOCH AWE.

"Loch Awe, upon the banks of which the scene of action took place, is thirty-four miles in length. The north side is bounded by wide muirs and inconsiderable hills, which occupy an extent of country from twelve to twenty miles in breadth, and the whole of this space is enclosed as by circumvallation. Upon the north it is barred by Loch Eitive, on the south by Loch Awe, and on the east by the dreadful pass of Brandir, through which an arm of the latter lake opens, at about four miles from its eastern extremity, and discharges the river Awe into the former. The pass is about three miles in length; its east side is bounded by the almost inaccessible steeps which form the base of the vast and rugged mountain of Cruachan. The crags rise in some places almost perpendicularly from the water, and for their chief extent show no space nor level at their feet, but a rough and narrow edge of stony beach. Upon the whole of these cliffs grows a thick and interwoven wood of all kinds of trees, both timber, dwarf, and coppice; no track existed through the wilderness, but a winding path, which sometimes crept along the precipitous height, and sometimes descended in a straight pass along the margin of the water. Near the extremity of the defile, a narrow level opened between the water and the crag; but a great part of this, as well as of the preceding steeps, was formerly enveloped in a thicket, which showed little facility to the feet of any but the martens and wild cats. Along the west side of the pass lies a wall of sheer and barren crags. From behind they rise in rough, uneven, and heathy declivities, out of the wide muir before mentioned, between Loch Eitive and Loch Awe; but in front they terminate abruptly in the most frightful precipices, which form the whole side of the pass, and descend at one fall into the water which fills its trough. At the north end of the barrier, and at the termination of the pass, lies that part of the cliff which is called Craiganuni; at its foot the arm of the lake gradually contracts its water to a very narrow space, and at length terminates at two rocks (called the Rocks of Brandir), which form a strait channel, something resembling the lock of a canal. From this outlet there is a continual descent towards Loch Eitive, and from hence the river Awe pours out its current in a furious stream, foaming over a bed broken with holes, and cumbered with masses of granite and whinstone.

"If ever there was a bridge near Craiganuni in ancient times, it must have been at the Rocks of Brandir. From the days of Wallace to those of General Wade, there were never passages of this kind but in places of great necessity, too narrow for a boat, and too wide for a leap; even then they were but an unsafe footway formed of the trunks of trees placed transversely from rock to rock, unstripped of their bark, and destitute of either plank or rail. For such a structure there is no place in the neighbourhood of Craiganuni but at the rocks above mentioned. In the lake and on the river the water is far too wide; but at the strait the space is not greater than might be crossed by a tall mountain pine, and the rocks on either side are formed by nature like a pier. That this point was always a place of passage is rendered probable by its facility and the use of recent times. It is not long since it was the common gate of the country on either side the river and the pass: the mode of crossing is yet in the memory of people living, and was performed by a little currach moored on either side the water, and a stout cable fixed across the stream from bank to bank, by which the passengers drew themselves across in the manner still practised in places of the same nature. It is no argument against the existence of a bridge in former times that the above method only existed in ours, rather than a passage of that kind, which would seem the more improved expedient. The contradiction is sufficiently accounted for by the decay of timber in the neighbourhood. Of old, both oaks and firs of an immense size abounded within a very inconsiderable distance; but it is now many years since the destruction of the forests of Glen Eitive and Glen Urcha has deprived the country of all the trees of sufficient size to cross the strait of Brandir; and it is probable that the currach was not introduced till the want of timber had disenabled the inhabitants of the country from maintaining a bridge. It only further remains to be noticed that at some distance below the Rocks of Brandir there was formerly a ford, which was used for cattle in the memory of people living; from the narrowness of the passage, the force of the stream, and the broken bed of the river, it was, however, a dangerous pass, and could only be attempted with safety at leisure and by experience."— NOTES TO THE BRIDAL OF CAOLCHAIRN.

Note 8.—BATTLE BETWIXT THE ARMIES OF THE BRUCE AND MACDOUGAL OF LORN.

"But the King, whose dear-bought experience in war had taught him extreme caution, remained in the Braes of Balquhidder till he had acquired by his spies and outskirries a perfect knowledge of the disposition of the army of Lorn, and the intention of its leader. He then divided his force into two columns, entrusting the command of the first, in which he placed his archers and lightest armed troops, to Sir James Douglas, whilst he himself took the leading of the other, which consisted principally of his knights and barons. On approaching the defile, Bruce dispatched Sir James Douglas by a pathway which the enemy had neglected to occupy, with directions to advance silently, and gain the heights above and in front of the hilly ground where the men of Lorn were concealed; and having ascertained that this movement had been executed with success, he put himself at the head of his own division, and fearlessly led his men into the defile. Here, prepared as he was for what was to take place, it was difficult to prevent a temporary panic when the yell which, to this day, invariably precedes the assault of the mountaineer, burst from the rugged bosom of Ben Cruachan; and the woods which, the moment before, had waved in silence and solitude, gave forth their birth of steel-clad warriors, and, in an instant, became instinct with the dreadful vitality of war. But although appalled and checked for a brief space by the suddenness of the assault, and the masses of rock which the enemy rolled down from the precipices, Bruce, at the head of his division, pressed up the side of the mountain. Whilst this party assaulted the men of Lorn with the utmost fury, Sir James Douglas and his party shouted suddenly upon the heights in their front, showering down their arrows upon them; and, when these missiles were exhausted, attacking them with their swords and battle-axes. The consequence of such an attack, both in front and rear, was the total discomfiture of the army of Lorn; and the circumstances to which this chief had so confidently looked forward, as rendering the destruction of Bruce almost inevitable, were now turned with fatal effect against himself. His great superiority of numbers cumbered and impeded his movements. Thrust by the double assault, and by the peculiar nature of the ground, into such narrow room as the pass afforded, and driven to fury by finding themselves cut to pieces in detail, without power of resistance, the men of Lorn fled towards Loch Eitive, where a bridge thrown over the Awe, and supported upon two immense rocks, known by the name of the Rocks of Brandir, formed the solitary communication between the side of the river where the battle took place and the country of Lorn. Their object was to gain the bridge, which was composed entirely of wood, and having availed themselves of it in their retreat, to destroy it, and thus throw the impassable torrent of the Awe between them and their enemies. But their intention was instantly detected by Douglas, who, rushing down from the high grounds at the head of his archers and light-armed foresters, attacked the body of the mountaineers, which had occupied the bridge, and drove them from it with great slaughter, so that Bruce and his division, on coming up, passed it without molestation; and this last resource being taken from them, the army of Lorn were, in a few hours, literally cut to pieces, whilst their chief, who occupied Loch Eitive with his fleet, saw, from his ships, the discomfiture of his men, and found it impossible to give them the least assistance."—TYTLER'S LIFE OF BRUCE.

Note 9.—MASSACRE OF GLENCOE.

The following succinct account of this too celebrated event, may be sufficient for this place:—

"In the beginning of the year 1692 an action of unexampled barbarity disgraced the government of King William III. in Scotland. In the August preceding, a proclamation had been issued, offering an indemnity to such insurgents as should take the oaths to the King and Queen, on or before the last day of December; and the chiefs of such tribes, as had been in arms for James, soon after took advantage of the proclamation. But Macdonald of Glencoe was prevented by accident, rather than design, from tendering his submission within the limited time. In the end of December he went to Colonel Hill, who commanded the garrison in Fort William, to take the oaths of allegiance to the government; and the latter having furnished him with a letter to Sir Colin Campbell, Sheriff of the county of Argyll, directed him to repair immediately to Inverary, to make his submission in a legal manner before that magistrate. But the way to Inverary lay through almost impassable mountains, the season was extremely rigorous, and the whole country was covered with a deep snow. So eager, however, was Macdonald to take the oaths before the limited time should expire, that, though the road lay within half a mile of his own house, he stopped not to visit his family, and, after various obstructions, arrived at Inverary. The time had elapsed, and the sheriff hesitated to receive his submission; but Macdonald prevailed by his importunities, and even tears, in inducing that functionary to administer to him the oath of allegiance, and to certify the cause of his delay. At this time Sir John Dalrymple, afterwards Earl of Stair, being in attendance upon William as Secretary of State for Scotland, took advantage of Macdonald's neglecting to take the oath within the time prescribed, and procured from the King a warrant of military execution against that chief and his whole clan. This was done at the instigation of the Earl of Breadalbane, whose lands the Glencoe men had plundered, and whose treachery to government in negotiating with the Highland clans Macdonald himself had exposed. The King was accordingly persuaded that Glencoe was the main obstacle to the pacification of the Highlands; and the fact of the unfortunate chief's submission having been concealed, the sanguinary orders for proceeding to military execution against his clan were in consequence obtained. The warrant was both signed and countersigned by the King's own hand, and the Secretary urged the officers who commanded in the Highlands to execute their orders with the utmost rigour. Campbell of Glenlyon, a captain in Argyll's regiment, and two subalterns, were ordered to repair to Glencoe on the first of February with a hundred and twenty men. Campbell being uncle to young Macdonald's wife, was received by the father with all manner of friendship and hospitality. The men were lodged at free quarters in the houses of his tenants, and received the kindest entertainment. Till the 13th of the month the troops lived in the utmost harmony and familiarity with the people, and on the very night of the massacre the officers passed the evening at cards in Macdonald's house. In the night Lieutenant Lindsay, with a party of soldiers, called in a friendly manner at his door, and was instantly admitted. Macdonald, while in the act of rising to receive his guest, was shot dead through the back with two bullets. His wife had already dressed; but she was stripped naked by the soldiers, who tore the rings off her fingers with their teeth. The slaughter now became general, and neither age nor infirmity was spared. Some women, in defending their children, were killed; boys, imploring mercy, were shot dead by officers on whose knees they hung. In one place nine persons, as they sat enjoying themselves at table, were butchered by the soldiers. In Inverriggon,

Campbell's own quarters, nine men were first bound by the soldiers, and then shot at intervals, one by one. Nearly forty persons were massacred by the troops, and several who fled to the mountains perished by famine and the inclemency of the season. Those who escaped owed their lives to a tempestuous night. Lieutenant-Colonel Hamilton, who had received the charge of the execution from Dalrymple, was on his march with four hundred men, to guard all the passes from the valley of Glencoe; but he was obliged to stop by the severity of the weather, which proved the safety of the unfortunate clan. Next day he entered the valley, laid the houses in ashes, and carried away the cattle and spoil, which were divided among the officers and soldiers."—ARTICLE "BRITAIN;" ENCYC. BRITANNICA—NEW EDITION.

Note 10.—FIDELITY OF THE HIGHLANDERS.

Of the strong, undeviating attachment of the Highlanders to the person, and their deference to the will or commands of their chiefs and superiors—their rigid adherence to duty and principle—and their chivalrous acts of self-devotion to these in the face of danger and death, there are many instances recorded in General Stewart of Garth's interesting Sketches of the Highlanders and Highland Regiments, which might not inaptly supply parallels to the deeds of the Romans themselves, at the era when Rome was in her glory. The following instances of such are worthy of being here quoted:—

"In the year 1795 a serious disturbance broke out in Glasgow among the Breadalbane Fencibles. Several men having been confined and threatened with corporal punishment, considerable discontent and irritation were excited among their comrades, which increased to such violence, that, when some men were confined in the guard-house, a great proportion of the regiment rushed out and forcibly released the prisoners. This violation of military discipline was not to be passed over, and accordingly measures were immediately taken to secure the ringleaders. But so many were equally concerned, that it was difficult, if not impossible, to fix the crime on any, as being more prominently guilty. And here was shown a trait of character worthy of a better cause, and which originated from a feeling alive to the disgrace of a degrading punishment. The soldiers being made sensible of the nature of their misconduct, and the consequent necessity of public example, SEVERAL MEN VOLUNTARILY OFFERED THEMSELVES TO STAND TRIAL, and suffer the sentence of the law as an atonement for the whole. These men were accordingly marched to Edinburgh Castle, tried, and four condemned to be shot. Three of them were afterwards reprieved, and the fourth, Alexander Sutherland, was shot on Musselburgh Sands.

"The following semi-official account of this unfortunate misunderstanding was published at the time:—

"'During the afternoon of Monday, when a private of the light company of the Breadalbane Fencibles, who had been confined for a MILITARY offence, was released by that company, and some other companies, who had assembled in a tumultuous manner before the guard-house, no person whatever was hurt, and no violence offered; and however unjustifiable the proceedings, it originated not from any disrespect or ill-will to their officers, but from a mistaken point of honour, in a particular set of men in the battalion, who thought themselves disgraced by the impending punishment of one of their number. The men have, in every respect, since that period conducted themselves with the greatest regularity, and strict subordination. The whole of the battalion seemed extremely sensible of the improper conduct of such as were concerned, whatever regret they might feel for the fate of the few individuals who had so readily given themselves up as prisoners, to be tried for their own and others' misconduct.'

"On the march to Edinburgh a circumstance occurred, the more worthy of notice, as it shows a strong principle of honour and fidelity to his word and to his officer in a common Highland soldier. One of the men stated to the officer commanding the party, that he knew what his fate would be, but that he had left business of the utmost importance to a friend in Glasgow, which he wished to transact before his death; that, as to himself, he was fully prepared to meet his fate; but with regard to his friend, he could not die in peace unless the business was settled, and that, if the officer would suffer him to return to Glasgow, a few hours there would be sufficient, and he would join him before he reached Edinburgh, and march as a prisoner with the party. The soldier added, 'You have known me since I was a child; you know my country and kindred; and you may believe I shall never bring you to any blame by a breach of the promise I now make, to be with you in full time to be delivered up in the Castle.' This was a startling proposal to the officer, who was a judicious, humane man, and knew perfectly his risk and responsibility in yielding to such an extraordinary application. However, his confidence was such, that he complied with the request of the prisoner, who returned to Glasgow at night, settled his business, and left the town before daylight to redeem his pledge. He took a long circuit to avoid being seen, apprehended as a deserter, and sent back to Glasgow, as probably his account of his officer's indulgence would not have been credited. In consequence of this caution, and the lengthened march through woods and over hills by an unfrequented route, there was no appearance of him at the hour appointed. The perplexity of the officer when he reached the neighbourhood of Edinburgh may be easily imagined. He moved forward slowly indeed, but no soldier appeared; and unable to delay any longer, he marched up to the Castle, and as he was delivering over the prisoners, but before any report was given in, Macmartin, the absent soldier, rushed in among his fellow prisoners, all pale with anxiety and fatigue, and breathless with apprehension of the consequences in which his delay might have involved his benefactor.

"In whatever light the conduct of the officer (my respectable friend, Major Colin Campbell) may be considered, either by military men or others, in this memorable exemplification of the characteristic principle of his countrymen, fidelity to their word, it cannot but be wished that the soldier's magnanimous self-devotion had been taken as an atonement for his own misconduct and that of the whole, who also had made a high sacrifice, in the voluntary offer of their lives for the conduct of their brother soldiers. Are these a people to be treated as malefactors, without regard to their feelings and principles? and might not a discipline, somewhat different from the usual mode, be, with advantage, applied to them?"—Vol.II. pp.413-15. 3rd Edit.

"A soldier of this regiment, (The Argyllshire Highlanders) deserted, and emigrated to America, where he settled. Several years after his desertion, a letter was received from him, with a sum of money, for the purpose of procuring one or two men to supply his place in the regiment, as the only recompense he could make for 'breaking his oath to his God and his allegiance to his King, which preyed on his conscience in such a manner, that he had no rest night nor day.'

"This man had had good principles early instilled into his mind, and the disgrace which he had been originally taught to believe would attach to a breach of faith now operated with full effect. The soldier who deserted from the 42nd Regiment at Gibraltar, in 1797, exhibited the same remorse of conscience after he had violated his allegiance. In countries where such principles prevail, and regulate the character of a people, the mass of the population may, on occasions of trial, be reckoned on as sound and trustworthy."—Vol.II., p.218. 3rd Edit.

"The late James Menzies of Culdares, having engaged in the rebellion of 1715, and been taken at Preston, in Lancashire, was carried to London, where he was tried and condemned, but afterwards reprieved. Grateful for this clemency, he remained at home in 1745, but, retaining a predilection for the old cause, he sent a handsome charger as a present to Prince Charles, when advancing through England. The servant who led and delivered the horse was taken prisoner, and carried to Carlisle, where he was tried and condemned. To extort a discovery of the person who sent the horse, threats of immediate execution in case of refusal, and offers of pardon on his giving information, were held out ineffectually to the faithful messenger. He knew, he said, what the consequence of a disclosure would be to his master, and his own life was nothing in the comparison. When brought out for execution, he was again pressed to inform on his master. He asked if they were serious in supposing him such a villain. If he did what they desired, and forgot his master and his trust, he could not return to his native country, for Glenlyon would be no home or country for him, as he would be despised and hunted out of the glen. Accordingly he kept steady to his trust, and was executed. This trusty servant's name was John Macnaughton, from Glenlyon, in Perthshire. He deserves to be mentioned, both on account of his incorruptible fidelity, and of his testimony to the honourable principles of the people, and to their detestation of a breach of trust to a kind and honourable master, however great might be the risk, or however fatal the consequences, to the individual himself."—Vol.1., pp. 52,53, 3rd Edit.

NOTE TO THE TWO DROVERS.

Note 11.—ROBERT DONN'S POEMS.

I cannot dismiss this story without resting attention for a moment on the light which has been thrown on the character of the Highland Drover since the time of its first appearance, by the account of a drover poet, by name Robert Mackay, or, as he was commonly called, Rob Donn—that is, Brown Robert—and certain specimens of his talents, published in the ninetieth number of the Quarterly Review. The picture which that paper gives of the habits and feelings of a class of persons with which the general reader would be apt to associate no ideas but those of wild superstition and rude manners, is in the highest degree interesting, and I cannot resist the temptation of quoting two of the songs of this hitherto unheard-of poet of humble life. They are thus introduced by the reviewer:—

"Upon one occasion, it seems, Rob's attendance upon his master's cattle business detained him a whole year from home, and at his return he found that a fair maiden to whom his troth had been plighted of yore had lost sight of her vows, and was on the eve of being married to a rival (a carpenter by trade), who had profited by the young drover's absence. The following song was composed during a sleepless night, in the neighbourhood of Creiff, in Perthshire, and the home sickness which it expresses appears to be almost as much that of the deer-hunter as of the loving swain.

'EASY IS MY BED, IT IS EASY,
 BUT IT IS NOT TO SLEEP THAT I INCLINE;
THE WIND WHISTLES NORTHWARDS, NORTHWARDS,
 AND MY THOUGHTS MOVE WITH IT.
More pleasant were it to be with thee
 In the little glen of calves,
Than to be counting of droves
 In the enclosures of Creiff.
          EASY IS MY BED, ETC.

'Great is my esteem of the maiden
　　Towards whose dwelling the north wind blows;
　She is ever cheerful, sportive, kindly,
　　Without folly, without vanity, without pride.
　True is her heart—were I under hiding,
　　And fifty men in pursuit of my footsteps,
　I should find protection, when they surrounded me most
　　　　closely,
　　In the secret recess of that shieling.
　　　　　EASY IS MY BED, ETC.

'Oh for the day for turning my face homeward,
　　That I may see the maiden of beauty—
Joyful will it be to me to be with thee,
　　Fair girl with the long heavy locks!
Choice of all places for deer-hunting
　　Are the brindled rock and the ridge!
How sweet at evening to be dragging the slain deer
　　Downwards along the piper's cairn!
　　　　　EASY IS MY BED, ETC.

'Great is my esteem for the maiden
　　Who parted from me by the west side of the enclosed field;
Late yet again will she linger in that fold,
　　Long after the kine are assembled.
It is I myself who have taken no dislike to thee,
　　Though far away from thee am I now.
It is for the thought of thee that sleep flies from me;
　　Great is the profit to me of thy parting kiss!
　　　　　EASY IS MY BED, ETC.

'Dear to me are the boundaries of the forest;
　　Far from Creiff is my heart;
My remembrance is of the hillocks of sheep,
　　And the heath of many knolls.
Oh for the red-streaked fissures of the rock,
　　Where in spring time the fawns leap;
Oh for the crags towards which the wind is blowing—
　　Cheap would be my bed to be there!
　　　　　EASY IS MY BED, ETC.'

"The following describes Rob's feelings on the first discovery of his damsel's infidelity. The airs of both these pieces are his own, and, the Highland ladies say, very beautiful.
　　'Heavy to me is the shieling, and the hum that is in it,
　　　Since the ear that was wont to listen is now no more on the
　　　　watch.
　　Where is Isabel, the courteous, the conversable, a sister in
　　　kindness?
　　Where is Anne, the slender-browed, the turret-breasted, whose

glossy hair pleased me when yet a boy?
HEICH! WHAT AN HOUR WAS MY RETURNING!
PAIN SUCH AS THAT SUNSET BROUGHT, WHAT AVAILETH ME TO TELL IT?

'I traversed the fold, and upward among the trees—
Each place, far and near, wherein I was wont to salute my
    love.
When I looked down from the crag, and beheld the fair-haired
    stranger dallying with his bride,
I wished I had never revisited the glen of my dreams.
SUCH THINGS CAME INTO MY HEART AS THAT SUN WAS GOING DOWN,
A PAIN OF WHICH I SHALL NEVER BE RID, WHAT AVAILETH ME TO TELL
    IT?

'Since it has been heard that the carpenter had persuaded thee,
My sleep is disturbed—busy is foolishness within me at
    midnight.
The kindness that has been between us, I cannot shake off that
    memory in visions;
Thou callest me not to thy side; but love is to me for a
    messenger.
THERE IS STRIFE WITHIN ME, AND I TOSS TO BE AT LIBERTY;
AND EVER THE CLOSER IT CLINGS, AND THE DELUSION IS GROWING TO
    ME AS A TREE.

'Anne, yellow-haired daughter of Donald, surely thou knowest
    not how it is with me—
That it is old love, unrepaid, which has worn down from me my
    strength;
That when far from thee, beyond many mountains, the wound in
    my heart was throbbing,
Stirring, and searching for ever, as when I sat beside thee on
    the turf.
NOW, THEN, HEAR ME THIS ONCE, IF FOR EVER I AM TO BE WITHOUT
    THEE,
    MY SPIRIT IS BROKEN—GIVE ME ONE KISS ERE I LEAVE THIS LAND!

'Haughtily and scornfully the maid looked upon me:—
Never will it be work for thy fingers to unloose the band from
    my curls.
Thou hast been absent a twelvemonth, and six were seeking me
    diligently;
Was thy superiority so high that there should be no end of

  abiding for thee?
 HA! HA! HA! HAST THOU AT LAST BECOME SICK?
 IS IT LOVE THAT IS TO GIVE DEATH TO THEE? SURELY THE ENEMY
  HAS BEEN IN NO HASTE.

 'But how shall I hate thee, even though towards me thou hast
  become cold?
 When my discourse is most angry concerning thy name in thine
  absence,
 Of sudden thine image, with its old dearness, comes visibly
  into my mind,
 And a secret voice whispers that love will yet prevail!
 AND I BECOME SURETY FOR IT ANEW, DARLING,
 AND IT SPRINGS UP AT THAT HOUR LOFTY AS A TOWER.'
"Rude and bald as these things appear in a verbal translation, and rough as they might possibly appear, even were the originals intelligible, we confess we are disposed to think they would of themselves justify Dr. Mackay (their Editor) in placing this herdsman-lover among the true sons of song."—QUARTERLY REVIEW, NO. XC., JULY 1831.

Printed in Great Britain
by Amazon